FAREWELL PHILADELPHIA

NANCY CARNEY

authorHOUSE®

AuthorHouse™
1663 Liberty Drive
Bloomington, IN 47403
www.authorhouse.com
Phone: 1-800-839-8640

First published by AuthorHouse 07/5/2011

ISBN: 978-1-4567-8543-7 (sc)
ISBN: 978-1-4567-8544-4 (ebk)

Printed in the United States of America

Contents

Rights

Proverb

Kind hearts are the gardens,
Kind thoughts are the roots,
Kind words are the flowers,
Kind deeds are the fruits.

. . . An excerpt from The Irish Sacred Heart Messenger

Chapter 1

Catherine's Alzheimers

I sat there watching the sun shining on my grandmother's fragile face. She still had a remarkable amount of her own natural brown hair with only a scattering of grey here and there. She was always very proud of her 'crowning glory.' Her eyes were listless and you could tell she did not know me.

As we sat in comfortable chairs in the conservatory of the nursing home, I wondered for the umpteenth time have I left it too late? The fact that she didn't recognise me every time I visited her was seriously affecting me. Alzheimers disease was beginning to steal the grandmother who reared my siblings and me, after the deaths of both our parents. This was always a time shrouded in secrecy. Nobody would ever talk about it. I was four years old at the time and hardly remember my parents at all. I had always known from snippets of conversation overheard, that they had died in tragic circumstances. I can remember whenever I asked Gran to tell me what happened to Mum and Dad, she would always remind me of Maggie Callaghan, who used to visit us on long winters nights, telling frightening stories before we went to bed. She had long grey hairs growing down from her *smig* and we used to whisper into Granddads ear 'is she a witch?'

'Do you want to be like Maggie with a *smig?* That's what she got for being inquisitive,' Gran would say. Of course I never noticed the twinkle in her eye. I was too busy looking in the mirror to see if any hairs had started to grow from my chin, so I gave up asking for fear of getting a goat-like chin like Maggie Callaghan.

As I looked around, primroses, daffodils and snowdrops caught my attention. I watched the little sparrows through the patio door, pecking at the bare patches at the edge of the well-kept lawn. Suddenly a robin appeared from nowhere. Gran always loved the robin. If one came close to the window she would say 'we'll have good news today.' Poor Gran doesn't see any of these things now.

To look at her you'd never believe she had a wonderful eventful life. She had talked about sailing to Philadelphia in a big liner from the fair cove of Cork to make her fortune when she was twenty-two. She often said, 'Sally one day when you are old enough I'll tell you all about it.' She had a habit of saying "ah sure tomorrow is another day, a gra." That put an end to that topic! You might as well forget about it. You'd get nothing more out of her that day! She could be very annoying!

As I reach out to take her hand, she slowly awakes from her secret world.

'Is that yourself Sally a gra?' she called out.

I nearly jumped out of my shoes! Oh my God, she knows me to day. I can't believe it!

'Yes Gran it's me, Sally,' I called out quickly in case she got distracted again. God knows I could be somebody else tomorrow! Gran's voyage into her secret world often produced amusing stories to anyone who would listen. Yesterday she claimed that an elderly gentleman had come into her room in the nursing home and asked her for a date. She said she turned him down, even before he had a chance to give her the flowers he was carrying. 'The cheek of him to have asked me out in the first place,' she exclaimed. 'Why I hardly knew him, and he wasn't nearly as nice as your granddad anyway.'

There were times when I enjoyed listening to her latest adventures, but I was running out of time here, and in no mood to humour her about silly stories that never happened. I had such an ache inside me to know what happened to my parents.

Today my Gran knows me! Not wanting to waste another minute of this precious time I quickly asked 'Gran tell me about the good old days.' I watched closely as her face transformed from the thin and listless look we have got accustomed to of late, into a mischievous smile. 'Ahh' she cackled, 'so you must have found out you won't grow whiskers for asking too many questions, young Sally. Do you think now you're old enough to hear what your Granny got up to with randy old men? Not that your Granddad was like that, or I'd never have married him. But I did run into some randy old buggers in my time. You might not think so now but I was very pretty when I was young. I was told my hair was chestnut brown and my Aunts would always pinch my rosy cheeks whenever they got the chance. I hated when they did that! They said it was all that fresh air coming across the bogs of Owenboy. I was only 22 when I left for Philadelphia to make my fortune. I intended to find an eligible bachelor when I returned to the west of Ireland. That was what I had my heart set on.

I couldn't believe my good fortune when Aunt Anne sent me a passage to America where she had a job waiting for me in Philadelphia. My mother scraped enough money to buy me a few decent things so I wouldn't be a disgrace to her. Everyone kept telling me I'd have a great time on the magnificent ship on the way to America. There would be an orchestra playing in the ballroom every night. Huh! Far from ballrooms we were reared, Sally!

We used to go to a few *hops* in the Town Hall, so I knew how to dance. The cinema was always the place to go on a Sunday night.'

'Gran, did you have many boys admiring you when you were young?' I ventured to ask.

There were a few lads, always hanging around corners to see if us innocent girls would stop and talk to them. My mother used to say; *they're corner boys and have nothing to do with them.* A fairly decent looking fellow might catch your eye, and you'd find yourself day-dreaming about him all the next day, but before you got chance to say hello to him, you'd hear he was sent off to be a Priest!

"Have you ever been in love me boys,
or have you felt the pain,
I'd rather be in jail I would,
than be in love again."

Sally waited while she sang her little verse of a song. She had become accustomed to hearing little ditties out of the blue, whenever the notion came over her Gran.

'Sally, a gra, would you search in there under the cushion and see can you lay your hands on a little baby bottle of brandy. I could do with a wee drop. It will give me courage. I have to go on a long journey.'

'Did you have a job at home before going to America Gran?' I asked quickly, not wanting her change from the subject.

'Oh I was very nifty with a needle and thread. I worked in a milliners shop in the local town. I was a dab hand at making hats and altering old ones. I changed designs from feathers to bows, or bows to buttons. It was quite an art. I hadn't ever graduated to making dresses or coats, but things were going to be different now. I was going to America. I had to be prepared for the dancing! I knew I would be able to hold my own well at least with the waltzing, but what to wear was a different kettle of fish! So with the help of Auntie Kate and an old foot sewing machine she kept under the stairs, I made a few dresses and a lovely red drindle skirt. Aunt Anne was so happy to know I was coming over. Her daughter May was getting married and the plans were already made for me to be her bridesmaid. They were going to make my dress for the wedding when I got there.'

Sally handed Catherine the little bottle of brandy and she crooked her bony hands around it and drank a good mouthful, replacing the cap, but still holding on to it in her lap. She had a far away look in her eyes and continued talking away as if she had never been interrupted.

'I was pretending not to be excited. Leaving my mother and father, my two sisters and a brother was going to be sad. We had it all planned out though. When I had enough money saved I was going to send home the fare for my sister Mary to come over too. Even though I was excited thinking of all that time on board a ship, I was a little apprehensive too. The *Titanic* disaster was still talked about. I was ten years old when it happened. We only had newspapers to tell us the news but the older people never stopped thinking about it. They had relations who drowned in it. It was such a tragedy.

Going to America was such a dream. I had all sorts of plans going on in my head and I wasn't going to spoil them by thinking of what might happen. So I said goodbye to all at home and without knowing it, this would be the last time I would ever see my father again. He died while I was enjoying myself sailing to Philadelphia.'

Chapter 2

Off to Philadelphia

Maurice Fitzgerald stood out on deck. He was bored and impatient to get back to America after spending six weeks at home in Cork waiting for his ailing father to die. Now the funeral was over he could return. His fiancé May was missing him. With his impending marriage drawing ever near he planned to have a jolly good time on board ship, for this may well be his last fling before tying the knot. It was jolly rotten luck that his young brother James was sent packing with him. James was always a weakling, and I daresay bound to be a nuisance, but with his father just buried he couldn't refuse his mothers pleas to look out for his younger brother. Surely there must be enough space on this ship to loose him when it was necessary to do so. He was going to be tied down long enough when he married May. Having a rich father-in-law ever watchful of his precious daughter, and an adoring mother who had always taken her side whenever there was an argument, he would have his hands full. This past six weeks apart gave Maurice time to reflect on their relationship. It wasn't that he did not love his fiancé. What man wouldn't fall for a pretty enough young girl, who was the only daughter of a very rich and generous businessman? May was the apple of her fathers' eye.

As he watched the passengers embark with their friends and relations, saying goodbye before coming on board, he realised he'd better make an effort to look out for May's young cousin coming over for the first time. The description of her by her Aunt was, a pretty girl with brown hair, grey-green eyes, rather shy and probably very naïve. She would be travelling alone. He'd have to make an effort to say hello at any rate, for May's sake, but he had no intention of wasting his precious time on a little brown mouse! Given the chance, his intentions were not going to be honourable for the next few days. He intended to enjoy himself at the first opportunity. Perhaps he could set her up with his brother James and be rid of the two of them in one go. He remembered his father often quoting 'to kill two birds with the one stone.' He had not always understood what it meant, but he smiled to himself now at having found the perfect solution.

'James, old buddy,' he called to his brother, who was also out on deck watching the sad scenes of families saying goodbye to their loved ones. 'Will you look out for a young girl of about twenty-two with mousy brown hair travelling alone? I think her name is Katy or Kitty.' Maurice felt he had done his duty and wandered off with an air of jauntiness about him, which could well be described as going fishing.

James himself was feeling sad at leaving home for the first time and watching such melancholy scenes, he could have done with a bit of comfort from his brother. He realised as he watched, that many parents might never see their children again. This had a most distressing effect on the young emigrants and their parents, who openly wept at the thought of being separated by a vast ocean. James already knew the feeling of the loss of a father. Although they did not always hit it off, he loved his father and knew his father loved him too.

It was a beautiful Harbour in Cobh with its scenic surroundings. The neat farmhouses and cottages, the herds of cattle and flocks of sheep were a sight to behold. Catherine Brennan was feeling a choking lump in her throat at what she was leaving behind and, vowed there and then, she would not be one of the emigrants who would never again see this beautiful sight. It was only a matter of time until she returned.

After stewards rang their bells, following several blasts of the ships mighty horn, they were on their way. Warmly clad passengers lined the rail to get their last look at the Irish coastline, as it receded into the distance. This was a misty-eyed moment for everyone.

It was spring; the sun was shining and the waters calm as they cruised down the Irish Sea. As they left Cobh, the fine weather still held and the mighty ship now set out into the Atlantic. By now the passengers who embarked at Liverpool had found their sea legs, but the Irish passengers who had just come on board, were tentatively testing their balance against the roll of the ship. The Irish people who embarked at Cobh were not only lonely, but also shy and hesitant and in no mood for laughter and games. Some passengers stayed below deck and unpacked. As they progressed towards America their spirits would pick up.

Catherine decided to explore the ship. Travelling alone had its advantages. You did not have to answer to anyone or be at a designated place at any particular time. There were arrays of cabins with two, three and four berths, fitted with the finest of bedding and wash cabinets. Looking down on the steerage passengers Catherine secretly thanked her Aunt Anne for sending her the passage for a second-class ticket. She was tempted to make do with steerage, and have more money in her pocket when she got to America. But her Aunt had warned her; first and second class were given perfunctory medical examinations and cleared in quarantine, while all steerage passengers had to go through Ellis Island to be cleared.

Going to America was such a dream, but the possibility of rejection passing through Ellis Island put fear into the healthiest of passengers. Her Aunt had written to her about the gruelling examinations by the medical doctors in the inspection rooms when she first sailed to America. The buttonhook for the eye exam was the most terrifying!

The orchestra was already playing in the first-class quarters, and there was a piano and a gramophone with a large selection of records provided in the dining salon. A large swimming pool looked very inviting but Catherine was in no mood yet to make so bold. She knew how to swim reasonably well, having taught herself in the lake at the back of her house when she was growing up. The only swimsuit she had was black and low cut at the back.

Her Aunt Anne had sent it in a parcel, amongst the many other garments her mother welcomed twice a year.

After dinner Catherine was feeling restless. She decided to go out on deck. Perhaps she'd meet someone to talk to and maybe meet someone from near home so they could exchange happenings in their town. There were a few couples with small children roaming around, some looking apprehensive, others drying a tear from their eyes. It was a starry night. The moon had been waiting in the wings, round and full, for the sun to disappear. Now the sky was black and velvety. It was the moons turn to give light. It began its journey across the sky running away from its white twin in the sea below.

Catherine noticed a solitary male figure at the far end of the deck. The bright full moon bathed him in light, but his face was in the shadow. She was touched by the dejected appearance of this young man, who seemed to be travelling alone, and thought to herself he must be as lonely as I am. She headed off in his direction but he was so absorbed in his own thoughts, he did not hear the approach of her footsteps.

'Hello,' she said. He jumped. 'Sorry, did I frighten you?' she said.

'No its okay,' he said. 'I was deep in thought. I needed some peace and quiet, I didn't sleep very well last night.'

'Were you excited about going to America too?'

'Kind of,' he said. 'By the way my name is James Fitzgerald. I'm from Cork.'

'I'm Catherine Brennan and I come from Mayo.' Reaching out her hand she said, 'I am pleased to meet you James Fitzgerald from Co. Cork!'

Catherine took an instant liking to this very young man, whom at first seemed to be a little prickly, but she wasn't prepared for the sadness in his eyes. She leaned on the rail beside him looking out to sea. They remained silent both engrossed in their own thoughts.

'You seem very young to be travelling alone James,' she commented quietly.

'Oh I'm not alone. My brother is here somewhere. I haven't seen him since we boarded. He's an awful man for the ladies! He came home when our father became very sick. That was six weeks ago. We buried him last week.

'Oh I am so sorry to hear that James,' she said.

Catherine had a great family relationship and felt loved, so her heart went out to this very nice young man, who seemed to be carrying a chip on his shoulder.

'Are you expecting to be called to the Army?' she asked.

'Hardly,' he said. She turned to look at him. She wasn't expecting such bitterness. 'I have no worries about conscription,' he said

'How can you be so sure James?'

Suddenly he reached down and pulled up one leg of his trousers.

'This is how sure I am,' he said.

Catherine was shocked to see he had an artificial left leg. 'I am sorry James, I wasn't prying, its just girls never have to worry about conscription and with you being just the right age, it was the first thing I thought of. Were you in an accident? Perhaps you don't want to talk about it. Tell me to mind my own business if you like.'

'It's okay, I've got used to it now. At first I was very bitter, but it helps to talk to someone.'

'Are you in pain?' she asked.

'Not the pain you are thinking of. But I am in pain all right—a pain that no pills can cure. This pain will never go away. You see when I was knocked down by a runaway pony and trap I was not alone. I was out taking a stroll with my girlfriend Teresa. I had just asked her to marry me and she had said she would. You see, every so often since she was fifteen I would jokingly ask her to marry me. She never took me seriously but would always give me the same answer. 'Ask me properly when I am eighteen and I'll tell you then James Fitzgerald.' We went to school together and she was the only girl I ever wanted.'

'What happened to her?' Catherine asked now intrigued.

'She was dragged along the road for half a mile before they got the pony under control. When I woke up in hospital I found my leg was gone and my girlfriend too.' Catherine wanted to throw her arms around this sad figure and cry her heart out with him, but she was afraid of rejection. For a moment she looked away. Tears, unexpected and sudden, sprang to her eyes. She felt an instant protective feeling for this sad young man who seemed only a few years younger than her. He was like a bird with a broken wing. She felt honoured that this stranger was able to pour out his heart to her. She was afraid to interrupt the silence by asking all the questions that sprang to mind. After a while she turned to him.

'At least James you wont have to be examined going through Ellis Island. I expect you already know from your brother how strict they are. Luckily my Aunt sent me the passage for second class. She said she would never forget the trip travelling in steerage and then the worry of rejection at Ellis Island.

James didn't make any comment. 'Do you mind if I ask you a personal question?' she asked.

He looked at her. 'Ask away,' he said as he rubbed the palm of his hand around the back of his neck.

'Have you ever cried since this happened to you?' she asked.

'Ah now Catherine, sure fellas aren't supposed to cry!' he answered.

If only I could alleviate this poor fellows suffering, Catherine thought. Then she realised she could help. By being a good listener and a shoulder to cry on. Sometimes that could make all the difference. If only she could find the right words of comfort. She knew it was impossible for the moment. She understood the anger that raged inside him and perceived *this is the first time he has confided in anyone!* Not that he had said all that much but she could tell it was wrenched out of him. Catherine wondered to herself, what sort of a man would leave his young brother all alone, onboard a ship bound for the unknown when he was clearly feeling so wretched after loosing both his sweetheart and his father.

Suddenly she realised there was traditional music coming from below deck. She desperately wanted this poor young man to come out of the depths of despair, even for an hour, before retiring for the night.

'James, do you by any chance play an instrument?' she asked him.

'Yes I do, I have a mouth organ here in my pocket, or maybe you call it a harmonica.

'Then let's go down and join the others. Can you hear them? Listen James they are singing 'off to Philadelphia in the morning.'

He smiled. 'Would you like me to play it for you?'

'Oh would you please. I'd love that.'

James removed the instrument from his inside pocket, rubbed it on his sleeve, licked his lips, ran his lips across it in a quick movement to get the right note and away he went. Catherine closed her eyes and though at least for a few moments this poor fellow's torture is forgotten in his music. She could see him playing to his sweetheart, as they took a stroll on a summers evening, his music as sweet as the birds singing. Her eyes filled with tears and she wondered why God saw fit to punish one so young.

Chapter 3

Sally's Mission

'Are you still there Sally, a gra? Did I dose off? I must have been dreaming. I met this nice young boy. I don't know where we were off to. He was such a nice boy but very sad. He was like a movie star. He would remind you of James Dean. Did I ever tell you Sally I went to school with James Dean?'

'Oh I thought it was John McCormack you went to school with Gran,' Sally replied good-humouredly.

Oh Danny Boy the pipes the pipes are calling,
From glen to glen, and down the mountain side.

Catherine was singing in an off-key chant.

Sally listened patiently as she chanted away. With regret she figured she would not hear any more about her trip today.

'Are you there Johnny? Mary will you reach up and take down that picture on the mantelpiece. Who are those people anyway and what are they doing in my house? Tell them to go home or I'll call the Garda. Will you go home now Mary like a good girl and let the men get on with their work? You can come again tomorrow.' Gran started her chanting once more.

'I'm as deep in love with Molly Bourke as an ass is fond of clover,
And when I get there I'll send for her, that's if she will come over.
So goodbye Mick, and goodbye Pat, and goodbye Kate and Mary.'

Sally couldn't take anymore to day! She was exhausted. 'Oh poor, poor Gran,' she thought. She took her worn hand in hers and kissed her on the forehead. She looked into the two eyes that no longer recognised her. Her grandmother had gone back into her secret world again.

As she made her way home she decided to give her herself a break from the nursing home. She was putting too much pressure on herself. She'd have to learn to be patient and relax. Growing up she heard comments from teachers in school 'Oh our Sally is like a dog with a bone.' They meant it in a complimentary way, because she was a very good and dedicated pupil.

But this was different and she was not in control of the situation herself. She would just have to be patient. Having come to this decision Sally drove home in a more relaxed mood and some of the tension started to ease. She put on a C.D. of Phil Coulter, which never failed to relax her. Thoughts of home soon started to set in and she felt a little guilty at neglecting her home and family. She'd make it up to them. Her husband Ian was indeed a pet and very understanding of her need to follow through this mission. He knew she yearned to know about her parents.

She parked the car in the driveway and prepared for the onslaught that would undoubtedly greet her on turning the key in the front door.

'Mummy, Mummy, Daddy she's home.' Jack, her little boy rushed into her arms. She hugged him fiercely.

'Hey, hey Lennon, down boy. Paddy, sit, sit now, down boys.' Sally scolded the two mutts.

Lennon the beautiful brown—black boxer licks Sally all over, while Paddy the black Labrador waits in the wings. He becomes impatient and pushes Lennon out of the way to get his turn. Jack jumps up on Lennon's back and shouts, 'giggy up Lemon, giggy up.'

'Hi honey,' Ian called out 'How did it go today?'

'Oh Ian it was wonderful for a while. Gran knew me to day. She started talking about her trip to Philadelphia. I'll tell you all after we have eaten.'

She reached out for her husband's hug of comfort. 'It's so good to come home and find you here she said. 'What would I do without you?'

'Well you'd have to get your own dinner for starters,' he laughed.

'Is it ready? I'd eat a horse. I didn't eat a bite all day. You know when Gran started talking about her journey to America I was afraid to interrupt. I was afraid to breathe in case it distracted her. When anybody walked by I was almost hushing them to keep quiet. It's so exhausting though. I'm wrecked tired and hungry too.'

During dinner Sally laughed out loud. 'What's so funny?' said Ian.

'Gran likes a little drop of the strong stuff. I never knew that before. Didn't she keep that well hidden? I'll have to take some with me the next time I go to visit. I've decided now I'm not going to see her tomorrow. Give myself a break and I'll be fresh for the next day. You know Ian she must have been a nice singer too. She was singing away to herself today.'

'Mummy was your Granny drunk today?' chirped Jack, out of the blue.

Sally and Ian had to laugh. Jack was only gone three. He was such a good little boy they forgot he was listening, so he often heard things not meant for his ears.

'Ian, I have an idea. Why don't you come with me the next time I'm going to the nursing home? If she doesn't recognise you I could say you are James Dean. That might trigger her mind back on board the ship again! But maybe she will recognise you, and sure I hope she does.' Sally was babbling away. 'God, I am being a selfish cow about all this. I never even asked how was your day and how did work go? Was there any breaking news that I should know about?'

'Nothing riveting this evening,' he said.

Sally was better pleased to hear that. Ian was the editor of the local weekly newspaper the 'Ballinamore Bulletin' and for most of the week would be under pressure to get the news ready for printing. The only day he could relax would be the date of issue. And even then he was too hard on himself, too critical reading between the lines, just because he felt responsible for the end product. He was a perfectionist and expected his staff to be the same. Sometimes he would come home in a foul mood because someone was too hung-over to pull his weight in an emergency. Working in a printing office has many such days and the word mistake was not yet invented in his vocabulary.

Ian was the strong silent type. He rarely contradicted his wife and she could do no wrong in his eyes. Therefore Sally was always free to do as she pleased.

Not that she was ever likely to do anything untoward in the first place. They were blissfully happily married for five years now, and had got over the hurdles of the earlier years of married life.

After dinner they sat comfortably in front of the fire with Jack playing on the floor with his toys. Lennon and Paddy were lying at their feet. The whole scene was one of pure bliss and contentment. This was a time of day Sally looked forward to. So relaxed, in fact she was rather hoping Ian wouldn't ask her again about the events of the day. She was content to keep them to herself for now and all things considered there wasn't much to tell just yet. She smiled to herself at remembering Gran's motto 'tomorrow is another day.'

Thinking of tomorrow, she realised she must prepare her show for Wednesday. Sally worked in the local radio station. She presented a woman's show twice weekly. She really enjoyed it. She was given the freedom of using any subject she wished, and she could use her own choice of music too. 'Country and Western' was her favourite but she varied it for she was well aware she had a mixed listnership. You had to be very broadminded on radio.

She could do a lot of her research at home while minding Jack, and had a choice of doing her show live or pre-record it. Her choice of subjects often depended on the seasons. The onset of spring could suggest a big revamp of your wardrobe, a clean out of make-up bag, or a diet for a new figure for summer clothes. Winter would be just as varied with recipes for hot meals and snacks for the colder days, the winter woolly fashions, sleeping problems, or health matters. Summertime could suggest a detox of your body, make-up tips, and the latest fashions for summer holidays. Giving up smoking and hair colours to suit individuals was always popular. Special occasions too gave Sally a huge amount of scope to work with. Christmas, Valentines Day, St. Patrick's Day, Easter, Mothers Day, special birthdays. The list was endless. Sally really enjoyed putting together a varied and enjoyable show.

Jack loved to listen to his Mummy on the radio. Sally of course would always play a request for him and he would sit through the whole show waiting for her to call out his name. One evening he met her at the door and said 'Mummy, why don't you say woof woof to Lemon and Paddy on the radio?'

Sally was dozing off, but knew she had better get her little mans bath ready. 'Come on you little rascal it's time for your bath and bedtime story,' Sally called out to Jack. 'Tidy up those toys now.' He was always willing when he heard the mention of his bath. Life would be so simple if everyone was as agreeable as Jack.

She was so looking forward to having a nice relaxing bath and an early night with her husband, and show him she was capable of putting him first occasionally!

She hoped he wasn't feeling neglected since she started spending so much time at the nursing home.

As she headed up the stairs with Jack in tow, she turned around and gave him one of her knowing winks and called out 'I feel like an early night to-night Ian, how about you?' She already knew what his answer was going to be. She got a thumb up sign and another wink back! Just for tonight she felt a selfish streak come over her. She knew her Gran would approve.

Chapter 4

Between Ourselves

It was amazing, she thought when the buzzer went off the next morning, just how obsessed I have become about this whole granny thing. With the onset of Alzheimers poor Catherine may not respond much more. It can be a very unpredictable disease and Sally knew in her heart that time could be running out.

She had woken at around six am when she heard Ian getting out of bed. He nearly always got up at that time. She had heard him getting dressed, making do with the light from the hallway, so as not to disturb her. He walked quietly down the stairs and she could hear his muffled voice greeting the dogs. Poor dogs, she thought to herself. This is the second time they were disturbed last night. She had not slept well. Her mind was racing with all sorts of thoughts spinning around in her head. She had got up quietly and slipped on her dressing gown and went downstairs to make a mug of hot chocolate. It might help her to relax. Lennon and Paddy greeted her from their baskets, but settled down again.

She settled into her comfortable armchair with her mug of chocolate and found herself drifting between sleep and wakefulness. She knew exactly where she was but images of the young Catherine Brennan on board the ship started to play around in her mind. She was conjuring up the vision of a beautiful looking girl with wavy brown hair, shoulder length, a white ruffled lace blouse and a long red drindle skirt to her ankles. Somewhere she must have seen a picture of her youthful grandmother. Where could she have seen this beautiful girl before?

She woke properly and shook herself out of this trance. 'God almighty I'm loosing it. Time might be against me with this Alzheimers disease, but I should not make this so stressful for myself. I should want to visit Gran without making it a 'This is your Life' scenario. So stop it Sally my girl!

Another idea came to her. She must get in touch with her sister in Australia. Tell her about her obsession to know about their grandmother's life. Perhaps she will not share her enthusiasm at all. After all she has left Ireland a long time ago, and people change over the years, but it can do no harm.

So with that decision, a blissful peace came over Sally. If she let herself relax one more second in the comfortable chair, she will end up sleeping there for the rest of the night. So she crept quietly up the stairs, like someone who was fearful of being found out, and snuggled down into the back of her sleeping husband. She wrapped her arm around him and knew he was blissfully unaware she had left his side unable to sleep.

Jack crept into the room and jumped up onto the bed hauling a mustard coloured bear he has since he was one year old. Sally was grateful for the interruption for she could well have continued sleeping especially after the disturbed night. Not that she was on a deadline or have to clock-in for work. That was such an advantage in her job. She yawned and stretched and gave Jack a big cuddle and of course Bobo the bear had to get the same affection too.

'Jack remind me to give that smelly old bear a bath at the weekend,' she yawned.

'Promise not to hang him on the line. Bobo is my best friend and I don't like to see him hanging Mummy,' he said.

After they had breakfast Jane the babysitter arrived to mind Jack. She was a very witty and good-humoured girl who adored him. And he adored her too. We were so lucky to find her, Sally thought to herself. She was like a breath of fresh air coming into the house. She also loved the dogs, and would always take them for a stroll with Jack in the pushchair. She would never stand on ceremony, but would go around the house treating it as if it were her own. And that is the way we like it, Sally thought. Protect me from someone who would have to be shown every chore that had to be done every day!

So with a kiss from Jack and a cheery goodbye from Jane and escorted to the door by Paddy and Lennon, she headed off to do some work for her next show 'Between Ourselves.'

Thursday morning Sally was free to go to the nursing home. She didn't ask Ian to come as she already knew it would not be a good day for him, and he would feel bad having to refuse her. Their work schedules were totally different. They rarely spent a day together except at the weekends. It will not always be this, Sally thought to herself! Things rarely remain the same for long and as they were both content with their lives there was no need to worry.

As she came in the side door where she usually found Gran sitting in the conservatory, she was approached by one of the nursing staff. 'Mrs Kirwan, your grandmother led us a right merry dance earlier on this morning. She nearly wandered off on us. A member of staff coming late to work spotted her out in the lawn in her dressing gown. She accompanied her back indoors. But don't worry dear; we have put a wee bell on her ankle now. This will alert the staff if she does decide to go on another excursion. She said she was going to America to make her fortune. Did you ever hear the likes?' And with that the nurse went off down the corridor chuckling away to herself.

As Sally drew nearer she could see Gran in her usual chair beside the window. She could hear her chanting a song she hadn't ever heard her sing before.

'Can anybody tell me where the blarney roses grow?
It may be down in Limerick town or over in Mayo.
It's somewhere in the Emerald Isle but this I'd like to know,
Can anybody tell me where the blarney roses grow?'

Sally sat down in the chair beside her grandmother. 'What will we do with you at all Gran?' she said, as she took the cold fragile hand in her own strong warm one. Just then Sally noticed the little robin outside again. 'Look Gran, look at the robin. Will we get good news today?'

'Oh I did a gra. I got a letter from America. They want me to go to Philadelphia,' she said.

Sally could not believe her luck. Quick as a flash she said 'but Gran you are already on the big liner and you met a nice boy like James Dean.'

Immediately her face transformed into a radiant smile. 'I was just on my way for a swim in the pool. I thought it might relax me before bedtime. I have only one swimsuit with me. It's very low cut. Will it be all right to wear it on my first night? Will people think I'm a brazen hussy?'

'Of course not Gran, you go ahead and enjoy your swim,' Sally humoured her.

Catherine Brennan walked out to the pool and slowly entered the water. She waded at first to find her depth and noticed only one other person at the far end of the pool. She sucked air into her lungs, held her nose and ducked beneath the surface. Thinking to herself how lovely and cool and relaxing this is. Oh this is heaven! She let herself come to the surface in a trance. When she opened her eyes she did not expect to find the only other occupant of the pool by her side. Before she could even contemplate what was about to happen next he reached out and grabbed her tightly around her waist. 'Are you okay, honey?' he said.

She pushed him from her and swam away. She was angry that a total stranger could get that close to her so easily. How dare he?' With long strokes he had caught up with her again in a few seconds.

‘My name is Maurice,’ he said. ‘I thought you were having problems. Can’t blame a man for coming to the rescue of a damsel in distress!’ he laughed mockingly.

‘If this damsel were in distress she’d prefer to drown than have a snake like you rescue her,’ she told him. Without another word he swam away as quickly as he had arrived.

Catherine made her way back to her cabin, smarting from the brief encounter with the very rude Maurice. How dare he think she was easy prey! She could still hear his mocking laughter. She showered and splashed her face with cold water, renewed her lipstick, ran a comb through her hair, chooses a red drindle skirt and a frilly white blouse, and emerged like a trooper refreshed for battle. But her mind was made up to avoid any contact with the insufferable Maurice—whoever he was.

Chapter 5

Danny Boy

Things had begun to liven up on board. Catherine could hear traditional music coming from below deck. She decided to wander down to join them. She recognised some of the old Irish airs played by the emigrants in steerage on fiddle, accordion and the flute. She noticed James Fitzgerald in the middle of the musicians playing his mouth organ, and she went over and sat beside him, companionably. She felt comfortable amongst these people. They took turns at playing their instruments, and one old 'seanachaidh' added a new dimension to storytelling, with his tales of fairies and ancient Irish heroes. Catherine was not found wanting when asked if she could sing. Her favourite was *Danny Boy*. As she started to sing '*Oh Danny Boy the pipes the pipes are calling*' she closed her eyes and lent herself to the words. She didn't realise the pretty picture she made there amongst the emigrants.

Maurice Fitzgerald was at a loose end. It was too early to retire. He would never be able to sleep. He had not seen his young brother since coming on board but he was not going to start worrying about him now. He was old enough to look after himself. He wandered below deck to where he could hear sounds of Irish music. It was not his kind of show. After nights out in the Drury Lane Theatre in Philadelphia, this will be just a bore, he thought. But it will help pass the time. As he drew nearer he could hear a female voice singing. He was not prepared for the sight that greeted him. The most beautiful, provocative girl he had ever seen, sitting in the centre of a bunch of burly, badly dressed emigrants. Could it be, or were his eyes playing tricks on him! Was that his brother James playing the harmonica while she sang *Danny Boy*? They looked so like a couple, so in tune with each other, he could not believe what he was hearing.

She was sleek and slim and so fresh looking. She looked like a princess in her red skirt and white blouse. He wanted to touch her. Here was a girl who was completely unaware of how attractive she was! Where had he seen her before? And how did this beautiful girl get to meet his cripple of a brother on board such a big ship? Typical of course, women always seem to fall for lame dogs! He never before thought he would wish to be in his brother's shoes.

He watched like a man in a trance while the emigrants cheered and applauded this beautiful rendition of such a popular song. He had often heard May's mother singing it to herself in the kitchen and he could see May joining in with her. He could never understand why native Irish made such a big deal of that particular song. But after hearing it sung tonight by this lovely stranger, something stirred in him.

He dragged his attention back to the musicians and watched while they played, and sang *It's a long way to Tipperary* and *When Irish eyes are smiling* and some others he had never heard before. He watched his brother James join in with all the singing and noticed how well he seemed to be liked. He would not have known any of these people before! How had he become so popular? He certainly had not mentioned knowing anyone as beautiful as this girl. His girlfriend, who had the misfortune of getting herself killed, was ordinary enough. Pleasant but nothing to write home about when it came to looks!

Maurice felt a determination he never felt before. He was going to have to get an introduction through his brother. Might as well make use of him someway! When he came back to visit his sick father he had not planned on having a young brother back with him. He could not refuse his mother's pleas but he was not going to be burdened with the tiresome task of being his brothers' keeper. He still could not help thinking he had seen this girl somewhere before! And for the first time in his life he thought, 'I wish I could sing.'

Catherine was enjoying herself like never before. She fitted in with these people, and everyone had cheered up enormously. She could not be happier at seeing James in such good spirits. They laughed and joked and compared songs with each other. She had not realised how easy it would to get acquainted with people. Her mother used to say, 'wherever there is a fiddle there will be a bow.' She was not sure even now she understood the meaning of it. There were plenty of fiddles and bows here, she though to herself. Oh she was going to have a great time on board this ship! She did not have to think of what was ahead of her yet. She would treat this just like it was a holiday, and that was something Catherine never experienced before. Holidays at home meant helping her father in the bog, saving the turf, digging potatoes and harvesting the oats.

Thinking of them now brought a lump to her throat as she though of her father and mother. She felt a peculiar shiver go through her whole body. Someone once described it like someone walking over your grave!

Suddenly Catherine felt very tired and decided she had enough for tonight. She felt a great desire to get to her bed. She said goodnight to James and the others and they all said, see you tomorrow for more of the same.

As she made her way back to her cabin she noticed the insufferable Maurice walking ahead of her. She had no wish to have another encounter with him. Taking her time not wanting to get abreast of him, she watched him go. She still smarted from his brassiness in the pool. She could see he was attractive, well muscled and tall, but all together a bit too perfect she thought, and far too opinionated!

Going to bed with such thoughts on her mind, it was not surprising she felt tired when she woke up. She had not slept so well. She had planned on some sun-worshipping today, so she would get the chance to relax again out on deck after breakfast. She also decided it was time to write a letter home, so she could post it when they docked. She had promised her parents she would post a letter at the first opportunity. She dressed in a white crochet top and a multi-coloured gathered skirt and a pair of white sandals. She piled her hair into a bun, added a touch of lipstick and was ready for another day.

As she made her way up on deck she noticed there were not many of last night's group up yet. Probably stayed a lot longer than she did before retiring! She smiled to herself at how very pleasant it all was. She felt like pinching herself, she was so lucky to be given this opportunity to see America.

Thoughts of her Aunt Anne and cousin May came to her and she wondered if she would settle into their ways. She hoped and prayed she would at least like the place—well enough to stay and save money, so that she would have a presentable dowry when she returned to her native Mayo, where she hoped to meet an eligible bachelor.

She settled down to write the letter while things were quiet, and vivid pictures of her parents came before her. She could see them now sitting looking out the half door and wondering where she is and what is she doing. As she rolled the pen between her fingers she thought to herself—there isn't a lot to tell them yet! Still she started to write—the voyage is lovely, the food is good, the weather is glorious and the craic is great with the other emigrants!

Just then a shadow crossed the page she was writing on. She looked up. The sun was blinding. She could not see properly only she knew it was a male figure. He was dressed in shorts with a pair of legs like an athlete, straight and well muscled. He just stood there without saying a word, staring at her. Reaching up to shade the sun from her eyes she noticed it was the arrogant Maurice.

‘Do I look like a damsel in distress?’ she asked him.

‘I don’t understand, have we met before? I think I would have remembered those legs.’ I’m Maurice Fitzgerald.’

‘So you keep saying,’ she answered.

He let his gaze wander over her figure. He noticed her narrow waist and her slim legs. What would it be like to wake up beside those legs every morning? he thought to himself.

She felt uneasy under the scrutiny of those two blue eyes that were capable of undressing her at a glance. She knew they were taking in every detail of her appearance travelling slowly over her slim form. She looked down at her breasts and wished she had chosen a less revealing top. But it was too late now. How dare he make her feel so uncomfortable! Of course she was flattered at such undisguised admiration! What girl wouldn’t? She had always felt comfortable with herself. Not because she thought she was beautiful, it was just how she felt! Suddenly she wanted to put as much space between this man and herself. She put away her writing and without another word walked quickly away. She had no idea where she was going and it did not matter. Just to get away from Mr Maurice Fitzgerald.

Four days out to sea a fancy dress was being organised in the ballroom after dinner. As Catherine bathed and dressed, she decided she would wear the long midnight blue gown she had made with the help of her Aunty Kate. It had taken hours to sew the glittery sequins. She felt quite fluttery with excitement. At last the time was here to wear it. She hoped it was not too daring. It had a shoestring detail across the swell of her breasts. She left her shoulder-length hair out loose and it curled at the ends when it was dry. She felt very daring as she stepped into the new black patent high-heeled sandals.

As she headed off for the ballroom humming to herself, she stopped and chatted several times to people she met during breakfast, or out on deck. Some people were wearing costumes. She noticed a priest, and there were a couple of bunny girls and a few nurses in uniform! They could hear the orchestra playing. Oh she was going to enjoy herself, she thought. She had just entered the ballroom when she heard 'would you like to dance?' She did not recognise this stranger but she was going to let her hair down tonight!

'That's what I'm here for,' she said cheerily.

Taking her by the hand he led her out on to the floor into the clusters of dancing couples. They had not got much further than exchange of names and customary 'where do you come from', when there was a tap on his shoulder and she heard 'excuse me mate.' Catherine was whirled away by another man. She now realised this must be a general excuse me dance! This allowed the fellows to tap in as often as they wished.

Catherine was having a ball! She recognised some of her partners from playing the sessions below deck last evening, others she had not seen before. But it did not matter. She was here to enjoy herself.

She suddenly noticed James. He was standing with a drink in his hand. He was nicely dressed in a jacket shirt and trousers but no tie. She was glad to see he was enjoying himself and noticed he had made lots of friends.

The orchestra was playing a slow dance. She walked up to him and asked him to take her out on the floor.

'You won't want to dance with me, surely,' he said.

'Why ever not James? Sure we can take it easy,' she answered. So hand in hand they moved out to the dance floor.

'This is the first time I have danced since the accident,' he told her.

Catherine was not surprised at that revelation. She felt comfortable and at ease with this young man. They danced on, smiling at each other and exchanging the odd comments, each knowing there was no physical attraction between them, so they could relax.

'I didn't know if I would be able to dance you know. I've made the break now, thanks to you. You are a very nice person Catherine,' he said.

'You're not so bad yourself James,' she answered. Suddenly she heard a voice behind her.

'James, old buddy, let me relieve you of your partner!'

'Oh hello Maurice,' said James. 'I was wondering what you were getting up to.'

Before she could object she was roughly navigated to a space in the middle of the ballroom. Lights, which encircled the floor, had dimmed and the orchestra was playing a slow smoochy number. Before she could contemplate his next action he wrapped his arms around her and rubbed his cheek against her hair. He pulled her closer in a vice-like hold, so that her breasts were against his chest. He pulled her hips closer to his and she could feel his hot, hard body against her. She shuddered with disgust. He lowered his head to kiss her but Catherine was too quick for him. With all the strength she could muster she lashed out and slapped him hard across the face.

'Get your filthy roaming hands off me,' she yelled.

'Oh gee honey aren't we having a swell time? Come on now don't be unreasonable. You're supposed to be enjoying it,' he smiled.

'Let go of my wrists,' she hissed. His grasp slackened, but his fingers started stroking her breast. She jerked free.

'Calm down,' he mocked with amusement in his eyes. His speech was distinctly slurred. 'I'm hardly going to jump on your bones right here, but we could go back to your cabin or would you prefer mine honey?'

'I'd rather jump overboard than go anywhere with you,' she said.

Catherine could not stay and listen to another word from this arrogant, ignorant, insensitive beast. Humiliation brought tears to her eyes. Why did this insufferable man humiliate her to the point of being almost physically sick? Her night was ruined. She hurried from the ballroom praying that no one had noticed her discomfort.

Chapter 6

Lonesome for home

Sally watched as the tears rolled down her grandmother's face. 'Its okay now Gran don't go getting yourself all upset. He's gone now and you won't have to meet him again,' she tried to console her.

'Oh if only that was so Sally a gra,' she said.

Sally felt she had made great headway today but she had to be careful not to wear out her grandmothers' strength. She loved to see her so happy reliving her life again, quite unaware of her surroundings. She hated to see her cry. 'Poor Gran,' she thought. 'I hope there weren't too many sad times in her life.' Of course it had to be a very traumatic time for Granny and Grandad when mother and father died, Sally thought. Strange how she couldn't remember any of it herself!

She got up and stretched herself. She could do with a cup of coffee. She had been sitting so still she had become stiff. She looked at her watch. She had another hour before having to return home. She was so afraid of Grans mind taking off on some tangent of its own and it might be days again before she recognised her. She took out a handkerchief and mopped her tears.

'You're grand again now Gran,' she said. 'We don't want you upsetting yourself.'

Just then a nursing sister came by on her rounds. 'Well, how are we now?' she asked. 'Has our Catherine arrived in America yet? I heard she was out in the lawn this morning on her way to Philadelphia.'

'What is she saying Sally? Who is she anyway and who asked her into my house. Tell her to be off home and stop poking around and going through my things,' said Catherine. 'Tell her I'll call the guards on her.'

The sister laughed as she headed off down the corridor. Sally decided it was time to give her Gran a little drop of the brandy she brought with her today. It might relax her, as she seemed to be getting rather agitated. Ian had bought it in town for Sally's next visit. He probably felt a bit guilty at not being able to get time off work to join her.

'Gran, tell me about meeting your Aunt Anne and cousin May when you arrived in Philadelphia,' Sally ventured again.

She started to smile. It was good to see her relaxed again. She seemed to have recovered from her agitation with the bold Maurice Fitzgerald, Sally thought.

'Oh, Sally it was lovely meeting them for the first time. Aunt Anne's husband Richard was waiting for me when the ship docked and he looked after my luggage and drove me to his home in a beautiful motor car,' said Catherine.

The windows of the McGlynn house were ablaze with lights welcoming her arrival. The front door opened and Aunt Anne came down the steps of their large very old-fashioned house to meet them. Dressed in a 'shower of hail' navy and white dress, her hair piled high, almost fully grey now. Catherine recognised her from photographs, even though her hair was different. The warm welcome was just as she had expected. She seemed to have all the characteristics of her own mother. A bubbly May was excitedly waiting for her mother to release Catherine. She too hugged her passionately and they both agreed that Catherine had blossomed into a beauty since the last photograph they had seen of her.

'Oh, this is so exciting,' May was saying. 'How was your trip and do tell us did you meet anyone nice? Did you go dancing in the ballroom? Oh I can't wait for you to tell me all about it. Is it just like they say it is? Did you get to meet the Captain? Did you by any chance meet my darling Reece?'

'May, May please' her mother said, 'Poor Catherine must be tired and hungry. Come inside dear, there will be plenty of time to tell us all. I'm looking forward to hearing all the news from home.'

'Oh, Catherine I can't wait for you to meet Reece. He's such a darling. And the wedding is only a month away. Its six weeks since I've seen him. He had to go home to Ireland as his father was very ill and he died while he was there. It's such a coincidence him coming over on the same ship as you. We told him to look out for you, but I guess it's a big ship.' May couldn't stop babbling on.

'Anyway you'll get to meet him tomorrow evening. We're having a dinner party to show you off. His brother was to travel over with him too. Wouldn't it be swell if you and his brother were to hit it off Catherine? I can't wait to show you my wedding dress. Mummy made it and I helped her sew on the dainty little buttons.'

A train of thought was developing in Catherine's mind. She was feeling a little heady. She couldn't take it all in now but she was beginning to weave several things together, and something was not feeling quite right. She asked Aunt Anne if she could lie down for a little while.

'I'm sorry,' she said, 'it must be because I was so long on the ship. I still feel quite giddy.'

She was shown to a beautifully furnished lilac and cream room. Apart from its inviting warmth, she remembered very little else. She couldn't wait to put her head on the pillow and just shut out all the thoughts circling around in her head.

She must have slept a good while because when she woke she felt so much better. She got up and washed and changed into the first things she could lay her hands on. She wasn't going to unpack tonight in this house. Tomorrow she was to meet her new employers and she understood from her Aunt the job had live-in accommodation. She was to be employed as a chambermaid in a large house with an array of servants. She was a little apprehensive at the thoughts of meeting her new employer.

She unpacked the gifts sent over by her parents. Her father sent a St. Bridget's cross, which he weaved himself. There were hand-made crochet lace bed jackets for Aunt Anne and May and a lace tablecloth as a wedding present, both made by her mother.

Four hours had passed since Catherine had climbed the long staircase. Now as she made her way down, the silver moon shed light on the pictures hanging on the walls. There were a lot of portraits. Tomorrow she must look at them properly and get Aunt Anne to tell her all about her relations in America. Suddenly she felt quite nervous. What if she didn't like living here? What if she didn't get along with the people who would be working with her? And what if they didn't take to her! It all seemed so exciting when she was at home, but now it was all very daunting.

As she sat on the stairs trying to make sense of why she was feeling so apprehensive, a delicious smell of cooking wafted up the stairs reaching her nostrils, and all of a sudden she realised a lot of her feelings were born of sheer hunger. She couldn't quite fathom out when she last had a meal. Slowly, she made her way down the stairs and could see the dining room just ahead. She paused outside the door. The scene was one of great happiness. May and her Dad were laughing at some joke and Aunt Anne was talking to a couple. The man was identical to Richard and she was to discover later he was in fact his twin brother Joseph, who was accompanied by his wife Ethel.

Seeing the closeness of the family scene in such luxurious surroundings brought a lump to Catherine's throat. She closed her eyes and conjured up a scene so different from the sight in front of her. A modest whitewashed thatched cottage, an open-hearth turf fire, a dresser with rows of willow pattern plates and red half door. The half door had many uses. It allowed daylight and fresh air to enter, as well as providing a suitable armrest whilst contemplating or chatting to passers-by. Its main use was to keep the children in and at the same time keep unwelcome animals out. Her father often said, 'a man standing at an open door was wasting time but a man leaning on a half-door would be passing time.'

She could picture her mother now, sitting by the fire darning her father's socks. He would be sitting opposite her in his wicker chair, so exhausted from his days work. Sleep would overcome him with his pipe still hanging from the side of his mouth. Catherine sighed. The only stairs at home were the steps leading up to the loft where they stored the grain for the winter.

The sound of her sighing must have carried downstairs, for they all turned towards her at the same time and gestured her to come in. 'We were going to let you sleep on dear for we thought it would do you good,' Aunt Anne greeted her. 'But we are so pleased you feel up to joining us. Dinner is almost ready. I hope you are hungry.'

'Oh I'm ravenous now and I feel much better after the nap. I don't know what came over me,' Catherine answered.

After introductions were made, Catherine produced her gifts from home. Richard and his brother were very interested in all the news from Ireland. They asked Catherine if there were still 'Knights of the Road' back home. Catherine laughed. 'That's a very fancy name for tramps,' she said. Yes they were still a common sight, she assured them. No house was too remote for them to pay a visit. Some of these tramps came on a regular basis, maybe once or twice a year, and everyone knew them by name. People never asked them where they came from or how they came to be penniless wanderers. They were accepted as they were. If a tramp was lucky enough to enter a house when the dinner was about to be served, an extra seat was provided at the table. They never asked a farmer for clothes or shoes. They knew his clothes were threadbare and patched and not worth anything. They got them instead, half worn from the towns or professional people. If one arrived late on a summer or autumn evening he was likely to ask for permission to be allowed to sleep in the barn or granary. Such a request would not be refused.

Catherine remembered one winter night when a tramp arrived in the middle of a storm and father brought in large armfuls of straw with which to make a 'shake down' at the end of the kitchen. If it were summer or autumn he would have slept in the granary, where it is likely he would have been much happier. Early next morning after breakfast, he would move on, and where he would stay that night nobody knew or cared. In fairness to those people they did not ask for lodgings from the same householder again for many years, if ever. They were never known to steal anything or do any kind of damage.

Richard and his brother found Catherine's descriptions of happenings at home quite hilarious. They were born in America and had never been to Ireland although their parents originally came from Donegal. At first Catherine was embarrassed by their laughter, but they assured her on noticing her discomfort, that she was the most refreshing person they had ever met and it was a pure delight talking to her and envied her natural ways. Her description of tales from home made it very easy for them to imagine the scenes. They were never fully convinced of stories overheard. They told her they were so looking forward to showing her off at May's wedding and were worried she would steal the show on the bride! May, was enjoying listening to her cousin, but still scolded the men folk, threatening if they didn't stop she wouldn't come to her own wedding!

Catherine felt she belonged here with these lovely people and felt a warm glow. Of course the glow could have come with the help of a glass of sherry! She wasn't used to drinking at home but this felt right here this evening. They all encouraged her and said it was a celebration of her arrival and to the future. Catherine was willing and toasted 'Slainte.' It might be the effects of the sherry that put her at ease, as she found herself obliging them with her usual rendition of *Danny Boy.* Aunt Anne and May joined in now and again but nobody could sing it like Catherine.

Before retiring for the night Richard McGlynn put an arm around her shoulder and said, 'Catherine you are a breath of fresh air.' She blushed profusely, but May assured her it was a compliment and to accept it gracefully. 'This will not be the last time you will hear it either,' Aunt Anne added. No matter what the future held for her, Catherine felt she would always remember her first evening in Philadelphia.

She slept like a log and when she woke it was almost mid-day. She showered and dressed. She pulled her hair back into a bun and just wore a hint of lipstick. Aunt Anne was in the kitchen preparing lunch. Catherine apologised for sleeping so late and hoped it didn't upset anyone's plans.

'Of course not my dear,' she answered. 'We would have let you sleep for the day if you wished. Travelling can take it out of you and it will probably be days before you get back to yourself. I hope you will be okay with us having a little dinner party tonight. May is so anxious for you to meet Reece and he is bringing his brother along for us to meet. I think she is secretly hoping you two will hit it off! But take no notice of her. She is such a romantic and just wants everyone to be as happy as she is,' she said.

'When will I meet my employer Aunt Anne? Catherine asked. 'Will I start work straight away and will I be living in their house?

'Oh yes dear, I was talking to Betsy this morning, and she said to keep you here today to completely recover from your journey. She will be quite happy to wait for you for another day. I was able to convince her you are worth waiting for.' As usual, compliments made Catherine blush.

'You can always come and stay with us whenever you wish. It's only a street away. The Park is not far away either. Whenever you have time off it's truly a beautiful place to go for recreation. I do hope you will be very happy here,' she said.

'What should I wear tonight for your dinner party? I have a lovely long midnight blue dress. Aunt Kitty helped me make it before I came over,' Catherine said.

'I expect that would be suitable, how is Kitty anyway and is she as gifted as ever with her sewing? Anne asked.

'She's great, but you know Aunt Anne I'm a dab hand myself with a needle and thread,' she said proudly.

'I don't doubt it for a minute. It's in your blood. We Brennans were all very good at craft. I'm afraid poor May must have taken the McGlynn side. She has no interest in anything like that. She helped a little making her wedding dress, and I mean a little! We must take your measurements Catherine, as I have to make your bridesmaid dress as soon as possible. I hope you are looking forward to the wedding,' she said.

'I suppose I am but I don't really know what to expect. I'll give you a hand with making my dress whenever you are doing it. What colour will it be?'

'May has chosen peach for the colour scheme, so the material is a lovely silk peach. I'll show it to you after lunch,' she said.

They spent the afternoon talking about home and Aunt Anne telling her all about America. May and her father had gone to work very early this morning. She worked for her dads Company in the accounts department. She was responsible for all the staffs' wages. This is where she met her fiancé eighteen months ago. They have been courting only six months, Aunt Anne informed her. Catherine was dying to ask more about him but decided to wait until this evening to see if her suspicions were correct. She prayed she would be wrong.

Aunt Anne suggested they take a stroll down to Fairmount Park. The sunshine would do them both good and at least Catherine would know how to get there when she had time off work. When they returned it would be time to prepare for dinner and May and Richard would be home.

It all seemed perfect but Catherine couldn't help feeling a pang of homesickness when she thought of her parents and sisters and brother. Aunt Anne was very understanding and comforted her, reminding her when her sister Mary comes over, it will all be different. Catherine couldn't wait to get working. She intended to save every penny to send for Mary as quickly as possible. Perhaps then she wouldn't feel so lonely for home.

Chapter 7

A Cruel Twist of Fate

Maurice Fitzgerald was leaning lazily against the opposite wall when Catherine walked into the dining room. Despite the fact her intuition had prepared her for the sight of this arrogant, insufferable, lean body enclosed in an immaculate dinner suit, she still got a shock. To discover she had been right in her calculations held no joy. His brother James was sitting in a chair by the window. Richard was talking to both men and when she entered he got up to make introductions. James smiled at her and she walked over to him and gave him a companionable hug.

'This is a small world, Catherine,' he laughed.

'Isn't it now, it's so good to see you again,' she smiled.

'Do you two know each other already?' asked Richard.

'We met on board the *'Carmania.'* We had many a good old sing song below deck, didn't we Catherine?' said James

Maurice looked twitchy and self-conscious. Catherine noticed the man seemed to have gone into some sort of a frozen limbo. There was no time to make any comments. The next instant May rushed in hurling herself into his arms and hugged and kissed him.

'Oh Reece I have missed you so much. Did you miss me darling?' she wailed.

He didn't seem to be able to speak at first, but it didn't take long to recover his composure.

'Of course I missed you May,' he replied looking into her eyes.

May suddenly remembered her manners and asked to be introduced to her future brother-in-law. She winked at Catherine discretely and whispered, 'He seems to be a swell guy, bet he'll want to date you.'

'Dinner is ready,' calls out Aunt Anne. 'I hope everyone is ravenous,' she added.

Now Catherine could look at this fiancé of Mays properly. She couldn't deny he was aggressively handsome and at least six foot tall. His eyes and hair were jet black. He bore no resemblance whatsoever to his brother James. There was no sign of softness in him at all. Stiff and untouchable—he could have been chiselled from stone. His eyes took in Catherine's appearance and somehow she felt he was undressing her with his glance. She was wondering how she came to dislike this man so much! From the moment he had caught her watching him she tried to avoid any further eye contact. She knew without looking that his dark eyes were levelled in her direction. Why in the world does May want to marry this man, she wondered. She seemed totally besotted by him. As Catherine nibbled at her own fruit cocktail she kept her eyes firmly fixed downwards. She wasn't too impressed with May's open affections for all to see. Nobody ever behaved like that at home!

The meal was wonderful and as one course followed another. Catherine realised her Aunt Anne was a great cook with a little help from Annette her housekeeper. She couldn't help wondering what it was going to be like in her employer's household. She had been told they were very wealthy people with huge interests in the shipping industry. But none of that need concern her. Her work would be co-operating with the other servants and seeing to the smooth running of the house.

She was anxious now to get started in her new job and was happy to know that tomorrow she would be introduced to the family. She was hoping she could soon escape to her room, but with the slow leisurely style of the meal and the chitchat around her, she realised she had to stay and be polite. After Annette brought in coffee, they all sat around discussing the day's events. James sat with Catherine. As they now knew each other they could talk about the forthcoming wedding. He was being the best man and she the bridesmaid!

'It was great we had that dance together on the ship. At least now we wont make a pigs foot of it with everyone watching us,' Catherine laughed. He told her he was going to work for May's father in their car manufacturing business. His brother Maurice was already working for them for the past two years. This is how he had met May. Catherine wished him good luck in his new job and hoped he would end up owning his own car one day, and she would expect to be the very first person he would take for a ride in it! They laughed totally at ease with each other.

Maurice positioned himself so he could see Catherine. Since his meeting her on the ship he couldn't get her out of his mind. It was a cruel twist of fate to meet up with her again in such circumstances. It wasn't that he didn't want to meet her again! He couldn't think of anything he wanted more. He watched as she laughed and chatted easily with James, yet she could barely be civil to him.

Maurice knew, and not for the first time that he was jealous of his brother. He knew he wasn't very good with people. But that wasn't his fault! His father was a school Principal and insisted Maurice attended the school he was teaching in. He had to go to school each morning and return home in the evening in his father's car. He envied the other pupils walking home in groups having fun. He knew the other pupils resented him and would never mix or allow him to play their games. The girls didn't want him either in their games. He always felt at odds with everyone. School was a very unhappy place for him. He never felt close to his brother or sister. When James started school he was allowed to attend the local school. He had all the village lads as pals and got on well with everyone. James was never resented because he was the teacher's son! Why couldn't he have been treated like that? He hated his father and he was glad he was dead. The only person he had real feelings for was his mother. But he didn't want to think of her right now. He had other ideas in his head. He would have to conjure up some way of getting an opportunity to be alone with May's lovely Irish cousin.

By nine thirty Catherine had enough. She rose to her feet. 'If you will all excuse me, I feel very sleepy. I really will have to be carried up those lovely stairs if I stay another minute. Thank you for a lovely meal Aunt Anne,' she said kissing her goodnight. With reassurances from everyone that they understood how exhausted she must be, she left the room. She was well aware of the cool scrutiny of the awful Maurice watching her across the room, but she ignored him. She knew they had got off on the wrong foot from their very first encounter, but as he was to become May's husband in less than a month, she would have to at least appear to be polite, but her intentions were to avoid his company at much as possible.

She had left the balcony windows open whilst she went down to dinner. She wandered over to the lace-curtained windows and sighed. Tomorrow I will leave here and start a new life, in a new job in a new home. It was a beautiful night and her mind wandered back to a little cottage in Owenboy and wondered if her family were missing her. She knew she was feeling the great loss of them. When Mary joins her, things will be better she told herself. I hope father is feeling well again. He wasn't himself lately. It was probably the long winter. I must write a letter when I have news of my new job.

She shook herself out of her revere as she heard voices below her balcony window, and realised it was May and Reece sitting in the seat beside the rose bed. May as usual was throwing her arms around him, and from where Catherine was standing it didn't look like Maurice was putting in much effort!

What in heaven's name did May see in him? They say love is blind. She hoped when she met her future husband, her heart would not rule her head! She decided to put that thought firmly at the back of her mind for the time being and got herself ready for bed.

When Catherine awoke to the sunlight streaming into her room through the balcony windows, she realised she had forgotten to close the drapes last night. Still she felt she had a great night's sleep. She was ready for anything today! She showered and dressed in blue cotton dress and a cardigan of the same colour and put her hair away in a bun. The only make-up she used was a pink lipstick. She felt it would be more suitable for the meeting with her new employer.

Aunt Anne greeted her cheerily and complimented her on her choice of dress. She assured her Mr and Mrs Michelson were very good friends of hers for years and knew she would be very well treated in their home. She was also happy recommending Catherine to them. They would love her. There was no need at all to be nervous!

After breakfast was over, they set off for the Michelson's house. While Catherine was very impressed with the beautiful home her Aunt Anne had, nothing could prepare her for what stood in front of her now. At her gasp, Aunt Anne laughed. 'Now you can see why so many servants are needed,' she said. As they made their way up the countless number of steps Catherine was aware of the scent of freesias and jasmine that was growing all around the door. The lawns were like a green carpet and she noticed a tennis court to the right of the house. Catherine felt butterflies in her stomach at the prospect of working for such rich people.

They were shown into a large room, which she later learned was the drawing room. When Betty Michelson walked into the room and greeted Aunt Anne with a hug, Catherine felt she was among friends and relaxed immediately. After Aunt Anne introduced them she said her goodbyes. She informed them Catherine's possessions would be brought around that evening.

Mrs Michelson said it was time to show her around the house. The staircase was so big and grand. Surely it would take ages to sweep and dust and polish it, Catherine thought. As if she could read her thoughts Mrs Michelson said it would not be her job to have to clean the stairs. She need not concern herself with the drawing room, library or the dining room. There were two housemaids, a housekeeper, a parlour maid, a cook and a kitchen maid. Her position here would be a chambermaid. That meant keeping all the bedrooms in order every day.

They entertained quite a lot and often guests stayed over, so it would mean changing bed clothing a lot. She would live-in, and have her meals with the other servants downstairs. She would be paid monthly and would have one day and two half days off in the week. Her evenings were her own to do as she wished, but the family would prefer if she told them where she was going, at least till she got her bearings. They felt responsible for her of course, her being so far away from home.

There were a few rules when working in service, Mrs Michelson told her. She would refer to her husband as Sir and herself Madam. She was to always speak slowly and quietly, never to shriek or laugh loudly, and to always hold your shoulders straight and head held high. She was to come to them if ever she needed to discuss anything or felt troubled. Catherine asked when would she start working and was told to be ready to commence in the morning.

She was shown her own bedroom situated at the back of the house and from there she could see a large swimming pool. Her room was beautifully decorated in cool pinks and pastel blues and lilacs. It resembled a bunch of sweet peas. There was a small balcony outside her window and as Catherine drew back the curtains, the heat hit her, reminding her she was in America now. She would have to get used to such heat.

She sat down for a few minutes taking in all around her. She couldn't help noticing the masses of white flowers and ivy winding over the wrought iron balcony, and the big tubs of red geraniums sitting around on a tiled veranda. These people are so wealthy, she thought. And I am so lucky to have got a job here. And tomorrow I will show them how much I appreciate it.

She decided she would write home this afternoon telling them all about this magnificent house she was going to work in. At least now she could describe it in detail and her mother would sit and picture it and boast about her to the neighbours. She would be so happy. Catherine reminisced, and could see them doing the ploughing now in the far field. She wouldn't miss the awful chore of helping to sow the potatoes! She hated that job in particular. She didn't mind working in the bog with the turf. She even enjoyed haymaking but setting the potatoes was a back-breaker, as well as ruining your finger nails with the cow manure that father would have spread in the drills.

She looked around her now and couldn't help feeling how different life was going to be here and once again felt a lump in her throat.

Chapter 8

An American Wedding

Catherine took to her new job like a duck to water. She got on well with the other members of staff and Mr. Michelson was such a pleasant gentleman. She hadn't heard from home yet although she had written three times. Aunt Anne and May were busy with the wedding preparations. They were having a marquee in their lawn for the reception and the gardener was very busy indeed.

Her bridesmaids dress was already hanging up having been made by Anne. Catherine had intended to help her but on her evenings off she found she was only in the way. May was occupied with invitation lists and menus and flower arrangements and last minute details. Even though the two cousins were very close and hit it off from their first meeting, there was an area in their relationship in which they were not totally honest with each other.

Having found Maurice quite repulsive on her first encounter with him, Catherine couldn't warm to him even though she knew he was to become family. May sensed it from the first evening they were introduced. Consequently, she was always guarded in most things concerning him when Catherine was around. And it didn't help either when Catherine asked her one night while they were chatting together, 'do you think Maurice is the right man for you?'

She avoided him like the plague and would make any excuse to May whenever it was suggested they make a foursome, with James as her partner. It could have been less of a problem if the wretched Maurice did not display so openly to Catherine that he fancied her, even though he was about to be married to her cousin. She held a private opinion that Maurice Fitzgerald would have no qualms about having a relationship with her, even while married to May! She hoped she was wrong, but there was nobody she could turn to, not even James. It was best she kept this to herself. She wished she never set eyes on him on that ship.

Her suspicions were confirmed the evening before the wedding. She called over to visit after her days work. She was also anxious to know if Aunt Anne had heard from home. But she assured her there was no mail for her. Feeling a little restless and also feeling uncomfortable because the arrogant Maurice arrived soon after her, she decided to get out into the sunshine and go to Fairmount Park and feed the ducks and be by herself.

Putting a jacket on over her shoulders she stepped out of the house without telling anyone. She'd have peace and time to think for herself. She was wearing a thin sleeveless lilac coloured dress, which she now hoisted up to her thighs, as she stretched out her long legs to the rays of sun. Letting her head relax over the back of the bench she shut her eyes. Such bliss, she thought as she gave a long sigh of contentment. This was heaven! She considered herself very lucky to be given such an opportunity here in America and must tell her Aunt how grateful she was. Suddenly she became aware of a shadow falling on her. She opened her eyes and as she glanced up she realised whose broad shoulders were blocking out the evening sun.

'Well now, so this is where you hideout,' Maurice said.

'Why are you following me?' Catherine asked

'Well it's the only way I can get to talk to you,' he said.

'I can't imagine what you and I have to talk about,' she answered as politely as she could.

Maurice settled himself on the grass at her feet. She presented a stunning image with her thick mane of chestnut hair shining in the sunshine and her long bare elegant legs. He savoured her like a predator. Catherine was aware of his staring and quickly wrapped her skirts neatly around her ankles. She looked around her and was grateful there were people walking in the park. She didn't feel comfortable at all alone with this man. She felt she would have to make an effort to be polite, at least for May's sake.

'Do you want to discuss something about the wedding with me?' she asked.

'No this is about us. You must know how I feel about you. Surely you have noticed,' and with that he grabbed her by the arms.

The suddenness of his declaration surprised Catherine and for a few moments she was stunned. She tried to pull away from him shaking and weak. She remembered James' remark about being an awful man for the ladies! Oh poor May she thought.

'Let go of my arms Maurice,' she said through clenched teeth. 'If you ever touch me again I will have to tell your fiancé. You pretend to love her but all you love are the possessions of her father.'

He let her go immediately, but she could see he wasn't one bit perturbed. He sauntered off along the path whistling *Dixie,* like he hadn't a care in the world! Catherine sat and watched as he went out of sight. 'What kind of an individual is he al all?' she asked herself. She looked around to see if anyone noticed, but everybody seemed to be minding his or her own business. She sat a while trying to figure out Maurice. He seems the kind of person who would demand everything and give little in return. May is so besotted she would be willing to give in to him! Love must certainly be blind!

It was so close to the wedding she didn't want to upset anyone and indeed who would believe her? It wasn't her place to try and change anything. They all thought the sun shone out of Mr Maurice Fitzgerald! She wasn't looking forward to this wedding day approaching at all. The quicker it comes and goes the better she thought. She would just have to be polite and grin and bear it, but under the polite surface, anger and resentment was festering. When Catherine went to bed that night she was very troubled by her own thoughts.

The wedding day dawned bright and sunny. The church was filling up nicely. The organ music was making its nice background drone. Gathering guests were greeting each other, and introductions were being made. Ladies were adorned with large boaters and brooches as big as sheriff's badges. There were great-uncles buttoned tightly into waistcoats. May's young cousin Peter was on duty at the door of the church giving out booklets for the service. At the front of the church Reverend William Murphy was pottering around the main alter, ensuring that everything was in order, and beamed at the congregation.

Catherine, being bridesmaid, walked into the church ahead of the bride and her father who was giving her away. She looked towards the alter, to where Maurice was waiting. He looked strikingly handsome and James, by his side looked as proud as punch. Aunt Anne was wearing a beige linen coatdress and a hat of the same colour. Maurice's mother wasn't expected of course having so recently buried her husband.

Suddenly the organ burst into 'Here comes the Bride.' There was a rumble as everyone stood up and turned to admire the bride. May looked a vision in a white full-length gown made of taffeta and lace, her veil arranged in puffs at the back of her head. Catherine looked radiant in peach silk.

Without further delay the ceremony began. Maurice mumbled his vows as if he didn't want to share them with anyone, which came as no surprise to Catherine! May said her vows in a clear voice that brought tears to many an eye. She was so besotted by this man she couldn't see further than her nose, Catherine thought.

May would have to find out for herself the kind of man she was married to in her own time. Catherine couldn't wait for this part to be over. After the signing of the register and the photographs were taken they emerged from the church to a hail of rice and confetti, driving back to May's home where the huge marquee had been erected in the lawn and the caterers were awaiting their arrival.

It was a beautiful day, magical, as most of the guests commented. The party went on with the small band playing and the champagne still flowing, into the early hours of the morning. No one seemed to want to go home. Catherine would have enjoyed it, if only she did not have such nagging doubts about the groom. Time would tell I suppose.

Her thoughts were interrupted as she suddenly noticed all the guests were rushing towards the driveway, where the going away car was waiting; all decorated with the usual 'Just Married' paraphernalia. May had changed into a pretty floral dress. She looked so happy and excited. Aunt Anne and Richard were hugging their daughter. Maurice sat behind the steering wheel looking the real *toff* in sunglasses. A basket of rose petals was being passed around and some guests had boxes of confetti. May suddenly turned her back on the waiting crowd, holding something high in the air. Of course, her wedding bouquet! There was a murmur from the crowd. Catherine turned away for she had no intention of catching it. It was all just a bit of fun of course, but she had other plans for the next few years at any rate.

'What's your reason for wanting to stay an old maid?' she heard a familiar voice beside her. It was James.

'I've no wish to remain an old maid. On the contrary, I'm looking forward to meeting a man I can love and have a family with. But for now, I want to make enough money to have a good dowry when I do marry. I'll be independent James. I will make my own decisions and will not be expected to toe the line for any man.

'Very strong stuff Catherine,' James replied, 'looks like the head will rule the heart.'

She didn't want to discuss this anymore and told James she was very tired. He said goodnight and she complimented him on doing a great job as best man. He even looked as if he was enjoying himself. What a different person from the sad dejected looking young man on their first evening on board the *Carmania*. Thank God she managed to avoid Maurice all day, she thought, as she made her way upstairs.

The tiredness had really descended on Catherine now. She had enough and couldn't wait for her head to hit the pillow. Mrs Michelson had given her the day off after the wedding to be with Aunt Anne who would be missing May. She was also going to help with tidying up. She was so looking forward to working with all the beautiful china and cutlery. She had never seen the likes at home. Not even when the priest came to say Mass in the house! Nobody could afford such luxury. Oh what a rich country this is, she was thinking. Once more thoughts of home stirred sadness in her. She hoped there would be a letter soon.

Chapter 9

A Letter Edged in Black

Aunt Anne seemed to be preoccupied. From the minute Catherine came down to breakfast, she seemed to be avoiding her. She did not think it was her imagination and it troubled her. Did I do something wrong yesterday? she pondered. Of course she would be missing May and is bound to be feeling very tired, but her Aunt was always so generous with her affection, it seemed odd to Catherine. Maybe she would prefer to be alone she thought to herself. I was so looking forward to having her to myself to day. With all the preparations for the wedding going on we had very little time lately to have a proper talk, she thought.

'Aunt Anne, are you okay with having me here today? Catherine asked. 'Perhaps you want to be on your own.'

'Come and sit down dear, I need to talk to you,' Anne replied sombrely.

Catherine felt a sense of uneasiness as Anne took both her hands in her own. She could see there was something troubling her Aunt.

'I don't know how to tell you this Catherine. You've been asking me if I heard from home. Well I have dear.

I got a letter from your mother before the wedding. I didn't tell you about it because I didn't want you upsetting yourself. I'm afraid I have bad news for you. Your father died six weeks ago. In fact he died while you were on board the ship coming here. He got pneumonia and it was too late to do anything for him. Your mother didn't want you to know till you settled in here so she didn't write about it straight away. No good would come of it. I took it upon myself not to tell you till the wedding was over. Your mother has a letter in with mine. Let me get it for you dear.'

Catherine was struck dumb. She had never contemplated this day would come! She knew her father was not feeling so good before she left home. He did not have much energy lately, but thought he was just run down. Poor father was not one to make a fuss and he was never a day sick in his life. It was so unfortunate this happened just after she left. Poor mother would be feeling sad enough at my leaving home.

Aunt Anne returned and handed her the letter from her mother. It was just as Anne had said. Pneumonia—nothing could be done. He hardly suffered and was well cared for and died peacefully. She hoped she wouldn't be too sad. Write home soon Catherine, she wrote.

Catherine almost devoured the letter. Her first time receiving a letter from home and the news was unbearable! They used to say at home 'God is good' no matter what happened or how cruel the blow. Well Catherine was not at home right now and she was not convinced that her God was good to her! She felt as if her heart would break. She decided to write a letter straight away. It would comfort her and she would feel close to all of them at home while she was writing. They would be expecting to hear from her too. She felt a little better after Aunt Anne brought a cup of hot sweet tea. 'Good for the shock you know, dear.'

They clung together and had a good cry, but after a while they both agreed that work was a good cure for feeling down and so they proceed to tackle the mess left after the wedding. Thank God Aunt Anne had the good sense not to tell me this till all was over, Catherine was thinking as she went about her chores.

She now became more obsessed about saving enough money to send for her sister Mary. As the months passed she was feeling confident she would soon have enough saved, so she wrote to Mary and told her to be making her plans for sailing with the Cunard Line. Mary was also very good at dressmaking and had gone to work in the milliners shop when Catherine left for America. She was very fond of minding children too so Catherine was on the lookout for suitable work for her. She had become friendly with a girl from Kilkelly whom she met by accident in the American Store. Catherine had been overcharged when making a purchase and when she drew attention to it she was ushered into an office where she met Katie McGreal who was a book-keeper there. They took an instant liking to each other and arranged to meet for a chat the following day in Fairmount Park.

Katie had two brothers Mick and Andy in Philadelphia. They had friends from Ballyhaunis who were great fun to be with. They tried to cheer her up when she told them she was feeling down over the death of her father.

She felt she was doing very well after the initial shock, but she experienced a further setback when she got the details of his death from home. He had been working in the field all day, preparing for setting the oats. He had completed his work and had to carry the harrow home across *the black hill.* He had not been feeling very well that morning, so when he did not arrive home by sunset, James, Catherine's brother, was sent out to look for him. He returned after an hour saying it was like a black hole out there! As darkness approached a mist would always descend over that hill. Neighbours eventually found him in the early morning light. He had fallen over and the harrow was on top of him. He had contracted pneumonia and nothing could be done for him.

Catherine was inconsolable when she heard the way he died. It was the darkest time of her life. She felt so lonesome and it took all her strength not to give in and return home. She considered using the money saved for Mary's passage over on a return ticket for herself, but she feared the poverty at home more, so she pulled herself out of the depths of loneliness with this sobering thought.

Aunt Anne and Richard were very comforting and to try and cheer her up they arranged a night out at the Drury Lane Theatre where John McCormack was topping the bill. They told her to bring her friend Katie along too. She pretended to enjoy herself but with songs like *The Wearing of the Green, I Hear You Calling Me, Annie Laurie* and *That Old Irish Mother of Mine* only served to make Catherine even sadder. As her Aunt and Richard made such an effort to arrange this outing she did not want to appear ungrateful. She was so glad Katie came too as she would brighten up the darkest day. She kept up a stream of chat about happenings at home. She told them about this bachelor fellow who cooked a feed of fish for himself on Good Friday, and sat down with a bottle of whiskey and cigarettes. During the night his brother heard him groaning and went out and woke up half the village, telling them his brother was dying. The ambulance was called but could not find the house and the neighbours had to go out with torches to the main road to show them the way. Everyone thought he would not last the night, but the next day when a relative called to see him in hospital, he was sitting up eating a big plate of scrambled eggs. It was stories such as this that helped keep Catherine's spirits up.

Katie was writing letters to a young man at home named Tommy Johnson. She too had planned to stay only long enough to make some money. He had written a letter recently asking her advice on purchasing a business in Ballyhaunis. It was coming on the market soon. Of course her advice was to go for it! Little did she know then but it would eventually become her home.

Catherine enjoyed her work, and in her spare time looked out for suitable work for Mary when she arrived. She often went to the movies with James. She always enjoyed his company and also felt the feeling was mutual. He made no demands on her and he told her he was now courting a girl from Donegal. Nothing heavy he would add jokingly. Not that he had to account to Catherine for his actions. They talked about their jobs and all in all he seemed fairly happy with his lot. He had lost the terrible sadness she noticed on their first meeting on the ship. There was a man-of-the-world look about him now. American life seemed to suit him and Catherine wondered if he had stayed at home after the tragedy, what would have become of him?

She felt it would serve no purpose at all to mention her great dislike of his brother. He never mentioned him either, which suited her. Now that May was no longer living with her mother, Catherine very seldom met him. She watched her change from a bright and sparkling bubbly creature, to a shadow of the person she first met when she arrived in Philadelphia. She had become quiet and somewhat cautious, with no mind of her own.

While she enjoyed the way of life in Philadelphia, Catherine always felt a terrible ache for home. Some days when she had an hour off, she would sit on the veranda outside her bedroom window in the Michelson's big house, and close her eyes and imagine she could smell the primroses growing wild along the hedges. She could see the white flowers in bloom on the hawthorn hedges, attracting the bees and insects, and the birds using it for nesting. She could almost hear the chorus of birdsong and see the arrival of butterflies. Her mother used to tell her to chase away the white ones, as they used to eat her cabbages!

Catherine loved chasing the red admiral butterfly and would try to gently catch one so that the colours of their wings would remain on the palms of her hands. She could almost hear the bleat of the lambs and picture their frolic as they played in the fields. The red sun setting in the West in the evening told us tomorrow would be a nice day. She could hear her father quoting 'A red sky at nigh is a farmer's delight, a red sky in the morning is a shepherd's warning.' Now she will never hear his voice again.

Their humble home in Owenboy was neither better nor worse than any other country thatched cottage in Ireland. The usual whitewashed walls surrounded the *Ramblers Rest.* It was the pilgrims making their way to Knock Shrine that affectionately called it that name. It was a welcome sight as you rounded the bend. You noticed two windows, placed high in the walls, directly under the thatch resembling two twinkling eyes, beckoning you to come inside.

Should you by chance arrive at this humble abode on a winter's night, the smell of pig's *crubeens* and cabbage, and the aroma of apple cake would arrest you. It might be the smell of treacle bread mingled with the fresh milk coming from the cow's teats, for it could be milking time. Or on another day if the wind was blowing from the North, it would bring with it the smell of the manure heap outside the back door!

The moon is full and there is a fox barking in the distance across the bog. The cows give a low contented moo, as they settle down for the night. The door of the barn closes and father makes his way indoors. He knows he has plenty to do yet tonight. 'Come on now everyone and kneel down and we will say the Rosary,' he could be heard saying as he made his way inside.

'Thou oh Lord wilt open my lips and my tongue shall announce thy praise.
Incline unto my aid of God. O Lord make haste to help me.
Glory be to the Father and to the Son and to the Holy Ghost'

The sheepdog rounds the corner barking furiously needing to inspect an intruder. On hearing the racket, Father gets up from his knees to look out the half-door. 'Goodnight to you whoever you are,' he calls out. 'Come on in we are just saying the Rosary. Kneel down there and say a decade with us.'

The atmosphere inside the cottage was a sight to behold. The turf fire was burning brightly and the kettle hung from the black shiny crane, simmering away ever ready with boiling water. A small child is peeping out from the *cailleach* bed, while another one is nursing a small bird with a splinter on its leg. A newborn lamb was asleep in a cardboard box at one side of the blazing fire, while a ginger cat sat washing his face the opposite side. A half pig hung up on one of the rafters beside a large piece of Ling fish. A horse's harness was lying on the floor looking like someone was in the middle of polishing it for going to Mass in the trap on Sunday. A bunch of sally rods stood against the wall ready to point for thatching. The *settle-bed* was in the corner and two children were kneeling down in front of it making shapes with their hands from the shadow of the oil lamp. They were passing the time till it was their turn to say a decade of the Rosary. In the middle of the prayers mother got up to look at the treacle cake in the cast oven by the fire, in case it was burning. She would need it later on tonight as they had promised a card game for the pig's head.

This was customary when a pig was slaughtered. People came from miles around to one of these games, and whoever won the prize was expected to host another game in their house the following week. Consequently, the pig's head went around the village for weeks until it smelled so fowl, it had to be buried. While the men were playing cards, Catherine would help her mother make the tea and cut up the treacle cake for them, for they sure had a healthy appetite and a filthy tongue when it came to playing cards. She loved to watch from behind their backs trying to pick up the skills, and would peep into several players' hands at the same time. Many a fright she got when one of them would give an almighty thump on the table with his fist and roar, 'the devil scald you.' It was all very innocent and no harm intended.

Lost in her reverie Catherine hadn't realised how quickly the time had gone and she jumped up as she looked at her watch. 'Glory be! I should be back at my work ages ago,' she told herself. 'I must have fallen asleep!

She felt good and alive and refreshed. She felt like she had just been home to Ireland for a visit and it felt great!

'Did I dream all that?' she asked herself. Whatever it was she hoped she would be able to do it again soon. At this moment she felt very close to home and to her father.

Chapter 10

A Bee in Sally's Bonnet

"Oh Danny Boy, the pipes the pipes are calling.
From glen to glen and down the mountain side"

Nurse, nurse, Sally. Are you there Sally? I want you to do something. Tell Johnny not be wasting his time chasing that mountainey *cailin.* I know what they get up to! Do you hear me Sally? That family of hers have no breeding! I don't want Johnny getting himself into trouble.'

'Don't worry Gran I'll tell him,' Sally humoured her. 'You have a nice nap now and I'll come again to see you tomorrow.'

Sally knew the time had come to give in for today. She was very happy with today's visit. 'I can't believe my luck, good old Gran.' She kissed Catherine's forehead before she left and was pleased to see she had already fallen asleep.

As she made her way home she knew she was exhausted but could not help feeling quite tremulous. She was getting places at last. She decided she was going to ring Pamela in Australia tonight. She was so excited at hearing so much of Gran's past she wanted to see if her older sister knew anything more. Ian was taking Jack to visit his granny tonight so she would have the house to herself. Of course it will be morning in Australia, so I'd better not ring too early, she told herself.

After she had made a quick sandwich and a cup of tea, she took the two mutts for a walk. Ian had left a note saying he had not got around to taking them for a trot across the green today. She needed the exercise herself anyway and definitely needed to inhale the fresh evening air into her lungs after a day in the nursing home. She was so looking forward to a quiet evening by herself, apart from Lennon and Paddy of course, but once they got their walk and had their dinner, there would not be a boo out of them for the rest of the night.

Sally was getting more excited at the thoughts of making this phone call to Australia. She had known that Pamela and Grans sister Mary had a close relationship. She used to visit her, and sometimes stayed for weeks during summer holidays from school. Pamela would be full of chat when she returned home telling us about Mary's time in Philadelphia.

She told her, after Catherine returned to Ireland, she stayed on to make a bit more money, but eventually she too came home to find a husband. Sally was always fascinated that Mary married her own cousin when she returned from Philadelphia. She did not think you were allowed to marry your cousin but didn't question it!

Matchmaking was rife in Ireland in the 1930's. This is how a girl got herself a husband. Yanks were considered a good catch in those days so the girls could be choosey enough. Sally smiled to herself. You'd think there wasn't a suitable man to be found in America!

Gran had a photo of herself and her sister Mary sitting in a park in Philadelphia in 1929. Standing behind them were two fine handsome men. They were tall and very well dressed in white shirts and ties and well-cut trousers. When Sally enquired about them she would just say they were two policemen they met in the park. They met them by accident one day when Mary was looking after the children. She was Governess to two little girls, Constance and Victoreen. They approached the policemen for help when young Constance had rambled off on them. Their black dog, Dubh was also missing. One blow of the policeman's whistle brought Dubh running back to them and young Constance trotting behind. A romance started through that encounter. But Gran would never elaborate, always putting a stop to any conversation with 'sure I'll tell you when you're older, a gra.' Well now she was old enough but it still wasn't easy to get it out of her! It was tough going!

After Sally gave the dogs their walk she decided to have a long soak in the bath. Lord knows she deserved it! It was a long day and she was tired but she was too excited to sleep yet. She had a bee in her bonnet to talk to her sister and see if she could remember things from the past. It was too soon to ring Australia just yet. Pamela wouldn't be out of bed and she won't be blessing me for waking her. Being a nurse she has unusual working hours, so it hasn't been easy over the years communicating with her. Their brother Rodger never came home again after going to America. Sally felt sure if she met him tomorrow in the street, she wouldn't know him! I suppose with no parents alive he lost interest. He certainly lost interest in Sally anyway, she thought to herself.

As she waited for her bath to fill up, she chatted away to Lennon and Paddy who were following her around everywhere she went. 'You're such good boys but ye will have to go to your baskets now. I'm not sharing my bath with either of you,' she told them, patting each in turn. Oh she did love those dogs!

She could not imagine the house without them now. Unless you were an animal lover you could not understand how people treated their pets as if they were humans. She grew up with all sorts of animals on the farm. Gran was always rearing little ducks and geese, baby chicks and little turkeys.

Soaking herself in the warm sudsy water she started reminiscing! Gran would tell her to go to the barn and take the hen off her nest and see if any of the eggs were chipped. If they were, it was a sign the little chicks were pecking from inside trying to come out. You could then help them along, by cracking the egg ever so carefully so they could wiggle out by themselves. It was such an exciting thing to watch. Very similar to watching a baby being born, Sally now thought to herself!

One very special time she remembered, a sheep had died leaving two baby lambs. They demanded to be fed each morning, so Sally looked forward to the job of feeding them a bottle of milk before going to school, and again every evening after milking the cows. They became pets and she christened them '*the bears*'. Of course the time came to sell them and no amount of begging made any difference. Grandad could not let them become sheep. They were to be sold as lamb for the table!

Sally felt very near to tears all over again at the thought. She pulled herself together and decided this was no frame of mind to be in when talking to Pamela. Hopefully some snippets of information would prove to be interesting, in case Gran could not remember the important things any more. With this Alzheimers you never could tell when total senility might take over.

She wrapped herself in a pink towelling dressing gown and headed downstairs to make a cup of hot chocolate. Lennon and Paddy were waiting outside the bathroom door for her. She patted them both telling them not to worry, they will not be sold off for meat. There was not much demand for boxer chops or spring leg of black Labrador. She chuckled to herself at the thought and sat down with the phone beside her. She looked at her watch. It would be 7a.m now in Australia. Pamela always said they have a very early start. She used to joke and say 'unlike you sleepy-heads in Ireland we believe in early to bed and early to rise.' Well Pamela my girl I'll be putting you to the test now she smiled as she picked up the phone to dial the number. Here goes, she thought.

Pamela was not sure if she heard the phone ringing. She had just come in from her night shift at the Hospital and was finishing her shower. She ran to her bedroom and sure enough the phone was ringing. She picked up the receiver and was overjoyed at hearing her young sisters' voice.

'Oh Sally, good day. I'm so pleased to hear from you? What's up is everything all right? Is our Gran okay?

'Hi Pam, yes everything is fine. Gran is ok. She eats like a horse but some days she tries to wander off. It's this Alzheimers thing that is the problem. Some days she's in a world of her own and does not know me at all. They have said she may get a lot worse. There's no knowing how soon. But Pamela today she was great. She talked all day about her time in Philadelphia. I have this obsession at the moment. I want to know what happened to our mother and father and how did it come about that she reared us. I want to know Pamela. You must remember the time it happened. Weren't you 12 years old? Gran has always fobbed me off whenever I asked questions.' Sally was getting agitated now.

'Wow Sally, there is a lot going on in that little head of yours! Where did all this come from now? It's a bit early in the morning to be hit with all this stuff! I can tell you some things about her stay in America but don't ask me to talk about our parent's deaths. If Gran hasn't told you herself, then I can't either. You were very young at the time and Gran made me promise not to talk about it. She would tell you herself in her own way and in her own time. Obviously she hasn't got around to it. But I promise you if she doesn't tell you before she dies, then I will tell you everything.

You know I spent a lot of time with Gran's sister Mary after our parents died. She was very good to me. I think Gran wanted me out of the way after the two tragedies. I was twelve at the time and I guess that was a very impressionable age. Poor Gran and Grandad had to take on the full responsibilities of grandchildren, and they were not getting any younger and had reared nine of their own.'

Sally listened. Two tragedies! Pamela rolled the words off her tongue so easily! God almighty she thought, why couldn't someone tell her what she wanted to hear? She had a right to know! She felt exasperated but tried not to show it when talking to Pamela on the telephone.

'She was in great talking form today. She talked a lot about her experiences in Philadelphia but she never said how many years she stayed, or how long Mary stayed after she went home. Do you know how they came to marry men in the West of Ireland in the 1930's when America was so rich and Ireland had nothing going for it? She did say she never meant to stay there. She only went to make her fortune so that she would have a dowry when she married a man with a home of his own. That way she would have a certain amount of independence when she married. Can you believe that Pamela or was that true at all?'

'Indeed it was true Sally. Seems a bit cold-hearted but they grew to love the man they married and stuck with him through thick and thin. Granny Catherine stayed in Philadelphia for six years, but before Mary joined her she had become very friendly with a girl from Kilkelly named Katie McGreal. When Katie went home to see her sick sister she never returned but married a man whom she had been seeing before she left Ireland. Granny became rather restless after that and could not settle. But you must remember too Sally, in those days the age of a girl was very important when it came to marriage. Ideally she should not be more than twenty-five. That was a time in our history when everybody wanted a large family, and if the women were around twenty five when they married, they would have a lot of childbearing years ahead of them, so you see it was a huge plus to be young. Gran probably felt time was against her because she was twenty-eight when she left Philadelphia. Anyway she was a home bird at heart and never intended to live in America. She was homesick a lot while she was there but was determined to save money.

She first saved enough to send for Mary and that took over a year. Mary stayed on when Catherine decided to return home, with high hopes of getting a husband of substance with a house and farm. You know, you can see why she could never live in America. She is by nature such an animal lover, isn't she Sally? Do you remember all the little furry creatures she always had around the farm? No animal or two-legged creature was ever allowed not to produce young! Not to mention babies, nearly one every year!

You know she married Grandad in a very short time after returning home. Now he was not the first man she *inspected*! She was fussy enough and did not take the first one that came along! Just under a year is all it took! Quick work in those days! By golly they didn't hang around, did they? she laughed.

Sally couldn't help laughing. She felt a lot better for having telephoned Pamela but not much wiser! They said their goodbyes. Sally was full of apologies for keeping her out of her bed after her hard nights work on duty, and Pamela for keeping her so long on the telephone—it must be costing a fortune!

Her last bit of advice was to try and get Catherine to tell her all about matchmaking in Ireland and how she came to meet Grandad. That would be a subject dear to her heart. And don't forget to give her a kiss and tons of love. And tell her she would love the wallabies and the kangaroos here in Australia.

Chapter 11

The Eccentric Visitors

Sally could not wait to ask Granny Catherine all about matchmaking. She often heard it mentioned when she was growing up, but had no interest. Snippets of conversation like Mary and Johnny were a match and didn't they turn out all right' or 'look at Kitty and Mike, sure they were a match made in Heaven.' Such a shame I had not tuned in to what they were saying, Sally thought. If only I had listened to all those stories Grandad and Granny and that auld witch Maggie Callaghan used to tell on long winters nights.

Sally closed her eyes and memories came flooding back. Simple, innocent times where people seemed to have all the time in the world! She remembers long winter's nights, after the Rosary was finished, a small little man named Walter coming visiting. He would always walk in the minute the prayers were ended. He came every full moon and never knew when to go home! Grandad used to try every which way to let him know it was getting late and we needed to go to bed. She can still hear him!

'Walter the morning won't be long coming.'

Walter would agree! Grandad would then try a different approach.

'How long now will it take you to get home?'

'About half an hour,' Walter would answer.

Grandad would get up and walk outside and come back in saying.

'It's a grand night out now Walter. The moon is out. You'll have a grand night going home.'

Still no move from Walter!

'How long did you say it would take you to get home?' Grandad would venture once more.

Still no move from Walter!

At this stage everyone was too tired to see the funny side of it and were dying to go to bed. Finally Grandad would start to get undressed right there in front of him. At last the penny dropped!

'I think it's time I was going home now,' says Walter.

When he was gone Grandad would say, 'I thought we'd have to get a Mass said to shift him.'

Sally could vividly remember another visitor called Paddy arriving on a wet Saturday for a haircut. Grandad was quite skilled at cutting men's hair. We would watch in wonder as the locks fell to the ground and wait for the usual 'mind that lump there Eddie' pointing to a giant boil hidden in the hair. The same boil was still there when he arrived for the next haircut! And at the end of the procedure we waited for the proverbial 'be God Eddie there's enough there to make an ass's collar,' Paddy would say as he picked up the shorn locks. And turning around to the fire he would always ask, 'do ye burn hair here?'

This man would also arrive if he ran short of tobacco for his pipe. Grandad smoked a pipe too and would share what he had with Paddy when he came begging. I think the favour was never returned! They would discuss ways of doing without a smoke if they ran short! Grandad might tell Paddy he had no tobacco since last Tuesday!

'Be God Eddie, why didn't you go to bed?' Paddy would say.

Sally often went to the shop for an ounce of *Bendigo*. 'I used to keep repeating it all the way in case I got it wrong! It was only a small chunk of tobacco about two inches long and about one inch wide. It was so small I was scared I would loose it coming back. It always seemed to be so precious. Grandad would make it last half a week. I would watch him tear away at it with his penknife, and pack it into his pipe and then set it alight with a match. Sometimes it did not always work for him and he would have to take some out and try to light it again. It was quite a skill and very interesting to watch.

He would always clean the pipe on a wet day. You would smell the tar like subsidence wafting all over the house. You would need a mask on! Pipe cleaners would come out black as soot, and if you picked them up with your bare hands you would have to get paraffin oil to clean them! Granny would shout at him to go outside with that dirty old pipe, but he pretended he did not hear her.

Sally felt sad thinking how this smell reminded her of her grandad. Times like this when she was on her own and have time to think, she could picture the scenes of her youth and how different times are now. Jack would love his great-grandad now if he were still alive. The pipe would hold a great fascination for him and no doubt the questions asked, and the answers given, would be worth eavesdropping on!

Sally loved to hear grandad describing the thatched cottage he grew up in. It had only two bedrooms and a large kitchen. It also had a *cailleach* or 'hag' bed. This form of bed was most common in the west of Ireland and originally designed to be used by an older member of the family, who may be bedridden. Projecting a section of the sidewall of the house when it was being built formed a recess. It was closed off by a curtain and contained a bed, usually a feather mattress. Three or four children would fit in this, moving out of it only when they grew too big and needed a bit more privacy. It was debatable if the next stage of bedroom accommodation was more private!

The *'settle-bed'* was the upgrade. It was a type of box made from timber and contained a feather mattress. It was situated in the kitchen, and was designed to fold for use as a seat during the day. At night it would be opened up and the feather mattress was rolled out and pillows added to make a very comfortable bed, sleeping a many as three people. Grandad said because he came from a family of ten, and he had nine children of his own, it was a godsend in small houses.

Sally often fantasised about living in that cottage with a large family. It would have been so different from her own time growing up with Granny and Grandad. Most nights were passed with Granny writing letters to her own children in England, and she would ask Sally to address the envelopes. She knew the geography of England better than Ireland because of this practice. She got used to the places where her uncles and aunties lived and knew that Hayes was in Middlesex, and Southampton in Hampshire, and St. Albans in Hertfordshire and Northampton was in the Midlands. Names like Fulham, Hammersmith, Kentish Town, Kensington were all in London and at school she excelled in English geography at *question time.*

Sally remembers staying up watching Granny create a new dress she had promised her for school in the morning, or for some other special occasion. She would thread the needle for her, as her sight was not a good as it used to be. She would tell her as she sewed about all the clothes she made for her own little girls, not to mention the horrible chore of darning the socks for the boys and Eddie that got worn thin by the Wellingtons boots. She said she hated the nights she had to darn the socks.

Sally stirred herself and stretched. She was feeling stiff from sitting so long. It was nice to have this time to her self to reminisce. Tomorrow when she visited Granny Cat she would see if she remembers Grandad's old pipe. And she decided to ask her straight out about matchmaking and how she met Grandad. But for tonight she would just chill out and decided to have an early night.

Tomorrow morning Ian and Jack would be coming home from their overnight stay with Ian's mother. She lived on her own now and so looked forward to having her son home for one night each week and she adored her grandson. He would be all excited tomorrow telling his little important stories and adventures, so Sally knew she had to be alert, or he would notice if she was not paying full attention.

She let the dogs out for their last toilet trip before bedtime and took herself off to bed with a magazine. She had next week's show to put together and she might get some ideas from the latest edition of *Pillow Talk.*

Chapter 12

The Skills of Matchmaking

'Who did I marry anyway Sally?' Granny Catherine asked when Sally mentioned matchmaking the following Sunday in the nursing home.

Oh dear Sally sighed to herself. This is going to be tougher than I thought. She looked around at the other patients. They all seemed to be in a little world of their own. Some of them never appeared to have anyone visit them. I suppose it's nice for Gran to have such a lot of memories, Sally thought to herself. Maybe in her own way she is enjoying reliving her past like this. What harm can it do anyway? She continued to humour her.

'Ah Gran do you not remember meeting Grandad? His name was Eddie Staunton. You met through a matchmaker? He arrived with his brother Martin who was taller, more handsome and was dressed up like a *toff*. You hoped he was the eligible bachelor! You said Grandad came with a patch in the knee of his trousers. You often told us about this first meeting, but never when Grandad was around.' Sally watched while Catherine pondered on this.

'I remember turning down a thin scrawny little man with soap in his locks. I told the matchmaker I met fine handsome men in Philadelphia and I didn't leave all that for a puny little man who couldn't wash himself properly! You know Sally when I came home from America I was considered a good catch. Indeed all yanks were at that time. The word would spread that a yank had returned home. The matchmaker would set about this highly skilled art of getting two suitable people to meet. A number of considerations had to be taken into account. The average match would be a man nearing thirty years of age—often the eldest son who would inherit the farm, with possibly one or both of his parents of pensionable age. The land may be in need of more stock because of shortage of money and so the woman chosen could be a yank or the daughter of a publican or shopkeeper—someone who could bring money into the home.

Good looks and intelligence played some part in getting the match fixed, but the main consideration from the point of view of the man, was the sum of money brought in. But of course it was of great importance too that the woman had good health. Often married men had to go to England to earn money and so the woman should be healthy and strong enough to carry on with the chores about the farm.

The age of the girl was a lot more important than that of the man. She should not be more than twenty-eight. This was a time when everybody wanted large families, so up to the age of twenty-eight it would be assumed she would have many years for childbearing. Even though times were hard and there was not much money to go around, they still wanted lots of sons and daughters. The parents looked forward to their young ones growing up and helping them on the farm for a few years, and then they would let them go to places like England, Canada, America and Australia. They hoped, and indeed expected, that dollars would arrive from them on a continual basis for the remainder of their lives.

'Did Grandad ever have to go to abroad when he was a young man?' Sally ventured to ask.

'He said he worked in the coalmines in Manchester for a short time in 1928 for twenty-eight shillings a week. His first introduction to the mines was to meet a dead man coming up on a stretcher! Needless to say he didn't stick that job long. He also worked in Liverpool on a farm. Every April he would reminisce about the Grand National race. He said they were setting potatoes in the field beside the racecourse and they were allowed to stop and watch while the race went by. Every year since we got married Eddie would come in from the fields to listen to it on the wireless.

He never cared much for England, so when his mother sent for him to come home as she wanted to sign over the place to him, he was a happy man. Martin, her younger son was putting pressure on her to sign it over to him, but Nora wanted Eddie to have it. He took another notion to go when the children were growing up but only stayed a week! He hated it and sure he missed us all, you can be sure. He had to put up with a lot of 'cajoling' when he returned home so soon. 'Did you go over to see the time Eddie?' they would ask when he went to mass the following Sunday. He used to be very embarrassed but sure it was no crime at all. You couldn't tell him though,' Catherine was laughing now to herself.

'How soon did you marry after meeting him? Sally probed once more.

'I suppose the younger generation would like to think it was love at first sight but there were a lot more things to be considered apart from the look of the man,' Granny answered. 'Other people had a say in it too. You wouldn't go against the matchmaker entirely. Once it was seen that the couple were not against the idea, the discussions would begin. The size of the man's farm and related matters such as the number of cattle, sheep and pigs he owned, and of course the amount of dowry required. He would then call on the girl and her parents with the information he had collected. If they were able to come up with the money, or part of it, the matchmaker would arrange a further meeting. Of course Sally, in my case I was more independent than most girls and I had more of a say in the matter, because I had gone to Philadelphia and earned my own dowry. Naturally I would have wanted my mother to be happy with my decision too.'

Catherine remained very quiet, thinking and frowning and occasionally humming a tune to herself. She was playing with the sheet on the bed, pulling it this way and that way and twisting it into a rope. Just as quickly she would spread it out with the palms of her hands as if to iron it smooth again. Sally remained quiet too not wanting to spoil her thoughts, whatever they were.

The other patients had dosed off so the ward was completely at peace. Sally could have dropped off too when Catherine suddenly said, 'you know some girls had very little say in the choice of man that was to become their husband. If her father, together with a close friend or uncle, inspected the prospective groom's farm and was satisfied with the findings, they would go to a solicitor to draw up the marriage agreement. They would then call to the priest and as no notice was required, the marriage often took place within a few weeks of the first meeting.

You know a certain amount of deception took place too. When showing the girl's father around the farm, an extra field or two belonging to a neighbour was sometimes included, with the permission of the obliging farmer, of course! And as the number of cattle were sometimes exaggerated when bargaining over the dowry, it was often necessary to borrow a few from the same farmer, just for the day, if you get my meaning.'

'That was very dishonest Gran,' Sally commented.

Catherine chuckled to herself. 'You might think that was bad but I'll tell you another thing that sometimes happened Sally. A young couple might only have met once before the marriage ceremony. The groom would be waiting in the church at the appointed time, while the bride availed of the customary privilege of being a few minutes late. The bride who arrived was not the girl to whom the groom had been introduced at all, but her ugly sister who might not be the full shilling! Or as the Americans would say, 'not too tightly wrapped.' The first girl would have less difficulty in finding another suitable man. If the groom noticed the difference he never disputed it and the marriage would take place.'

'You're pulling my leg now Gran aren't you?' Sally asked.

'Oh no it's true but this didn't happen very often of course.' Catherine laughed.

'Gran were people always happy with that kind of a marriage?' Sally asked.

'Not every couple were happy of course. You accepted your lot mainly because of a deep simple faith. You wouldn't dream of walking away from a marriage because in those days, there was nowhere else to go. There was no state allowance for separated people, and other members of the family were unable to accommodate them for they lived in poverty themselves. There was no going back to the home place, so their only hope of survival was to remain together regardless of unhappiness.

Sure many a good blazing row I had with your Grandad! He'd come in from the fair after selling cattle, half stupid with drink. The money from the sales would be in little bundles in several different pockets. It's a wonder he didn't loose the half of it! It wouldn't do at all to let a man out with holes in the pockets on a fair day! I used always be very careful and would mend any holes the day before. You never knew which trousers Grandad would chose to wear that morning so you had to go over all of them. We would try to add up different prices he got for each animal. They didn't always add up, so we would have another search in the trousers pockets! Usually we would find the missing notes along with 'bull's eye' sweets for the young ones, bless him.'

Sally was reminiscing now too. 'I remember the black and white striped sweets all right Gran. It was only on fair days he would buy sweets. I remember too he always brought home lamb chops and they had to be fried straight away for he was starving. I kind of remember some of the arguments too, but you would always send me off down the fields to collect kindling for the fire or get a bucket of water from the river. I knew well it was an excuse to get me out of the way so I wouldn't hear what you had to say to him,' said Sally.

'Well you know things had to be said, but if we had our disputes they were minor ones, and we kept them within the four walls of the house,' said Catherine. 'All in all we had a very good life together and if I could turn back the clock I'd do it all over again.'

Sally had to be content with her visit for today, for as she looked around her she noticed the Nurse coming down the corridor. She was dishing out the patient's medication. She knew from past visits, as soon as Gran got hers she was out like a light. So she kissed her grandmother goodbye and promised her she would be back real soon. And she would.

Chapter 13

Shy Eddie

Eddie Staunton sat on top of the hill enjoying the evening breeze coming across the bog. The countryside had so many aromas to offer but as Eddie had such a lot on his mind right now he did not notice. He was busy surveying his surroundings. The fields looked in good condition and the cows were grazing peacefully in the far field. The brown mare Fanny was in the next field with the only donkey he owned. He had a nice scattering of sheep in the field beside the river.

As he smoked his pipe he pondered to himself. He could do with a few more cattle in the herd and maybe another horse. Then he would have a team for ploughing. It was very hard on one mare to pull a plough on her own. Eddie felt his life might be about to change. He might be soon taking a wife. Lately he had been getting a lot of hints from people 'isn't it time you took yourself a wife Eddie?'

There was a tremor of excitement running through him. He had never before contemplated marriage seriously. He was thirty-five years of age and in the very comfortable position of having the farm in his name.

The last remaining brother at home was soon to make a home for himself about a hundred yards away in the same village, so there would be just his mother and himself in the home place.

His mother Nora was now seventy-five. He knew a younger woman would soon be needed to carry on the household chores among other things. Some of his older brothers and one sister had emigrated and had not returned. Martin and John Joe stayed at home and his two other sisters had got married lately. He tried England himself but working in the coalmines would kill a man! And besides the farm was a nice cushy and healthy living, especially after a spell down the coalmines no one knew that better than Eddie!

The local matchmaker had been on the lookout for a suitable girl. A week ago he came to Eddie and told him he had spoken with a girl home from America in Owenboy. She was the right age and was willing to meet him. She should have a fairly tidy dowry. She had spent six years in Philadelphia. Next Sunday was to be the day.

On this beautiful spring evening with the sun going down behind the hill, the birds singing their chorus of song, content with their day you could feel the peace and tranquillity, but Eddie was not feeling very tranquil! He was very apprehensive and nervous but with a certain amount of excitement too, as the all-important day was approaching.

His first thoughts every morning and his last thoughts at night were of this meeting. It was a big step and meeting a prospective bride for the first time, it was going to be nerve racking. 'The sooner it comes now the better I will like it,' Eddie told himself.

His faithful sheepdog Sailor sat at his feet pretending to be asleep, but cocking his ears at the slightest move from Eddie. He was ready to obey any command. This evening there was nothing for him to do and he sensed his master was unusually quiet and did not even notice he was there.

Eddie was surveying the half-acre field freshly ploughed the last two days. His arms ached with the newness of the work. It was a year since the last ploughing and when you are on a farm you are always changing the pattern of work, so you can expect new aches and pains. It comes with the territory! Next week the cutting of the turf will bring its own share of backbreaking aches, for the first day anyway, but the next day the muscles will right themselves once more as they become accustomed to the work.

He must get out the goose grease jar when he got back to the house he thought to himself. His mother always kept the greasy fat from the inside of the goose at Christmas and put it in a jar. It was the cure for all aches and pains that goes with farming.

As he sat on the stile filling his pipe with tobacco he smiled to himself. What would the yank do with the goose grease jar I wonder? Probably chuck it out with a lot more rubbish around the house. But that's all right if she can offer me a better rub! Eddie blushed at such thoughts. If Father Gibbons knew what I'm thinking he'd make me kneel down this minute in front of him and hear my confessions'.

He did worry about that side of things. He had very little experience with women up to this. The nearest he ever got to a girl would be giving a ride home to one of the locals on the cross-bar of his bicycle coming from a dance. Fellows boasted about it the next day to each other.

As he puffed away contentedly on his pipe his thoughts returned to the meeting next Sunday. He would have to think about presenting himself nicely if he was to make any impression on this yank. He would have to buy a new white shirt and tie. It never mattered much up to this how he dressed himself although his brother Martin was always very fussy about what he wore.

'I'll have to ask Julia Walsh in the next village to buy a white shirt and a new tie when she goes to town. Sure my best suit will be grand. She'll hardly notice the patch on the left knee. I'll put my right knee over it when I sit down he thought to himself. He had one good pair of brown shoes and his hat was nearly brand new. He'd ask Paddy Mullen to give him a haircut. Its many a haircut I gave him and he's always borrowing a fill of tobacco when he runs out, but I never get one back.'

He patted the dog and said sure maybe my new wife might cut my hair when she gets used to me and she might give you a bit of grooming too. 'What do you think about that Sailor?'

He walked purposefully back to the house. He started to see his possessions with new eyes, the eyes of his prospective bride to be! How will she take to all this? The matchmaker said she spent six years in Philadelphia.

After all the glamour of America I wonder what she will think of my small modest thatched cottage.

He crossed the stile and surveyed the scene in front of him. The roof needed repairs over the end room where the leak was coming in last February in the heavy rain. He must thatch that at the first opportunity and certainly before the first inspection of his place by the matchmaker and the yanks family. It wouldn't do to have a leak over the bed on their wedding night either!

The front door and the half-door could do with a new coat of paint. I think I'll change the colour to red this year. It will be cheerful and welcoming and it will go well with the whitewashed walls and the green boxwood. I don't know why Mother always painted the door brown anyway, he told himself.

The door was flanked on either side by two small windows with pink geraniums in full bloom. The old skillet pot of bluebells looked cheerful and if she likes flowers at all she will admire the rambling red rose bush at the end of the house. That timber water barrel with its rusty bands around its middle will have to go behind the house where no one will see it.

Damn those bloody weeds and grass. They never stop growing out in the yard. Christ there's so much to do he thought. But sure she knows it's not a hotel she's coming to! God I'd better do something about that gate too—it's past fixing anymore. It's off its hinges for months now. I'll ask the blacksmith to make a nice new one. It will make a great first impression on the yank. It will also keep out those bloody geese and that long necked gander. He's always hissing and honking making sure everyone knows he's in charge. That will stop them sneaking up to the half door leaving their droppings all over the place!

Eddie was starting to relax a bit now happy with his decisions and glad he took the time to notice what needed doing. It might be harder to improve on things inside the house with mother having the last say he thought to himself frowning.

He had never mentioned a word about his plans for marriage to her yet. He felt they would be welcomed with opened arms. She had approached the subject a couple of times but Eddie was not always receptive to such ideas. He either changed the subject tactfully or walked out with the pretence he had chores to do. It would not be the easiest of conversations to have with his mother. But he knew he would have to prepare her for the big step he was about to take soon. 'I suppose if I start making a few improvements around the house she'll put two and two together and maybe with a bit of luck she'll broach the subject first,' he told himself as he lay in bed that night.

The older generation were very shrewd and did not miss much. It would make it a lot easier on him now if she did start talking about it again. 'I'll wait till I meet this Catherine Brennan before saying anything at all to mother. Sure I mightn't take to her at all,' he said to himself. 'How am I going to know from one meeting anyway? I'll have to ask Martin to come with me. At least two heads will be better than one,' he told himself.

Content with these decisions and pleased about the changes he was about to make around the house, he fell into a deep contented trouble free sleep.

Chapter 14

The Introduction

The following Sunday dawned bright and sunny. Catherine was awake early. She had slept very well having decided, on retiring, that this was after all only another meeting with a prospective husband. The last two such occasions had not gone too well. There could be many such occasions if this Eddie Staunton was not suitable either.

She had to smile at the last arranged meeting with a little man named Johnny Kelly. He was a stiff built little man with a 'gimp' on him, squaring his shoulders trying to make himself taller than he was, and stretching himself up to about five feet four inches tall. Catherine had arranged with the matchmaker to meet him on a Saturday in town. She brought her sister along too. They noticed this little man with the matchmaker, and I suppose the poor fellow must have felt their eyes on him, because he put on more of a 'gimp' than ever trying to impress them, squaring his shoulders making out he was a great man altogether, and that the main street was hardly big enough for him.

As luck would have it, a shopkeeper had just hung out a net bag of footballs. As Johnny passed by, in his excitement he gave an extra swagger of his shoulders, and hit against the net of footballs sending the whole pile onto the ground and rolling all over the street. They were bouncing and rolling all over the place and everyone was turning around and laughing and young children running to get a ball. If she had any doubts about this little man going to be her future husband this surely was a sign from heaven. 'I wouldn't marry that guy if he had a hundred acres,' she whispered to Bridget.

Catherine decided that whatever she wore for Mass was good enough for this meeting too. She chose a brown dress with cream polka dots and a cream frill around the neck. It had a mid-length pleated skirt, which showed off her long slender legs. She wore a shade of mink nylons and brown court shoes. She wore her wavy brown hair parted in the middle and coiled at the nape of her neck in a chignon style. Her favourite pond's cold cream, pink lipstick and a touch of rouge on her cheeks for colour, was all the make-up she needed. Crossing her fingers and giving a last glance in the mirror, she winked at herself and whispered, 'Good-luck Cat, this could be the first day of the rest of your life.'

She set off for Mass with her mother. She had arranged for Lavan's hackney car to take her and her brother James to *Drumoneen* when Mass was over. She had not mentioned about her arranged meeting to her mother and indeed had not told her about the previous dates either. It was soon enough to tell her all when she had actually chosen a partner. She knew her mother well enough to know she believed in her, and would choose wisely. After all she had let her go to Philadelphia six years ago and trusted her good judgment then.

It was one o clock when Catherine and her brother James arrived outside Mannions Hotel in *Drumoneen.* They told the Hackney driver to return in two hours. James went inside to see if the matchmaker had arrived. While Catherine was waiting outside she looked down the street and noticed three men walking towards her. She already recognised the matchmaker so one of these other men must be her prospective husband!

She suddenly felt a tremor running through her body. One of the men was tall and good looking and very well dressed indeed. The smaller man was not as good looking and even though he wore a hat, he was not turned out as well at all. She noticed a patch in the knee of his trousers. She closed her eyes as she whispered to herself, 'Please, let it be the taller one.' Just then James returned to her side.

'You look a bit pale Catherine. Are you feeling all right?' He enquired.

'I'm fine James. I just suddenly felt a little shaky. You know this is a big step I'm taking and I've only just realised it.' she said.

Just then the trio reached their side. The matchmaker introduced them. First the smaller man with the hat, 'this is Eddie Staunton, my dear, and he brought his brother Martin with him.' Then he introduced Catherine and they all shook hands. Catherine noticed Eddie had a very nice firm handshake, while his bigger, more handsome brother was like a wet fish. Her first thought was to remember to ask her mother about a man's handshake! She used to say, 'You could tell a lot by a man's handshake.'

They all went inside the Hotel and ordered drinks and a pot of tea and some 'spotted dick' cake for Catherine. She let the men do the talking while she observed. Eddie seemed to be a very shy man, serious in his ways but could still laugh at his own mistakes. His brother on the other hand was the complete opposite, very outspoken, a real 'jester' telling stories of other peoples misfortunes. Everything seemed a great big joke to him. He seemed to want to steal the limelight, often making remarks that would make another man feel small, but Eddie did not seem to take offence at all. She hoped James was taking notice so they could compare later. But when a man got a pint of Guinness in his hand he could easily forget his reasons for being here at all!

'Why am I comparing these two brothers?' she asked herself. 'It's not as if I have a choice anyway. Eddie is the one looking for a wife.' She scolded herself for thinking she preferred Martin at first sight. From what she had seen so far she certainly would not be considering another meeting with Martin! He was far too opinionated and she did not like the way he seemed to be putting Eddie down at every opportunity.

He reminded her somewhat of the bold Maurice Fitzgerald. It would not do to go thinking of that 'philanderer' right now or it would turn her off marriage altogether. Her thoughts went to poor May who had discovered for herself, after a very short time that the sun did not actually shine out of her Reece! She was very disillusioned with her marriage, having discovered he was unfaithful to her from the very beginning. She even told Catherine before leaving for home that her marriage was on the rocks, and wished she had given more thought to Catherine's words of wisdom when they had first met.

Eddie was watching the frown on Catherine's face. He wondered what she was thinking. He was not altogether listening to what the men were talking about. He was too much on edge. He was not sure how he should approach the subject of another meeting—if indeed there would be another such meeting. He did not feel he was making much headway at the moment. There was no doubt he certainly liked the look of her. What man would not? She was a fine looking woman. Should he tell her his thoughts he wondered? He often heard the lads joking saying they asked a girl to marry them last night. They would say, 'Would you like to be buried with my people.' Of course that always got a laugh from the lads but this was no laughing matter! He decided to go and sit next to her.

'Is everything all right Catherine?' he asked. 'You don't look too happy.'

She smiled then and Eddie noticed how pretty her face was when she smiled.

'I'm fine. I was just reminded of someone in America who is a lot like your brother.' Catherine answered.

Poor Eddie had no idea how to read into that! Was that good or was she frowning because she missed a boyfriend over there? This isn't going to be easy.' he thought to himself.

'Would you like to go outside for a walk and we'll see if we have anything to talk about?' he said.

She nodded and as they stood up they told the others they would go up the street for a stroll and get a bit more acquainted with each other.

'If we don't come back you'll know we have eloped,' Eddie laughingly joked.

Martin shouted after them 'Sure if she doesn't want you I'll have her myself!'

They walked outside to the beautiful sunshine. They headed up towards the Church and Eddie commented that if it were fair day in the town she would not be able to walk with those dainty shoes.

'Did you ever go to town on a fair day?' Eddie asked.

'When I was younger my father would allow us to go into town in the evening when all the animals were gone. We would dress up and parade up and down the street, while the boys were in the pubs, having a few drinks after their long day. I think the smell of the manure stayed in our nostrils for days afterwards, but that didn't stop us from wanting to go again,' Catherine told him.

'Have you done this before?' they both asked at the same time. They both laughed out loud.

'You first,' Eddie said.

'I met a couple of men a few weeks ago but I couldn't take to either of them. My sister Mary and I used to date two policemen in Philadelphia for a while on and off, but we were just passing the time. That's all gone by the wayside now.'

'Do you think you could take to me Catherine?'

'Oh, I've met worse,' she laughed.

She felt quite comfortable in this mans company. He was very easy to get along with and as they continued to walk around the grounds of the Church, she admired the shrubs and flowers. She was anxious to know did he have a garden with flowers and a yard with fowl and animals.

Catherine loved animals and Eddie told her there were geese and a gander, ducks, chickens, a cat and his beloved dog 'Sailor.' He added there were cows, calves, sheep, a mare and a donkey. The garden could do with a woman's touch, as his mother was not able to be bending her back now. He told her his mother loved fowl and still tended to them and when Catherine assured him she too was crazy about animals and we should get along just fine he could not believe his luck!

'Does mean you will consider taking things a step further?' He asked her excitedly.

'It does if you think you could put up with me. How do you know now Eddie Staunton that I'm not a lazy old bag, no good at cooking, washing, ironing, cleaning, milking a cow, and keeping a man happy?'

'Can you milk a cow?' He asked with a smile.

'Sure if I can't maybe you'd teach me,' she teased. 'I must say I didn't milk many cows in Philadelphia in the last six years.'

'Oh I'll teach you all right and maybe you'll teach me some things too!' He said with a knowing wink.

This man had a good sense of humour Catherine thought to herself and she liked it. She felt things were going very well and she could see herself liking him more and more. Can it be possible that this will be my future husband she asked herself? She would first wait to see what his farm was like before getting too used to the idea. She still had to know how he felt about her. What if he didn't take to her? How far would it go before he said so? Catherine was beginning to get a bit panicky at the thought. Eddie noticed her frowning and once again he wished he knew what she was thinking and suddenly Catherine blurted out,

'What about you Eddie, will I pass the test?' She asked almost defiantly.

He paused in his steps looking straight at her. He knew he was no good with words but at the same time he would like to let this lovely homely girl know that any man, who would get her, would indeed be the luckiest man alive!

'I'll take my chances whether you can milk a cow or not,' he said. 'If you'll return with me now we'll tell the matchmaker to go ahead with the next stage of the procedure.'

As they walked down the street of *Drumoneen* Eddie took Catherine's hand in his own. They both felt they had taken the first step towards making definite plans to become man and wife.

Chapter 15

Hot-headed Martin

Eddie woke the following morning feeling like a new man. He had made great headway yesterday and he knew he never felt so good about anything before. He could not wait to get started on the alterations to the house. His whole future depended on it and he was not going to be rushed into anything until he was good and ready! To day he would put out the dung heap in the drills as fertiliser for the potatoes. At least it is a good time of year I'm preparing for a wife, he thought. With the cow manure gone from outside the back door at least the place would not smell too bad. He would get a couple of gallons of Jeyes Fluid to disinfect the area when it was empty, and now that the cows are out in the fields there will be no more of that again till the winter months. By then he hoped his new wife would be accustomed to the ways of the farmyard.

Eddie kept forgetting that this girl came from a farm before she went to Philadelphia. Still six years looking at the big lights could change a girl, and he heard she was not home from America very long, so it might take a while to get used to things here again.

'Well do you think she'll have you?' Martin shouted from the stile. Eddie was so engrossed in his own thoughts, he never heard his brother approaching and he nearly jumped out of his trousers.

'Jesus, Martin do you have to frighten the life out of a man. Why are you creeping around like that?' Eddie asked.

'Ah fuck you sure I'm not creeping at all. You were miles away there. I called out but you didn't hear me. She a fine looking woman anyway! You'll be a lucky man to get her. I suppose you won't want to go to the barn dance next Friday night in Murphy's now that you think you have a chance of a woman,' Martin said.

'I can still go if you're going Martin. Did you hear Maggie is going to America with the other yanks when they are going back next week? I thought you might make it up with her, but I suppose you are waiting for a returned yank! Poor Maggie. I don't wonder at her going. She's mad about you, but not having two cents to rub together sure she knows she doesn't stand a chance with you! A yank would have the money you are looking for to put up that house you keep talking about building.'

'Well that's exactly what I'm going to make a start on today. After seeing you hitting it off yesterday with the yank from Owenboy, it's time I built my own place or make a start anyway in case you do bring in a woman! I'll take the ass and cart and start clearing the foundation. Will you give me a hand after a while when you have all the jobs done Eddie?' Martin asked.

'Ah Jayus Martin will you give a man a break! I'd need a *meitheal* of men myself for all the things I need to do! I was going using the bloody ass and cart to put out the dung heap in the drills. You know yourself I have to make the place look presentable. The matchmaker and someone from Catherine's family are coming to look it over. I have a feeling she'll come herself too and take a look at my holding of land. I wouldn't blame her either. She's a smart girl and it's her money we'll be bargaining over.' Eddie said.

'All right sure I'll give you a hand so to-day, just to get ahead of yourself, but I'll expect you to return the favour to-morrow,' Martin said. 'I mentioned to mother about your matchmaking plans this morning Eddie,' he added.

'Martin what sort of a bloody man are you at all? Could you not leave that for me to do myself? That big mouth on you will get you into trouble one day,' Eddie was very annoyed.

'Ah, calm down man, will you? She was okay about it. She said it won't stop you're growth anyway! Sure haven't I done you a favour? Haven't I broken the ice for you now! You can do the same for me when I get a wife. It's easier coming from someone else. She'll be delighted to welcome another woman into the house, and you can be sure she'll want grandchildren around her too. If you need any help in that department give me a shout!' He laughed mockingly.

Eddie blushed. He had enough on his mind without worrying about that side of things. He would broach the subject of marriage to night to mother. No point in prolonging it now that she got a hint of it. It will be better to get it out in the open anyway and give her time to think about it before meeting the girl in question.

To take his mind off the ordeal ahead of him Eddie let his mind wander to the forthcoming barn dance. Since he was about fifteen he was introduced to these dances because elderly people liked to host these *sprees*, as they called them, but they needed help to prepare for them. He and a few other local lads would arrive at the house a day or so before the dance and give it a good complete overhaul. Even though the house would be kept neat and clean at all times, it was an excuse to give it a fresh look. A coat of whitewash would be painted on the cottage inside and out. A number of women took over the washing and ironing and cleaning. The cat and the dog were evicted while the local women were busy baking all kinds of cakes and pies, and roasting chickens. Eddie would be asked to fetch and carry baskets of turf from the shed and buckets of water from the spring well. When the finishing touches were put to the parlour with the table laid out with a white tablecloth and fancy china tea-sets, they would tell him he could go home and wash and change his clothes, and he could come back later for some of the refreshments. That's the bit Eddie enjoyed best.

Even in those days Eddie was fascinated with the arrival of the yanks. It was customary to give a *spree* for them before they returned to America, and sometimes they might meet a man the night before their departure, were offered a proposal of marriage at the barn dance and would never return to America again.

They would arrive in all their glory. They made an exquisite picture climbing down from the shaky old sidecar in their beautiful long evening dresses, with swirling skirts and high-heeled shoes and nylons. They spoke in a distinct American accent and were guessing everything!

His thoughts went to Catherine again and now that he was on his own he was able to think more clearly. He hadn't noticed her accent yesterday or that she was guessing everything. Maybe that's because she wasn't doing it!

He was looking forward to meeting up with her again. He felt they would have a lot more to say to each other the next time they met up. Surely that must be a good sign. Martin seemed to think well of her too. Although you never could tell with him! He liked every girl he ever met! It must be the fact he was in the army and was starved for female company.

Eddie believed Maggie Murphy would be a good choice of wife for Martin. She never made any secret of the fact she was besotted by him but he was such a devil-may-care sort of fellow. He heard she was to join the nuns in Texas when she went over with her sister and the Bourke girls next week. So she must have given up on Martin! Unless he might see the light before she left and now with this barn dance, maybe things would change.

Eddie laughed to himself. There I am plotting to get a wife for Marin and I have to get a matchmaker to find one for myself! I suppose I am eager to get him settled so I will be rid of him before I take in my own wife. Who could blame me? What would I want a young red-blooded man in the house with my new wife and me! I wouldn't think she'd want to come in under those terms. He was reminded of the words of a song 'I won't come in while he's there.'

Eddie started whistling to himself as he shovelled the manure into the cart. He had hardly stopped all morning and had not felt the work much at all; so busy was he with his thoughts and plans for his future. To night, he said to himself, I would have a heart-to-heart with mother! She is a good sort and sure maybe she will be delighted with some help coming into the house.

After emptying his load of cow manure in the far field, he was making his way back for another cartload when he decided to stop for a few minutes and have a puff of his pipe. No point in killing myself trying to do it all in one day he thought. He was glad he smoked the pipe for it made him sit down and rest a few minutes. Martin never smoked so would not let a man stop for a break at all. Kept going hammer-and-tongs till the job was finished!

Eddie never believed in that kind of hard labour. It was time to give the poor donkey a break to have a drink and a rest. If Martin wanted to keep working in the field spreading out the manure, well then let him, Eddie told the dog Sailor, who had trotted back and forth all morning after the cart. 'We'll sit down here a few minutes at the headland old boy and have a rest,' he patted Sailors head and lit his pipe and lay back contentedly puffing away.

'So this is where you are, sleeping away while my back is nearly broke spreading out your bloody dung heap,' roared Martin while prodding Eddie with the fork to wake him.

'Ah calm down man will you and take that bloody fork out of my face! I only sat a minute to have a smoke and must have dosed off. Can't you sit down yourself and rest a minute and we'll make up for it again when we get going? It's not peace-work we're on you know and the pay isn't too good either,' Eddie said laughing.

'You can lie there all day if you like. It's not my dung heap that has to be shifted! One thing I will tell you. I want that ass and cart tomorrow, so if you haven't finished you can scratch yourself all day for all I care,' Martin shouted as he walked away home.

Eddie knew that was the end of the help for to day. It didn't surprise him, as he always knew Martin was a hot-headed bastard. No good in a crisis. If he wanted to get out of doing a job he would create an excuse to get away. He had seen it often enough before. He probably has a date to night and doesn't want to be too tired. He's an awful man for the ladies, thought Eddie. I don't know how he does it.

That night, Eddie and his mother were sitting by the open fire, each holding a cup of tea, each deep in their own thoughts. The grandfather clock was about to chime. Eddie planned to wait till it struck its nine melodious ding-dongs. He did not want anything to interrupt them when he finally got the courage to tell his mother about his meeting last Sunday with a yank from Owenboy, who was making herself available for marriage.

She sat with her knees spread like a man, holding her cup by the bottom and pouring the tea into the saucer to cool it and tipping it back into the cup again. She had to spare the milk for the porridge in the morning and this performance would cool the tea down so she could drink it. She leaned her elbow on her knee and looked across at Eddie.

'You have something on your mind son. Spit it out like a good man. Tis no use bottling things up,' she said.

'You don't miss much Ma,' he answered her smiling.

'Sure I have eyes in my head and don't I know my own son by now. I wouldn't be much of a mother if I didn't,' she added.

So without any more hesitation Eddie told her from the beginning how it came about his meeting with Catherine Brennan, and that if she was willing to take him on after seeing his house and farm, then there was going to be a wedding. His mother was very happy and told him she would help all she could to prepare for the meeting.

It was with a happy heart he retired for the night after his mother reassurance him, that if she were not going to be help, then she would not be a hindrance either, and would gladly give him her blessing. He now knew it was all up to the lovely Catherine. He said a little prayer to St. Anthony to help her find it in her heart, when next they met, to accept himself, his house and holding of land and his mother into the bargain!

Chapter 16

Murphy's Barn Dance

Friday dawned bright and sunny. By the time Catherine woke, yawned and stretched herself she felt it must be time to get up, as the sun was well high in the sky. She had not intended sleeping so late, but she had worked a long hard day yesterday in the *black hill* setting the potatoes with her mother and brother Jimmy.

This was the first time she worked in the fields without her father by her side. She knew this was the exact field he was working in when he fell after his days work, and was unable to make it back to the house. Even though six years had passed she still missed him. Sometimes she felt she had not grieved properly for him while in Philadelphia.

There was not alot of work on today thank God so she could prepare herself for the barn dance in Drumoneen tonight. It was planned as a farewell hooley for some yanks returning to America. When Catherine met them in town during the week they asked her to come along too. The more the merrier they said and after all she was a yank, although not a returning one.

She was so looking forward to it for she loved dancing. She washed her hair and arranged the waves to frame her oval face and curl the ends with curlers. She left it like that all day to dry. She took out a midnight blue dress, showed it to her mother and then arranged it on the bed alongside her undies, nylons and high-heeled patent shoes. She would wear her nice blue glitter earrings and the blue cross and chain.

She must remember to take her camera with her for they were as scarce as hen's teeth here at home. She remembered the day she bought it and wondered could she afford such a luxury with her saving so hard to take Mary out. There was not much chance to use it since coming home. Her gramophone too was just sitting on the dresser. She must play her records of John McCormack for her mother.

Since her meeting with Eddie Staunton her mind was in turmoil. She realised he was a very nice man and was looking forward to their next meeting, but he did not seem to be in any hurry showing his possessions. She had a tidy dowry saved and would not like to see it squandered on the wrong man. It would be nice if his homestead and farm were in a fairly healthy state. Naturally I won't mind splashing out on some items for my own personal touch around the house, she thought to herself.

With an old woman in the house there will hardly be any modern things. There could be some nice antiques. She had a great passion for such things. For the present she was going to concentrate on the night ahead. She had not been to a barn dance for over six years and even then she wasn't too sure if she enjoyed it or not. She hadn't any fancy clothes to wear and envied the yanks arriving in all their glory as they climbed down from the shaky old sidecar, with their beautiful long evening frocks. The spoke in a distinct American accent and took photographs of everyone and everything.

After they had dined they sat by the kitchen fire and talked non-stop about their voyage, telling everyone the great place America was, with everyone busy making money. Everyone was rich and wore beautiful clothes. It seemed like a fairy-tale then with America only a name. At least now Catherine knew for herself what they were talking about, and tonight I'll be one of those yanks, she chuckled to herself!

Later that evening there was a lot of activity in the small *Drumoneen* town. All roads were leading to Murphy's house near the crossroads. Word had fairly got around about the barn dance. It was no wonder as they were held only very occasionally. The musician had arrived in his ass and cart with a fiddle wrapped in a canvas bag. As he would be playing until the early hours of the morning, he was given a good meal, after which he proceeded to play a selection of favourite tunes on the fiddle, while they were waiting for the crowd to arrive. *The Geese in the Bog* and *The Connaught Mans Ramble* were among the most favourite tunes with everybody.

A younger member of the family, who were holding the dance, gave a few steps of a reel to the great strains of *Miss McLeod's Reel* to a rapturous audience. As the dusk was falling the local girls and lads were gathering into the barn. The girls wore their best summer dresses. The lads looked very smart in their dark suits and white shirts and of course were freshly shaved and their hair shone with brilliantine.

Finally the yanks arrived and soon the dance began in real earnest. Feet clattered on the hard floor as they danced the sets. The threshing barn shook with excitement and the lanterns hanging on the beams swayed to-and-fro. Catherine was finding herself in great demand and was enjoying herself immensely.

During one dance, the *Siege of Ennis* she met up with Eddie's brother Martin. It was so fleeting she hadn't time to speak at all and she was not sure if he realised it was her. It would be nice if Eddie were here too, she thought. The more times they met up the better chance she would have of making up her mind about him.

The next dance was called. This time it was the *Haymaker Jig.* 'We need seven facing seven. Come on folks get in line.' Catherine loved this next dance, but she felt very warm after the exertion of the last one and decided to take a walk outside to cool herself. As she closed her eyes and inhaled the fresh evening air she was greeted with 'well now isn't it a small world' as someone spoke behind Catherine's ear. She looked around and found the very man she was just thinking about. She blushed like someone caught doing something wrong. It was from pleasure too she realised. She noticed Eddie was shaved to the bone and his hair was well groomed, but she couldn't help noticing the same trousers with the patch in the left knee. It must be the only good trousers he owns, she thought.

'Hello Eddie, I didn't realise you were here. I met up with your brother in the *Siege of Ennis* a while ago. I don't think he knew me. I'm glad to see you haven't forgotten me,' Catherine babbled away nervously.

'No fear of that now at all Catherine. I'd put a bet on it that Martin knew you too. He probably has his eye on someone else, knowing Martin,' he said.

'Are you coming inside to the dance?' she asked hoping he was a good dancer.

'Ah, sure I have two left feet Catherine,' he answered.

'I guess I'll have to teach you how to dance so among other things,' she laughed, even though she felt disappointed at this revelation. She hoped he was joking.

Eddie liked the sound of that. It was looking promising and they only having met just once! He decided to ask her to take a stroll down the '*boreen*' with him. He had his mind made up before to night. He would like this lovely colleen to become his wife. He couldn't wish for anything better. There was no way he could say this to her yet. It was hard to tell if the feeling was mutual, after only one meeting. So he was on his guard not to give anything away too soon.

'Would you like to go for a stroll before you go inside again? He asked. Catherine was disappointed for she would have much preferred to go inside to dance some more, but it looks like Eddie was not joking when he said he could not dance. She wondered if she would be happy with a man who couldn't dance. She would have to see if he had other compensations! She may as well go for a stroll anyway and get more acquainted. This was a great opportunity.

'Okay so but you'll have to walk slowly. I have a pair of high heel shoes on to night and I don't want to ruin them,' she answered.

'Don't worry I'll take it easy. Here give me your hand and I'll guide you out over the stile.'

Catherine liked the feel of his hand holding hers! Should she say anything personal? I suppose it's better to wait and see the size of his farm of land, in case it's only a small patch. It would be easier to get out of the situation if neither had been too personal.

'What would the matchmaker say if he saw us now Catherine?' Eddie interrupted her thoughts.

'There's no law against taking a stroll together is there? Anyway he doesn't have to know. Tell me Eddie how come your brother can dance and you say you cannot?' Catherine asked.

'Ah, he must have learned in the army. That fellow would be game for anything.'

'How many are in your family Eddie?' Catherine wanted to know.

'There were ten in all, three girls and seven lads, but there are only nine now. Tommy died when he was twenty-one.'

'What happened to him?' asked Catherine.

'He was working with a gang of labourers on a building site and one evening after work they went on a drinking spree. They fed him alot of *poiteen*—you know making a man out of him! It must have been too much for his heart as he died that night.'

Eddie fell silent and Catherine noticed the tears glistening in his eyes.

'That must have been a terrible time for all the family. How did your poor mother get over it?' she asked sympathetically.

'She doesn't talk about it at all but I know she is still very sad,' he answered.

Suddenly Eddie wanted to change the subject.

'What about yourself Catherine, are you a great dancer?'

'I guess you could say I am. I certainly enjoy dancing whenever I get the chance. Would you like me to show you a few steps of the waltz Eddie? This is a nice smooth field and there's no one looking at us. Ah come on, please. You might like it,' she pleaded.

Eddie was embarrassed. He knew he would have to put his arm around her. He was already holding her hand so he supposed there wasn't a lot more to do except move his feet and hope he wouldn't step all over hers. That would be a bad start. She started humming to herself and he realised she was serious. 'One, two, three—one, two, three,' she was repeating.

"Daisy, daisy, give me your answer, do. I'm half crazy all for the love of you.
It won't be a stylish marriage; we can't afford a carriage,
But you'll look neat upon the seat, of a bicycle made for two."

He realised she had led him along by the headland of the small field before he knew what was happening. This girl is a right charmer he thought to himself and couldn't help laughing. In fact they were both laughing and Eddie felt it was a long time since he enjoyed himself like this. This girl made him feel for the first time he was missing out on the fun side of things. Maybe his brother Martin had the right idea he thought. Playing pitch-and-toss with the lads was all right for an odd night but he was enjoying himself in a more exciting way tonight.

Suddenly he realised he was still holding Catherine but they weren't dancing now. He liked the feel of her body against his and she made no move to leave the circle of his arms either. The moon had come up from behind the hill and you could hear the corncrake in the meadow field beside them. The bark of a fox could be heard in the distance and the grass was becoming wet with dew. Catherine was aware of the joy she was experiencing at this moment, and she knew she would never compare it to the bright lights of America. It served its purpose at the time, and she knew when she said farewell to Philadelphia, she would not be returning.

In the distance you could hear a singing session starting up which meant the *hooley* was coming to an end. Catherine broke the silence between them as she realised she had better return or she might miss her seat home to Owenboy. She had not realised when she walked out for a breath of fresh air she would be so long gone.

They walked back companionably hand in hand both wrapped up in their own thoughts, neither one wanting to break the silence. They were both happy with their own thoughts. Years from now, they would vividly recall this night and tell their grand children, for little did they know now, that it was the first night of the rest of their lives together.

Chapter 17

A Future Mother-in-law

A month had passed since the night of the barn dance. With new determination Eddie had done Trojan work around the farmhouse and on the farm. He wanted to get things in ship shape for the inspection of his holding. He now felt he was ready and would be happy to take things further and as quickly as possible. He had his mind made up about the woman he wanted to marry. It was now up to Catherine.

He would go to confessions next Saturday night, and Sunday morning when he received communion he would say a special prayer for things to work out in his favour. The next step was to contact the matchmaker and he would do that tomorrow. He would tell him he was ready to make the final arrangements to meet on his farm. Sunday would be the best day. He would still be dressed up after Mass and when things were straightened up after the dinner, he would be ready for the meeting. His mother would be wearing her Sunday best too.

He was very happy now that Martin was making shapes to move out of the homestead. He had bought the field adjacent. It was all he could afford for now but he had his eye on 'Mouse' McGowan's fields. Eddie knew well that when his new wife came in with her dowry, he would have to give Martin enough to buy that holding.

The foundation for the house was dug out a few weeks ago and with the help of some handy men in the locality the house was now taking shape. Tom Fallon from *Drumoneen* was coming next Monday morning to put the roof on. Altogether things were looking up.

Sunday morning arrived and as Eddie woke his first thoughts was, of his impending meeting at his farmhouse with Pat Killeen the matchmaker, and whomever he brought with him. He had not met Catherine since the night of the barn dance but he was hoping she might come along today. He left it up to the matchmaker to make his own arrangements about who should be present. Eddie didn't care at this moment. He was relieved the day had come and as he was well prepared he felt he had something worthwhile to offer a woman.

He had already told his mother Nora about his plans. She had made a special effort to tidy up the parlour. The table was laid with her best white damask linen tablecloth and napkins—the only fancy china tea set she owned was taken out and the best cutlery placed on the table. The only time Eddie had ever seen his mother go to such trouble before was when the priest was coming to say Mass in the house. She wore her black silk dress with its white crochet collar and cuffs that she made herself, and kept it for what she described as 'state occasions.' Eddie was so proud of his mother going to such trouble and quite honoured that she considered this an occasion to unveil the black dress that smelled of camphor from the mothballs. These were a Godsend for protecting clothes not used very often. Moths could ruin a garment when it was stored away. You could always rely on the travellers or gypsies to have supplies when they called around selling their wares.

Earlier that morning she cautioned him to make sure he wore his white shirt and see if he could find a pair of trousers that didn't have a patch on the knee. Her heart was broken mending for him! From a young age Eddie always seemed to fall on one knee, with the result he now appeared to have a sharper bone in that knee and it was always coming through his trousers. She checked behind his ears making sure he hadn't left any soap in the creases. She was very pleased this day had come at last.

This was the first time Eddie brought a woman to the house and she had often prayed for it to happen. Please God this will be a good day for us all she whispered to herself. Eddie is a good living man and deserves a good woman. Please God she will have a nice dowry too. Then Martin can finish his house and be in a good position to take in a wife. What more could a mother ask but to have two of her sons living beside her. God knows there are enough of my children gone abroad. She considered herself a lucky woman indeed.

Eddie was sitting on the stile smoking his pipe looking up the '*boreen*' with Sailor sitting on the ground beside him. They were to be here at four o'clock and it was now ten after four. He noticed a small black car going back the road and hoped it would be his expected guests. It looked like the matchmakers but he couldn't be sure. It would take a minute or so yet before coming around the corner. Even though he was expecting them he still jumped when it arrived. His heart was pounding not knowing whom to expect. As they drew nearer he noticed Catherine in the back seat and her brother in the front. He wasn't sure now if he wanted her to be here or not. He emptied his pipe and climbed down from the stile and welcomed his party.

The first thing Catherine did was to pat the dog on the top of his head. Sailor brushed his thick tail on the ground and looked as if he was laughing up to her. They made a lovely picture. This is great start thought Eddie, she likes dogs! As the men commented about the weather Catherine got chance to take in the appearance of the place. She noticed the freshly whitewashed cottage with the red door. She also noticed it was at the end of the *boreen* so there would be no traffic going by their door. This was very pleasant as she lived on the main road to Knock Shrine where there was very little privacy. This is a haven of peace she thought.

She realised Eddie was speaking to her, asking her to come in and meet his mother while the men folk went down the fields.

They entered through the half-door and arrived in a large room with a beamed ceiling. The window was very small with very little light coming in. Most of the brightness came from the open doorway. The flagstone floor was well swept. Eddie's mother Nora sat by the fireside but stood up when Catherine entered. She reached out her hand to welcome her. The handshake was feeble enough but Catherine understood, as she was an old lady. Her smile was very welcoming and Catherine felt at ease with this woman who may well be her future mother-in-law! She was a lot like her own mother in statue but bigger boned. She could smell camphor from her clothes so Catherine guessed she must have gone to the trouble of taking out her special occasion dress, as she had often seen her own mother do. This greatly endeared her to the old lady.

After the introductions Eddie said he would leave them and catch up with the others down the fields. He said he would not be too long. He told his mother to make a cup of tea for herself and Catherine and to have the kettle boiled when they returned. 'Although you'd never know we might have something stronger than tea if things go well,' he said shyly winking at Catherine as he headed out the door.

Nora bent over to stoke the fire and lower the kettle, which was high up on the crane. This gave Catherine a chance to look around her. The table was filled with all sorts of nick-knacks with very little room to work on. The first thing she would do was clear it up. She would need a lot more space than that to make bread. The dresser over in the opposite wall was real nice indeed. The large platter plates with the blue '*willow pattern*' were lined up along the back of the top shelf, while the dinner plates were stacked in the middle row with the mugs hanging on hooks. The bottom shelf had a row of jugs in different sizes and patterns. Its flat surface was crammed with letters, medicine bottles, tablets, hairbrush, comb, photos and a jam jar filled with screws, nails, buttons, and pencils. Catherine noticed another jar filled with goose grease and hoped it wasn't Eddie who used it. She did not fancy going to bed with a man smelling of goose-grease!

The *settle bed* was on the far wall beside the back door. Catherine knew what it was used for even though they did not have one at home. Eddie said he came from a big family. Usually the boys in the family slept in the *settle bed* in the kitchen. It could accommodate anything up to four youngsters at a time. Catherine felt bold enough to question the old lady while she was busy making the tea.

'Did you have a large family yourself Mrs Staunton?' she enquired.

'I did indeed a gra. I had ten in all. I had seven boys and three girls, she answered.

'Where are they all now?' Catherine asked happy to be able to make a comfortable conversation with this dear old lady.

'There are four in Chicago, and the others are scattered around Ireland. They are all doing well except my poor Tommy who died at the age of twenty one.'

Catherine could see she was finding it hard to talk about it so she decided not to pursue it and instead commented on the nice cottage. She took the cup of tea offered to her and busied herself with putting in a spoon of sugar and stirring it. As she looked around she noticed the paraffin oil lamp hanging from the rafters. It was made of brass with clear glass globe but Catherine felt it could do with a good clean. She knew the glass was very fine and delicate and could be broken easily. She also knew it wasn't easy to get your hand into the globe. She had often cleaned her mothers when she was a child when her hands were small enough to do a good job. Of course there was nobody here now to do little chores like that.

As she sipped her tea she could see the garden through the open doorway. When they had finished Catherine asked Nora if she would walk with her out to see the garden. Nora was very pleased at such interest, as she had always enjoyed keeping it looking nice. Now of course she wasn't fit to keep ahead of things like that. Eddie kept it as best he could but he had more pressing things to do on the farm, which was making a living for them.

Rows of boxwood hedging were trimmed so neat even a small child could see over them. They were designed like a maze and she could picture little children playing *hide and seek.* There were roses and large white daisies growing inside the sections of boxwood. In other sections, there were sweet Williams and masses of different coloured flowers mingling together with no apparent pattern. A murmur of bees could be heard as they darted in and out of the honeysuckle that seemed to grow wild across the stonewall, and the lovely smell of the flowers was like a rare perfume. Catherine could see herself working amongst the flowerbeds, carefully weeding around the new shoots, investigating plants that she didn't recognise. She was so busy looking at the wonderful display she had not noticed Nora watching her. She was so pleased with the open admiration Catherine had for her garden, she could only say a secret prayer that this fine young girl would take a liking to her Eddie. Now she could see why he had made such a big effort to make the place look so presentable.

So engrossed were they in their own individual thoughts, that neither heard the approach of footsteps till the three men were beside them. They both noticed they were very jubilant. It was a good sign. Nora decided to take herself inside and told the men she would make the tea and to come inside within a few minutes. Eddie walked to Catherine's side and asked her if she would like to see the yard with the fowl. He knew she liked animals.

Catherine was not prepared for the sight that greeted her. Eddie had walked a few steps ahead of her and had reached for a basin of grain, and was scattering it on the ground. Without a word or sound from him, a clutch of chickens seemed to arrive from nowhere, scurrying to get their share of the feed before it had disappeared as quickly as it had arrived. There were at least a dozen beautiful *Rhode Island Red* chickens and just as many black ones. A bunch of white ones came from nowhere to join in the party! A red Cockerel sauntered amongst them proud as punch. There was an unusual looking bird amongst them that Catherine never seen at home. Eddie informed her it was a *Guinea* hen. He was never sure where it came from but always seemed to be there. A bit like a goat amongst the cattle he mused.

He took her to see the two pigs in the sty and the mare *Fanny* in the haggard eating hay from the haystack. The geese were making a great racket in a small garden a little distance away and Catherine noticed a gander amongst them. There were at least a dozen half-size geese and Eddie told her they were the goslings hatched out six weeks ago. They must have noticed it was feeding time.

She could hear ducks quacking some distance away and Eddie told her they were swimming in a small brook at the far end of the next field.

In that field she could see three cows with small calves beside each one. Catherine could only come to the conclusion that every creature was put to work around this place. It must be a great breeding ground and as she smiled to herself she thought, 'I wonder if I come to live here will I be producing in such abundance?'

Catherine wasn't opposed to the idea at all. Far from it! She hoped to have a large family and be blessed with sons and daughters. Eddie noticed the twinkle in her eyes and wondered what she was thinking. He left her to her own thoughts, as he was very busy with his own. So far things had gone very well indeed and Catherine's brother and the matchmaker were indeed very impressed with their findings on his farm. Watching Catherine he could see her fitting in very comfortably here amongst the poultry and animals. He secretly hoped she was feeling the same.

They made their way back to the house, each deep in their own thoughts and both wanting to say what was on their minds. Catherine was secretly hugging the notion that she could not wait for the day to come, when she would be as busy as a bee, working amongst all these lovely creatures. She had definitely made up her mind that Eddie Staunton was the man she wanted to marry. She hoped they would come to a settlement today.

When they returned to the kitchen they found her brother, the matchmaker and Nora, laughing and joking and drinking tea from large mugs. A bottle of whiskey was standing half empty on the kitchen table. It looked like there was a bit of bargaining going on in a jovial way.

'Come in Eddie, a gra and bring in the young lady and have a cup of tea,' Nora called out to him. 'It looks like we might have a match made while the two of you were outside. What do you think yourselves?'

Eddie blushed but was secretly pleased it had come to a head at last. There was no point in beating about the bush anymore. Catherine too was very pleased at how quickly it all happened, and the next step was to draw up a marriage agreement with a solicitor, and settle the date with the parish priest for the marriage.

The date they all agreed upon was 8th September. The corn would be harvested by then and there was a lull for a couple of weeks before the potato digging commenced. Nora hugged Catherine and told her if she wasn't going to be a help, then she wouldn't be a hindrance! They all shook hands and agreed it was indeed a fine days work. They felt sure it would be lucky when it was done on the Lord's Day. They sealed it with another drink!

Chapter 18

An Irish Wedding

The week before the wedding day, something happened leaving Catherine very disillusioned about men and marriage. A letter arrived from May in Philadelphia with the terrible news that her marriage was on the rocks. Her wonderful Maurice was not behaving like an adoring husband. He had started to ramble very shortly after their wedding day. Now why was Catherine not surprised at this news? Did she not try to warn May when she first arrived in America?

Poor May was apologising in her letter for not listening to Catherine when she had offered advice. She was so besotted by him at the time she didn't want to hear a bad word against him. Luckily they did not have children but poor May was devastated. She also said Aunt Anne and Richard were terribly disappointed. Her letter was heart rendering. She was so unhappy and wasn't holding anything back. She said it was really swell having Mary for company. Of course she wished Catherine were still there. It was not the same without her. The whole family could do with cheering up and she was the one person who had the gift to do that. They had heard about her forthcoming marriage to Eddie Staunton. They sent her their love and wished her the best of Irish luck.

Catherine's thoughts hurled themselves back in time to the first meeting with Maurice Fitzgerald on board the *Carmania*. She never liked him and hoped her good judge of character was going to prove itself once again, with her own choice of husband. She had a good feeling about this man who was to share her future, and she could not wait for the day to arrive. She put the letter aside for now and decided a reply could wait, until she had more time to devote to it. You could not write a letter at a time like this, without pouring enormous feeling into it.

She decided to concentrate on what had to be done. Her wedding suit was hanging on the door of the wardrobe covered with plastic. It was a powder blue two-piece made from taffeta, with very fine chiffon scarf that could be worn as a bow. She found a hat of the same colour and she was planning to wear her strappy black patent sandals and a patent clutch bag. All in all that side of things were up to date.

Packing up her possessions in the two trunks she brought home from Philadelphia was a difficult task. There were a lot of things she had not unpacked at all. Trunks were very handy storage compartments and her own mother had taken such a fancy to them. They may not look much from the outside but were indeed very beautiful inside. Blue brocade lined the walls and there were drawers inside with secret compartments. She kept her fox fur inside the trunk at all times. She remembered the day she purchased it and wondered should she be so extravagant. Catherine wasn't a wasteful person by any means but did feel a little reckless that day. She hoped there would be plenty of occasions to wear it. The first would be on her wedding day, if it showed any signs of getting cold.

Her sister Bridget was going to be her bridesmaid and her navy blue dress was ready too. Mary was still in Philadelphia and didn't want to come home just yet. She too had planned that whenever she came home to Ireland it would be to stay. She was going to be looking out for a husband with the assistance of a matchmaker. For the present though, she was enjoying her job as governess to the two little girls.

Catherine was bitterly disappointed at not having Mary at home for her wedding. She would dearly love to have her as her bridesmaid. Mary too was wishing she could be home to see her beloved sister on her big day, but it was too costly to travel. She wrote a letter on hearing the news of her intention to marry a farmer called Eddie. She sent a beautiful set of white sheets and pillowcases, cleverly embroidered with a little message pinned on them saying '*to be used only on special occasions.*' Also, she hinted she hoped there would be plenty of little ones running around by the time she returned. For years afterwards Catherine would pin the little message to the freshly laundered sheets, smiling to herself before putting them away for the next special occasion.

The sun was shining so brightly on the morning of 8th September that Catherine had to shield her eyes as she peeped through the net curtains of her bedroom window. She felt a little apprehensive and also a little sad. This was the last morning she would be waking up as Catherine

Brennan. She could hear the birds singing and wondered was Eddie waking up to a similar scene. She closed her eyes and pictured him. She felt he would be very nervous at what was ahead of him.

She wandered outside and inhaled the fresh air coming across the bogs of Owenboy. She also needed this time to herself to reflect. Marriage was a big step and Catherine had no intention of taking it lightly. Even though she did not know her future husband very long, she prided herself at having great insight into the future. Her mother often said she could foretell things when she was young. Just now she felt Eddie was a good man and was quite happy at the way things had turned out.

She had no regrets since saying farewell to Philadelphia although at this moment she could not help herself thinking, if she were to have married in the States, her wedding day would be so different from what she was experiencing now. She could see her Aunt Anne and Richard giving a huge party to all their friends and telling her how proud they were and how much they loved her.

She heard her mother calling out from the back door 'Come in Catherine and put some clothes on or you'll get your death of cold out there. The car will be here for you and you won't be ready! Did you eat anything at all this morning? I'll put on an egg to boil for you now. Can't have you fainting at the priest's feet,' she finished.

Catherine smiled and gave her mother a hug. 'I'm going to miss you Mam. I am doing the right thing, aren't I?'

'Of course you are and may God's blessing be on you. I'll miss you too, but as long as you are happy, what more could a mother ask for *a 'gra*?'

By the time the car arrived in the street outside everyone was ready. It was going to be a long day. They drove in silence to the Church to be greeted by the Parish Priest Father Killen. He told them Eddie was waiting inside for them. 'Here we go then in the name of God' said Catherine to her brother James who was going to walk her down the aisle, "wish me luck!"

It was a simple ceremony and was over in half an hour. Eddie had scrubbed up well and was turned out very nicely indeed. His mother must have made a special effort ironing his shirt. The collar seemed to be stiff with starch and every so often Eddie rubbed his finger along the inside of it as if it was annoying him. Apart from that and the nervous cough that could be heard in the silence of the big Church, he seemed to be very happy. He whispered to Catherine that she looked pretty as a picture and said his mother and the neighbours were busy getting food ready for a *hooley* tonight in the house. He had ordered a barrel and a half of Guinness, and there would be plenty of bacon and cabbage and *Golden Wonder* potatoes for everyone.

The mare and trap was waiting for them outside and after the priest showered his blessings on them, Eddie told her he was going to drive them to *Portacloy* for the day. Catherine was in her element and was glad to see Eddie had thought of spending time alone with her, before returning to his home to start their new life together. God only knows when I'll get away again, she thought to herself. She was prepared for life on a farm and she fully intended to buckle down to the tasks that had to be done.

As Eddie skilfully handled the reins pulling this way and that way as they approached each bend in the road, Catherine could not help feeling very proud of this new husband of hers. She hoped by the end of their first full day on their own, he would be a little less shy. Still, she thought to herself it's better than being a ladies man, with smart remarks and compliments flying and no weight at all to them. She felt very nervous herself at the thoughts of their first night together and said a little prayer to the Virgin Mary to come to her aid.

'Well Mrs Staunton, how are we doing now?' Eddie asked, making her jump in her seat beside him. She was so carried away with her own thoughts that she felt herself blushing like someone caught in the act. He noticed her confusion and reached for her hand.

'Sure maybe we were thinking about the same thing,' he smiled and gave her a knowing wink, which only added to Catherine's confusion and made her blush even more profusely. Eddie pulled over the mare calling out "whoa there *Fanny* girl whoa." The mare came to a halt and was very quick to make use of the moment to grab a big mouthful of luscious green grass from the roadside.

Eddie put an arm around Catherine's shoulders and looked into her green eyes. She leaned over to him and they kissed for the first time, right there in the side of the road. She felt a warm glow inside her and she could feel Eddie too was very stirred by the embrace. Oh it was a lovely start to their marriage she thought to herself!

They were now much more at ease having broken the ice with each other and as the day progressed they found they had a lot in common. Their tastes were similar and their love of all things furry and feathered was heartening. The day went quickly by with all the chatting they were doing and all the questions that had to be answered. They bathed their hot feet in the salt water and lay down on the fine sand and dosed away, both busy with their thoughts. After, they had a nice snack in Katie Kelly's teashop near the beach, and they both agreed they couldn't wait to get back to the house that was now going to be their home.

They arrived back around six o'clock to a tremulous welcome from the neighbours, who were dying to see Eddie's new wife. They had everything prepared for a great *hooley.* A bonfire was burning outside and between the smell of the smoke and the food, Catherine now felt ravenous. Eddie went to check on the barrel of porter and see if all the other chores were done. It wasn't very often he left to go anywhere for a full day. He checked the animals and as he was about to see to the fowl, Nora came out to have a quiet word with him before things got too busy with the celebrations.

'This is a proud day for me Eddie,' she said putting a hand on his arm. 'I only hope you will be fierce happy. You have picked a lovely colleen there my boy. God's blessings be on you and Catherine.'

Eddie felt such a glow at this demonstration of affection from his Mother. It wasn't often she showed him she cared. Most people he knew were like that anyway. They didn't wear their hearts on their sleeves.

'Come on in now *a 'gra* and we will have a good evening. I see the Atkinson's have arrived with their fiddles and they wont start the dancing till you and Catherine are ready to give a few steps together. You know well now Eddie 'tis expected of you even though you'd rather the ground opened up and swallowed you. It will be over before you know it,' she coaxed.

Like every mother, Nora knew her son very well and she knew he was not the kind of man who would enjoy such a demonstration. She knew if it was Martin he wouldn't need to be told twice. He loved to show off. They were as different as chalk and cheese, she mused to herself.

When they arrived inside things was looking very good. The food was being handed out and the drinks were flowing. Old Billy Moran was telling a story to Catherine about the night he got married and the bed was rigged by some smart *buckoos.* It collapsed as soon as they both put their weight on it. Catherine was laughing with the others but Nora noticed with affection she had blushed to her hairline, so she came to her rescue.

'Come on you old *codjure* and stop making the poor girl uncomfortable on her first night with us. Sup up and give us a tune on that old rusty violin,' Nora said.

And so the night began with more fiddlers joining in and the dancers made up sets of four for the half set. The barn dance and the polka was called for and you could see sparks rising from the concrete floor, as the heel tips from the studs of the men's boots connected with it, as they swung with their partners while set dancing. They took a break to listen to some stories about the *banshee* and the fairies, and a few were called on to sing a verse of a song. They enquired if the new bride could sing at all, and Catherine assured them she could sing—better than the crows anyway! That's all the encouragement they needed, and before she knew what was happening they had her singing. She shyly gave them her favourite *Danny Boy* and while she was singing you could hear a pin drop. She noticed Eddie watching her from the far side of the room, but was not able to make out his expression in the poor lighting. When she had finished Catherine got a rapturous applaud. She was having a great time and loved meeting these lovely friends and relations of Eddie's.

Now they had got a song out of Catherine they were not going to rest till they got one from Eddie too. At first he was shy and hesitant and you would swear that nobody would be able to persuade him to sing. As soon as Catherine suggested to him to sing just one verse, he suddenly took a deep breath and started singing

Bold Robert Emmet, the darling of Erin,
Bold Robert Emmet, who died with a smile,
Farewell companions, both loyal and daring,
I gave up my life for the Emerald Isle.

Suddenly there was great commotion outside and before anyone had a chance to find out what was going on, a bunch of straw boys arrived at the door. They barged in dancing and started to take everyone in turn around the floor. Catherine had heard of this custom, if people weren't asked to a wedding, they would dress up in straw and come anyway. Of course the fiddle players needed no introductions to them and started up playing once more.

By midnight Eddie and Catherine were sent to bed, amid cheers and good wishes and were told, 'don't do anything we wouldn't do.' Martin, now worse for wear, having been busy all night handing out mugs of Guinness but did not leave himself short, called out with a big laugh, 'I wont be far away if you need any help Eddie. I'll be happy to oblige. You know me I'm a very obliging man!'

'Shut up Martin,' called Nora giving him a look that would kill.

Eddie looked at his new wife and they shared a knowing smile. Nothing Martin would say could spoil this night. This was to be the biggest moment of their lives and they both knew it. In the privacy of their own room they shared a very tender kiss, which was to seal the happiness they both felt after the big step they had taken today. As they snuggled down together they could hear the music and dancing still going on. They were so exhausted after the events of the day; they both fell asleep as soon as their heads hit the pillow.

Chapter 19

World's Apart

Catherine awoke to find herself alone in a strange bed. It took her some moments before she could focus on anything around her or even where she was. She leaned on one elbow and took in the room around her. She was in a feather bed with brass railings at the head and foot. Her eyes drew to something in the corner of the small room and suddenly she focused on her trunk, which she had sent ahead of her before her wedding day. Quick as a flash it all came back to her and she woke herself properly, already getting excited at the prospects of all the discoveries that were ahead of her. She felt like a child on Christmas morning with anticipation.

Eddie must have got up early to do the milking. Having been brought up on a farm she knew the first chore of the morning was to milk the cows. She prided herself on knowing how to do this tedious task. She reminisced at the first time her father showed her, but she could not get the hang of it at all! The next time she had better luck and as with most things, once you got the knack you never lost it. Most people would joke and say 'it's like riding a bicycle, once you know how you will never forget.'

There was a jug of water in an aluminium basin for washing herself. She was not wildly excited at the thoughts of washing in cold water, but soon discovered it was comfortably tepid. Eddie must have boiled the kettle and crept into the room with some warm water. How thoughtful of him, she smiled, sure he knew I would be lost in my new surroundings this morning. She had plenty of time to make it up to him when she got used to the ways around her new home.

She dressed quickly and choose her clothes wisely—neither too fancy nor too frumpy. She had no idea what type of work was to be done today. She would take a walk around the farmyard with Nora after she had some breakfast. She was so looking forward to seeing all the fowl that Eddie had in abundance in the yard.

She made her way to the kitchen and found Nora up and dressed and tidying up after the *hooley* last evening. Nora greeted her good-humouredly and had the kettle boiling over the fire. A saucepan of porridge was cooking in the double burner beside the fire. She had a couple of fresh duck eggs in a saucepan waiting to add boiling water to them when Eddie came in.

'Eddie is up and gone out without eating a bite this fine morning. He said to tell you he will be in to have his breakfast with his new wife later,' Nora said with a twinkle in her eye. At this Catherine blushed up to the hairline. She didn't know what to say but Nora made her feel at ease by saying, 'It's a grand thing to have another woman in the house again Catherine. I had three girls in and out amongst the seven lads, but they are gone now a few years. Judy is married to a Cork man. She met him in Galway and it didn't take her long to make up her mind to marry him. Mary is over in Chicago and will hardly get married now, and Ellen is married with a little girl back near Mulranny.'

Catherine decided now was as good a time as any to ask the question she knew had to be asked, for her own peace of mind.

'Can I ask you what name you would like me to call you?' she asked shyly.

'Ah sure Catherine *agra* Nora will do fine till a better name comes along! Sure that's what everyone calls me. As the older generation used to say 'you can call me anything but don't call me too early in the morning.'

They both laughed together and after a nice cup of tea Catherine said she couldn't wait a moment longer to see all the fowl, and get to know the routine of the different chores outside. So herself and Nora wandered out and were just in time to see Eddie throw the last fistful of grain to the chickens, with the geese and gander trying to grab it too.

On seeing them, Sailor the sheepdog left Eddie's side to check out the newcomer. He tentatively approached Catherine's side with his tail between his hind legs. She reached out and patted his head and immediately he sat up on his back legs and gave her his two front paws. She was so chuffed at this and Eddie was so happy to see his beloved dog take to Catherine so quickly. It was a good sign. Sailor was a good judge of humans throughout his life with Eddie.

He waved to them and called out to Catherine to come and see all the eggs the chickens had laid already. She was well accustomed to doing this chore for her mother. It was such a rewarding job collecting the eggs and she always felt it was like the hens were saying thank you for all the food. Eddie had finished all the chores around the house for this morning, and so they all went inside to have breakfast together. Eddie said he was ravenous. Nora said she would dish up this morning as it was Catherine's first day and sure she would be more used to things in a strange house by tomorrow morning.

While Nora was busy arranging hot coals under the saucepan of boiling water for the eggs at the open fire, Eddie quietly came up beside Catherine, put a hand on her shoulder and surprised her with a quick kiss on her cheek. As Catherine looked up shyly he quietly said in a voice low enough for only her to hear 'the next time I'll spend longer at it.'

'Is that a promise Eddie? She laughed quietly. 'I might keep you longer too.'

There was a definite twinkle in Eddie's eye this morning, and Catherine felt she was the one that put it there, and it was such a good feeling. She felt confident she would make this marriage work, and so far Eddie was nothing but a gentleman. There was much to discuss and so many things they had to compare with each other, but all in good time. They had the rest of their lives to do it.

For the present though she couldn't wait to go outside and take in all her surroundings. Eddie had said there was a brook for the ducks and geese to swim in. A river at the bottom of the far field had trout and eel, which he caught regularly for their dinner on Fridays. If you stood outside late in the evenings you could hear the gulls over the lake about half a mile away. This was what she had wanted for as long as she could remember!

The only reminder of America now was the trunk with all her clothes in the bedroom. She hoped she would get use for all the fancy garments that were stored inside. If Eddie's brother got a wife soon there would surely be a *hooley* in the house and she would get a chance to air her finery!

She felt a long way from life in Philadelphia now, and it would be foolish to even compare. They were worlds apart. She had no regrets. She quietly whispered 'thanks be to God.'

Chapter 20

A Cradle for the Babóg

It was 8th December and thoughts of Christmas were entering Catherine's head. They were three months married now, but apart from an odd 'fly in the ointment' they were very content with their lives. It had been such a learning process she felt in more ways than one. Even though she was reared on a farm, it took a while to get accustomed to the routine of life on Eddie's farm.

Nora was a delightful mother-in-law and Catherine knew she was the luckiest girl to have found one she could get on so well with. It was one of the drawbacks when marrying into a farm! You married his mother as well! This could be detrimental to a young couple trying to work at their marriage. Catherine did not have any problems there at all, but the same could not be said for Eddie's brother Martin. He was worse than a difficult mother-in-law! She soon discovered he was overbearing and inconsiderate and very selfish. He had finished building his house and had moved into it when they got married, but Catherine was not long finding out, he took advantage of all Eddie's possessions, using the mare and donkey and all the tools whenever the mood was on him. It didn't matter if Eddie had plans for that day; he would arrive first thing in the morning and take what he wanted without asking.

One morning Eddie came bursting into the house muttering. 'That bloody bastard is gone off with the mare and I needed her for myself today. I want to get the rest of the spuds in before they rot in the ground.'

Catherine was surprised by his manner. This was the first time she had seen her husband so agitated and it upset her. More times than she could count in the past three months, she had wondered why he was so acceptable of Martin's behaviour. She wished he would stand up for himself more where that man was concerned.

'Come here *agrá* and tell me what's wrong,' she coaxed.

He sat down and took out his pipe and started to kindle it. Catherine thought she never seen him look so vulnerable and her heart went out to him.

'Sure isn't tomorrow another day Eddie and I know you'll find plenty to occupy you yet today. I've never seen you idle yet. Make sure you let him know that you'll be needing the mare tomorrow.' said Catherine.

'Ah Catherine I'm fed up with it. I'd just like for once to be able to do what I had in mind. That bloody man would break your heart, and when I say anything to him he just laughs it off.' Eddie said.

Catherine thought this might be a good time to tell him the news she was savouring to herself all week. She pulled up a chair beside his and reached out and took his hand in hers.

'Eddie love, sure maybe what I'm about to tell you will take your mind off Martin. What would you say if I told you we'll be having our own little helper for picking the spuds with you,' Catherine smiled up to him.

'Ah come here to me you grand girl! Are you telling me I'm going to be a father?' Eddie beamed down at her.

'You are to be sure. Isn't it a grand surprise now for you today? Sure I wouldn't get the chance to tell you if you had gone off with the mare! So now *Dad* wont that put a smile on your face all day?'

'It surely will *me darling* and thank you. Tell me when will we break the good news to mother?' he asked her.

'Any time you like Eddie. Do you want to tell her she's going to be a grandmother or will I?' she asked.

Eddie scratched the back of his neck for a while then started to scrape the ashes out of his pipe thinking deeply. Catherine had seen him doing this when he was deep in thought. She prided herself that she knew him well enough to know he'd find it uncomfortable breaking this news to his mother.

Times like this, she realised, she had grown so fond of this nice easygoing man. She told him that she would tell Nora as soon as the opportunity presented itself. She could see Eddie was relieved and the smile returned to his face again. He leaned over and kissed her and said 'I suppose now you'll not be able to come out picking the spuds with me tomorrow,' he said sheepishly glancing down at her waist.

'Ah come on now Eddie, being pregnant is not an illness. I'm not a delicate *will-o-the-wisp* you know,' she said. 'I was told I had good childbearing hips, whatever that means. Hadn't you noticed Eddie?' she teased.

Eddie blushed a little at this. He was never any good at this side of things, and no good at all with compliments, so Catherine wasn't expecting any. She had long since noticed these traits in him! But she didn't mind that at all as Eddie was a good man. Even though she had preferred Martin's good looks to Eddie's on the day they met, it hadn't taken her long to realise she would have made a terrible mistake if she married a man like him. Each day Catherine would say 'thanks be to God' for all his goodness to her.

'Eddie I think I'll keep the news to myself yet. It will be a nice Christmas present for Nora to hear she will be a grandmother again.' she said.

'Sure that's grand with me too. I'll keep it to myself so and not mention it to Martin till you tell mother. He'd be sure to blurt it out to her before you tell her yourself, if he got the wing of it. It will be a happy day for her, as she hasn't much contact with Julia's kids down in Cork. Sure she has never seen her grandsons in America and probably never will either. She'll be a great help to you when the time comes, you know Catherine. I know she's very fond of children but it's a good while since there was a child running around in this house,' Eddie said.

Catherine had never heard him so talkative. She knew he was excited. 'Sure it's like riding a bicycle. Once you know how, you never forget it! And talking about bicycles my love, how would you like to take a ride into town? Just the two of us and make a day out of it, by way of a little celebration, and we could get some laths of timber on the way home in McEllins and on wet days I could be making a cradle for the *babóg.*'

She wasn't wildly enthusiastic about the idea, as like Eddie she too had plans for the day, but sure she could do catch up tomorrow. Having Eddie in this mood was better than anything she could have wished for. They had never discussed having children, so Catherine had no idea how he felt about them. But nature will have its way and it's not that there isn't enough pro-creation going on in the farm to remind him of it! Every animal and fowl was hard at work! That was the first thing she noticed when she came to see Eddie's farm!

When Nora got up they told her they were going to town and asked her to keep an eye on things. They would be back by evening to do the milking and put the animals and fowl to bed for the night. She never bothered them with questions only agreed with everything they wanted to do. Not many were as lucky as that. Catherine often thought about it to herself and mentioned it to Eddie too. And once again she thanked God for giving her such a wonderful husband and mother-in-law.

Chapter 21

The Black Sheep

A few days before Christmas a letter arrived from Chicago from Eddie's older brother Anthony. He was coming home for the holidays. Catherine noticed a change in both Nora and Eddie. They weren't very enthusiastic about the news, and she wondered why. Not having heard his name ever mentioned before, she asked Nora was he a married man or had he any family.

'Ah no *agra*, sure he never bothered with the ladies. He was too fond of the 'golden lady,' she said sadly.

'Will we make up the *cailleach*, or should we let him sleep in the *settle bed*? she ventures to ask Nora as she was giving the house a good clean for Christmas.

'It might be better to let him sleep in the *settle bed*, he might not be in form to climb up to bed some nights,' Nora answered quietly. 'Sure Martin might keep him a few nights now he has his own place. They used to get on well together when they were young. Thick as thieves they were; always plotting and planning, and causing mayhem between them. But a lot has happened since then, and it will do no good raking up old ashes! Don't be killing yourself doing up the house for his homecoming

Catherine. Sure he won't take a bit of notice. He'll be hoping there'll be plenty of drink in the house,' she said quietly.

Catherine was coming to her own conclusions about their visitor. She had never heard Eddie mention his name since they met, but then he never told her much at all about his siblings. She found that a little disturbing, as she was missing her brother James a lot, and never a day passed that she didn't give a thought to Mary in Philadelphia. Bridget was a home bird, and it didn't look much like she would leave home now. Her mother was glad of the help around the house, but there wasn't much future in that.

Of course, with only four in her family, compared to ten in Eddie's, you could imagine why there would not be the same closeness. By the time the last one was born, the first ones were ready to leave the nest, Catherine mused to herself! Anyway there's plenty of time for Eddie to tell her all about them and he would do it in his own good time.

Lately he had grown quieter. Catherine knew he was happy about her pregnancy, but she wondered was he worrying about how to tell Nora the news. Maybe it was his brothers impending visit that was bothering him now.

Certainly he was quieter since the letter came. As it was now Christmas Eve, she decided she would break the good news to Nora and not have poor Eddie on edge any longer. It was almost dark. He had finished putting all the animals in for the night and was standing at the gate having a last smoke of his pipe, when Catherine came out to secure all the fowl for the night. She closed up all the henhouses but left one door open for the last remaining straggler to go in by herself, while she went to put up the galvanise sheets in front of the geese and ducks in the far garden. Eddie had told her of the odd fox raid in the past, so she put a good heavy stone in front of each of the doors.

From inside, where Nora was putting the finishing touches to the evening meal, you could smell the aroma of freshly made bread, mingled with the smell of pig's *crubeens* and cabbage. As Catherine came in by the stack of turf, she filled her apron with small clods of stone turf, to have a nice bright welcoming fire for their guest. He should be arriving soon, and she hoped he would be good and hungry. They decided to have cabbage and bacon especially for Anthony's homecoming, and they had invited Martin to join them, as this was his first Christmas on his own in his new house.

Perhaps next year he too would have a wife. Catherine couldn't wait for the day. It would be so good to have another woman living nearby for company and advice when the baby came. It wasn't that Nora wasn't good company, but a woman of her own age would be great. Also she wouldn't have the extra work of giving his house an odd going over, and changing his sheets occasionally. Not that he had ever asked her to do it, and indeed there were little thanks from him when she did! Nora had hinted that Martin wasn't any good at any of that, and would stay in the same sheets till they stood up and took a walk by themselves! They used to laugh at Nora's fondness for straight talking! It was like water off a ducks back with Martin. You couldn't insult him!

As she passed by Eddie she reached out for his hand and told him she was going inside now to tell Nora their good news. Instantly, Eddie looked all shy, like a schoolboy, and Catherine laughed up at him and gave him a kiss. He laughed then too, and said, 'Will you do all the talking then? I'm a bit on the hungry side now.' Catherine knew well it was a cover up for his shyness with this particular subject.

Thankfully Nora had everything ready and was sitting down waiting for them to come in. Catherine was glad also that Martin hadn't come yet, as they wanted Nora to be the first to hear the good news. The delight was soon obvious, when Nora stood up to throw her arms around Catherine and say 'I knew the minute I clapped eyes on you, there would be happiness in this house again. May God's blessing be on you and the child.'

There was tears in her eyes and Catherine laughed and said 'I didn't do it all on my own, Granny! Your son here had a lot to do with it.' Poor Eddie was mortified but Nora put him at his ease again by saying 'Sure Eddie *agra* I didn't have ten children myself without knowing how they came about! You were always a shy boy,' she added, giving him an affectionate little thump on his arm. 'This is a great time to celebrate. Get the bottle of sherry for Catherine. A small drop won't do the child one bit of harm, and Eddie you and me will have a drop of whiskey. Martin should be down now any minute and he can hear the wonderful news too.' She laughed again saying, 'this will be a great excuse for Anthony to wet the babys head. He'll always find a good reason to celebrate.'

Catherine could see it was a great time to share the news. It took a lot of the tension off Anthony's visit. Just then she realised, its time he was coming as the dinner would be spoiled for them all. Maybe they should start to eat theirs, for there was no telling what time he'd come. He might have a while to wait for a car to bring him here. She looked out the half door to see if there was any light in the distance, but all she could see was Martin just outside the door. It looked like he was just caught in the act of doing something wrong. She could not help wondering was he standing outside a while, listening. And if so how long has this been going on!

'Are you there long Martin?' Catherine called out. She didn't care at all for snoopers and wanted to let him know she was on to him. 'Is there any sign of your brother coming? I was just saying maybe we'd better get on with our own meal. You're probably as ravenous as the rest of us, and who knows maybe Anthony wont want dinner at all.'

'Oh, sure I'd eat a horse now this minute. Anyway if he comes in the middle of it, what harm,' Martin said.

'Happy Christmas Martin, come on in we have great news to tell you,' Nora calls out to him.

'Oh I don't think our announcement will be news to Martin,' says Catherine. 'He's been loitering outside like a corner boy before he came in,' she chided meaningfully.

'I heard enough all right. Leave it there Eddie,' reaching out to shake hands with his older brother. 'I didn't think you had it in you, man. I thought you'd have to get help!' He guffawed, making poor Eddie blush like a schoolboy. 'When will the great occasion be?' he asked. 'What sort of work will be going on at the time?'

Once again Eddie was embarrassed. He had never thought to ask Catherine. It did not seem to matter when she told him, but now that Martin brought it up he too was curious. He looked at Catherine across the room and lifted one eyebrow as if to say 'help me out here.'

She quickly answered that the hay would be saved and the corn would not be ready yet. Without any calculations at all the pair of men and Nora chirped up together 'That must be end of July so.' They all laughed out loud together.

It was at that moment Anthony stumbled out of the hackney car. The smell of freshly cooked food, and the happy laughter coming from inside the thatched cottage, sobered him momentarily. It was a long journey and with little food inside him, the few drinks he had on the journey took effect on his senses rather quickly. He had slept a good while, on and off, but this was such a welcoming sight.

Through the half door, he could see his mother looking so happy, her arm around a very attractive brown haired girl. 'This must be Eddie's new wife,' he thought. 'By golly she sure is some looker! Martin and Eddie hadn't changed anyway! He would know them in a pot of cally! They were all laughing together. He stood for a moment taking in the scene, feeling like an intruder, rather than a son coming home for the Christmas. The smell of the food, mingling with the smell of smoke from the turf fire, and the low lowing from the cows in the barn nearby, and the stillness of the night brought all his childhood memories back. He had been through such hardship in Chicago since he left, that this was a balm to his bruised feelings. Oh he knew well it was all self-inflicted. He had nobody to blame but himself for his wayward ways. He was not expecting sympathy from anyone, but he was feeling rather nervous, wondering what kind of a reception he would get after all the years not keeping in touch.

Suddenly the dog gave a few low barks beside him, and everyone inside turned towards the half door. Eddie came out quickly calling 'is that you Anthony?' Come in man, come in till we take a look at you.' He put his hand out to welcome his brother. 'You're just in time for our Christmas Eve supper. I hope you are hungry. It's great to see you again, man,' he was babbling with his nervousness, Catherine noticed.

As Anthony entered, Nora rushed up to throw her arms around her long lost son. She cried as he held her, and Catherine never saw her so vulnerable before. She could understand how heartbreaking it must be, fearful you may never see one of your children again, and there was nothing you could about it. Martin was also very emotional too, and finally when they all had their moment with him, Eddie finally introduced him to Catherine.

He was a fine tall handsome man, so beautifully dressed in a well-cut dark grey suit, that he put the other two brothers to shame. Even Eddie on his wedding day was not turned out as good as this. Catherine could not help thinking, what have they been saying about this poor man; sure he's very respectable.

The sound of a horn blowing outside interrupted her thoughts, and while Eddie went outside to see what the racket was all about, they set about dishing up the dinner. With everyone in high spirits each one happy with there own individual feelings on this night, they all wished each other a very happy Christmas.

When Eddie returned and sat down to the table without a word, Catherine noticed he was gone all subdued and very quiet again! She was so ravenous she just had to forget about it for the moment. She was eating for two now, so best get that food where it belonged. This was her first Christmas in her own home, with her new husband and a baby on the way. Her heart was so full with happiness, she silently thanked God.

Nora called on them all to join her in a little prayer. She said 'let us be thankful for this night and pray that we will all be alive this time next year.'

To which they all answered "Amen."

Chapter 22

Murder Most Fowl

Catherine woke with a start! She noticed it was brighter than other mornings, and then she realised it was Christmas morning and they had all slept late. As she peeped out the window there was a coating of snow all around. She put on her dressing gown and slipped into an old pair of shoes and quietly crept outside to take in this scene, before anyone else woke up. She was like a child wanting this all to herself! She stood drinking in the scene and knew she would never forget this first Christmas of her new life.

She was making her way around the house to let out the dog, when the sight that met her eyes as she rounded the corner, froze her to the ground. One of the henhouse doors was opened wide and there were feathers and hens scattered all around the yard. There were bloodstains covering the snow, and suddenly Catherine realised she had made it very easy for the fox to raid the henhouse. She remembered she left the door open for the last hen to go in, and never returned to close it. She had so much on her mind last evening she completely forgot.

'Oh my poor hens,' she wailed to herself. What will Eddie say to her? No wonder they slept late. There was no cock crowing to wake them! She started to cry at the great loss of her beautiful hens. The cold was making her shiver and she realised she was in her nightclothes. She ran back into the house, and down to the room to prepare Eddie for the sight that would greet him on Christmas morning. He had awakened a few minutes before and wondered where she was. He felt a very lucky man this Christmas morning and he knew Catherine was the reason for such happiness.

'I thought maybe you were getting me a mug of tea in bed for Christmas morning,' he laughed. At the sight of her tearstained face, he leaped out of bed and held her to him. His first thought was has something happened the baby! She was crying and babbling something like 'its all my fault Eddie, you're going to kill me. It's all ruined now. You'll never forgive me.'

Eddie was really worried now. This was not like Catherine at all. He had never seen her cry before. She was always so in control unlike some girls he had noticed. He could hear Nora raking out the ashes and putting on the fire in the kitchen, so he said 'Come on now Catherine and tell me what is wrong, you have me worried sick. You have to tell me sooner or later, no matter how bad it is. Is it the baby or are you not feeling well?'

She brightened up a little then 'No the baby is fine Eddie,' she said.

'Well thank God for that anyway. Now will you just tell me what's upsetting you and get it over with,' he said.

'It's the hens Eddie, the fox was in the henhouse last night and has them killed, and it's all my fault,' she started crying again.

Eddie was shocked to hear this. He had such a hatred of the fox. The bloody fox was a nightmare. He had seen many a slaughter by him and each time was still a shock. Poor Catherine had never seen it before, so he knew how she must have been feeling. He knew she cared for those hens, as she did with all the fowl around the farm. He would try to make light of it just for her sake.

'Come on now it's not the end of the world. We'll get more chickens in the factory next week and start building up the numbers again. It's not your fault at all. How could it be your fault love?' he said soothingly.

'I never went back to close the door. I was waiting for that black devil to go in by herself, and forgot to go back to close the door. Do you remember Eddie you were outside and we came in together?' she was saying through her tears.

'Well then it was as much my fault as yours,' he comforted her. Lets leave it at that and we'll make a start on the day. Its Christmas morning and there's a lot to be done. You get some clothes on you now and go down to the kitchen and make us a nice big saucepan of porridge. I'll go and see what's to be done outside and take care of the massacre. Sure it's not the first time I've had to tidy up after a fox, and I suppose it won't be the last. It's a good job we went to midnight Mass last night anyway.'

'Eddie do you know there's snow everywhere?' she laughed up to him. He could see she was excited about it, but God knows he wasn't! It was not good news. It meant nothing but extra work for him. He hoped it would melt away by dinnertime, but he did not want to spoil her excitement by saying so. He was dreading going out at all knowing what was before him.

As he passed Nora in the kitchen he called out 'happy Christmas mother' and kept going. She was bending over the fire and making a pot of tea. She called after him to have a cup of tea but he pretended not to hear. He wanted to get out before her to tidy up the mess. He was glad there was no sign of Anthony either.

As he rounded the corner he stopped in his tracks! The brightness of the white snow only seemed to emphasise the slaughter scene. There were red bloodstains and black and brown feathers everywhere. Heads were torn off the bodies and scattered around. There must be ten hens lying dead and the poor old cockerel was dead too. It turned his stomach. He had never seen so much destruction by a fox before, but the door was wide open for him!

He pulled himself together and tackled the chore putting all the dead hens in the wheelbarrow for now. He would bury them later in the day. He swept up the mess and poured water all over the yard. Satisfied it looked presentable again, he tackled the usual chores. The dog came out to greet him, but soon sniffed the blood and busied himself nosing around curiously. Eddie went to milk the cow and feed the pigs, and let out the rest of the hens in the other henhouse. They were okay and did not appear to have been too traumatised after the night. We should still be ok for a few fresh eggs from them, Eddie thought to himself.

'It's a wonder we never heard the racket in the night,' Eddie announced as he made his way into the house. He felt it was better to get it over and done with straight away for everyone's sake.

'What racket?' asks Nora.

'The fox attacked the henhouse,' he replied.

'Well the devil scald him,' cursed Nora. 'He'll be around again tonight if he didn't get in to any of the hens, especially with the snow. Did you see where he came in Eddie? It should be easy to track him in the snow. You could set a trap for him and we might have him got by the morning. You'd get a pound in the Barracks now if you caught a fox.'

Eddie decided to say no more about it. He could see Catherine cringing, hoping the ground would swallow her. After all it was Christmas Day and with the weather so cold now Nora would not be going outside and wouldn't notice a lot of the hens missing. She need not know everything that was happening.

'Is there no sign of Anthony getting up yet? Did ye check to see is he dead or alive?' Eddie asked, just to change the subject and lighten the atmosphere, as they were all around the table having the porridge.

'Ah, sure he needs a good sleep this morning after the long journey, and maybe not much to eat on the way,' said Nora good-humouredly. It was nice to see her happy about having him home, thought Catherine, as it was a different story yesterday! Her mother used to say "blood is thicker than water," and this certainly was an example of it.

She did not get the same feeling about Eddie though. With all that happened this morning, and with all the banter last night after the dinner was over, she did not get a chance to ask why he was disgruntled last night.

'Eddie, why was that person blowing the horn last night when Anthony came inside?' she asked quietly, as soon as she got Nora's back turned. He shook his head, but said in a voice so low she could hardly hear him. 'He hadn't the price of the Hackney car, would you believe that?' he shook his head once again.

Catherine found it hard to take in. 'Sure he's dressed like a toff he looks the picture of wealth, Eddie. There must be a reason he couldn't pay. Maybe he had large notes and the Hackney man had no change.'

'We'll wait and see, love and say nothing to Nora for now. But I have my doubts about something. I wonder how he heard I got a wife! When he gets up I'll have it out with him. If he came home thinking he'll get something from the place, he's out of luck. He's gone so long it owes him nothing! Anyway Catherine I've all straightened up again outside, and try not to blame yourself, these thing happen.' He gave her a knowing wink, and hoped Nora could not hear over the noise of washing the cups.

Catherine felt a lot better now Eddie was so forgiving about it, and she could not help feeling that once again, this man of hers was proving to be very kind. She felt so lucky and thankful. She was going to make such an effort to have a really scrumptious Christmas dinner today for all of them, and forget about the awful start to the day. She was hoping they might have a singsong. Apart from her wedding day when Eddie shyly sang a bit of a song, she had no idea if the others could sing or not. Surely between the three brothers, Nora and herself, they should be able to exchange lots of songs.

A game of cards would also help to pass the long evening, and of course she would take out the gramophone she bought in Philadelphia last year. John McCormick's records were her favourite. If only she knew Anthony was coming sooner, she would have loved a new record. There was little chance of getting one now. She would have to wait till Mary was coming home and put in an order in good time. That could be a long wait but she was patient, and in the meantime she would keep her memories of Philadelphia alive by playing the records she bought while she was there.

It seems such a long time ago but Catherine had no regrets. She had plenty to look forward to now. Soon she would be feeling the stirrings of new life inside her, and by the end of the summer she would be a mother. Once again she thanked the Lord for his goodness to her.

Chapter 23

Grace Summerfield

It was New Years Eve. Martin Staunton took down the *Old Moore Almanac* from the mantelpiece. This little gem of a book predicted the weather forecast, the changes in the moon and the tides, dates of fair days, and would even predict air or sea disasters in many parts of the world. They may not be all disasters. Some good things may be ahead. Martin thought it might predict events meaningful to him in the coming year. He liked to plan ahead. Actually it would be more accurate to say he liked to be ahead of everyone else. Lately he was becoming very disgruntled. He was slipping up. He always had a way with the women. He liked them all alot and they liked him, but still it was Eddie, the plain, unassuming, quiet man that hooked the loveliest girl Martin had ever met. She had all the qualities he liked in a woman. How could he hope to find someone like her?

When they first met in the street of *Drumoneen* with the matchmaker, he noticed she was looking at him more than Eddie! He was well used to it and was flattered. It was a boost to his ego as always. He was not in the mood to settle down then and anyway the introduction was for

Eddie, but seeing him now with a lovely wife and a child on the way, Martin recognised his feelings of jealousy of his brother! He also noticed she had eyes for no one but Eddie. The lucky bugger, Martin thought. He felt of late she was very offhanded with him. This was foreign to him; he prided himself that he had a way with the ladies.

Of course Eddie had an advantage over him. He had a house and a good holding of land! Martin had his eye on a little farm belonging to 'Mouse' McGowan that was bordering his own few measly fields that surrounded his house. It was for sale since 'Mouse' died over a year ago, but Martin hadn't any money left since he finished the house. It was very basic and could do with a woman's touch badly. Lately he was thinking alot about a returned yank named Grace Summerfield, whom he met at a crossroads dance one night, but had not seen her since. He heard she had alot of money having been a good few years in Chicago.

'She has one drawback. She's a good few years older than me.' Martin was thinking to himself as he scratched his head. 'That might not be such a bad thing in the long run. There would be an old age pension coming in when I'd still be young enough to enjoy it.'

He overheard two auld *codgers* talking that night and of course Martin was never shy about eavesdropping. They were saying she was a head cook in a big house in Chicago, and was well healed! Martin liked his grub and things were starting to take shape in his head. Age or not she was starting to look good in his eyes. He wondered if he might swing this one himself, without the help of a matchmaker! If she liked him enough maybe his small farm would not be a drawback at all. He knew he could charm her, it was just a case of getting the timing right. If a matchmaker was not involved, then he had a better chance to snare her, and it would not cost anything.

He decided he wouldn't do any work at all today. He had bigger fish to fry! While the right mood was on him he'd head for town and sure maybe he'd meet someone who would know her. He washed and shaved himself and dressed in his best suit. He had more confidence in his suit. He never knew how Eddie could go out dressed like he did. If Catherine didn't notice the patch on his knee in his good trousers the day she met him, then she must be half blind, he thought to himself.

He contemplated telling Anthony his plans and bring him along, but sure he'd probably start drinking too much and disgrace him. No need to introduce the 'black sheep' if he got lucky enough to meet up with this yank today. Anthony was a handsome dog and sure she might fall for his good looks. Lucky enough he wasn't a charmer, like him! He needed the drink to give him support. He might go telling the others when they got home, and Martin wanted to surprise them. Soon enough telling them if he had any luck. Anthony was returning to Chicago tomorrow and Martin knew well they would be glad to see the back of him.

He had noticed a lot of tension between them when he wandered in a few times. His mother was pretending there was nothing wrong, but Martin could read between the lines! The atmosphere was very chilly indeed. He asked Eddie one evening when they were rounding up the sheep if everything was all right between him and the bold Anthony.

'Did he ask you for money since he came home Martin?' asked Eddie.

'Jayus, Eddie are you having me on? A man all these years in America, coming home and asking for money from a poor farmer in the west of Ireland!' Martin was shocked.

He had noticed all right he hadn't gone out or spent a penny since he came, only eating and drinking everything Catherine and Nora put before him. 'No Eddie, because he knows I haven't any to give him. But I have the feeling he has asked you for some,' answered Martin.

'He hasn't the bloody price of a ticket back to America, can you believe that?' Eddie said downheartedly. Between us, we have collected up enough to buy a ticket. Poor Catherine wont have a penny left of her hard earned money,' Eddie was saying. 'Do you know Martin I won't be sorry to see him go and neither will Catherine. I hate to see poor mother so worried about him though.'

'When he arrived I thought he was the picture of wealth.' Martin said. 'That suit of clothes must set him back a week's wages,' he added.

'Aah Martin, God knows where he got it. There's probably some sort of a poor house over there too, but he wont tell you,' Eddie answered.

Martin was remembering that conversation when he set off to town, so he felt he was doing the right thing not asking him to go with him. 'He'd only be spending the few pounds I have, and I'd never get it back,' he thought to himself.

In all the years Anthony was gone, Martin never seen a letter coming with a few dollars in it for his mother. She never complained or spoke badly of him. Except little remarks here and there about his drinking. 'Sure when he goes back we'll probably never see him again,' she would say. Martin was pondering away to himself as he cycled the miles to town.

The first person he ran into when he arrived was Willie Jack, one of the *codgers* he overheard talking about this Grace Summerfield. He was glad to see him for he might just come in useful today.

'What are you doing in town Willie?' he asked him.

'Minding my own business.' he answered, quick as a flash.

Martin pretended not to be offended by his manner. If this were another time he wouldn't bid him the time of day! He could have sworn the *codger* knew that too, but he was here on an important errand and he was going to give as good as he got!

'Come here to me Willie and tell me have you seen the new yank around these times?' he asked him good-humouredly.

'Ah ha, Mairteen, you buckoo, you're sniffing after her, are you?' He smirked crookedly, showing his gapped, black teeth and rubbing the two palms of his hands together. 'I'll tell you where she went if you buy me a pint,' he laughed wickedly.

'You're a hard auld codger Willeen but you're on!' Martin told him.

'She's below in Stewarts ice cream parlour now and has a few people with her. It looked like they were on some kind of business,' he answered.

Martin went to his pocket and handed Willeen the price of a pint. He walked off with his head sideways against the wind, heading straight for Nolan's pub. Martin stood thinking. 'How the devil am I going to go into an ice cream parlour? Only a child would want ice cream this time of year?'

He pondered this for a while. 'Maybe that's an idea,' he thought to himself. 'It would look good too in front of the women.'

He sat on a windowsill, watching people go by. He noticed children with their parents, but he was hoping to see one or two on their own. He stooped down and undid the lace of his shoe. No harm to be ready anyway, he thought. He had not too long to wait. He spotted a young girl and a little boy skipping along beside her, coming towards him. As they were just approaching, he called out and asked the girl to please tie his shoe for him, as he could not bend down with a bad back. She looked warily until he said, 'I'll buy you an ice cream in Stewarts.' She pondered this a few seconds and then asked 'Will you buy one for my brother too? And will you buy one in a tall glass with fruit in it?' she added. Martin thought to himself 'this little witch drives a hard bargain!' But he did not mind in this case. 'Go on then you little rascal and tie my shoe for me. May God help the man you're going to marry,' he joked. As she bends down to tie his shoe, he pinched her little bottom and guffawed.

It did not take her long to complete the task, and off they went together down to the corner shop that sold the mouth-watering ices. Mary and Johnny were their names and he told them he was Martin. Mary was a chatty little lady and told him their mother always bought a three-penny cone. She used to wish for a fruit ice in a tall glass but mother said she had no money for such luxuries.

When they got inside he ordered the ice cream they wanted, and got a chance to look around. Sure enough Grace was there in the middle of a group of girls. You could pick her out of the group by the clothes she was wearing and her hair was done differently than the local girls. They had no money to spend on themselves. The atmosphere around the table was one of pure jovialarity. He'd fit in there among them like a glove, he thought to himself as he watched them. He had never set eyes on any of them before. From the distance he thought that Grace was on the small side, but he loved merriment and sure they say *there's good things in small parcels.'*

As Grace threw back her head laughing she looked his way. She stopped laughing and stared at him. Martin was well used to this admiration from girls. He quickly gave her a wink and a nod of his head, and he was chuffed to see her blush at his acknowledgement. 'Martin, my lad you're in there' he mused to himself.

He decided to be rid of the two children, so he told them to be off home now and to say thanks for the ice cream. He felt they had served their purpose and it had been worth the few pence he spent on them. He made his way over to the table and said, 'How are the ladies doing and can anyone join in the party?'

Some of them giggled—a habit he hated in girls, others nodded to him but Grace said 'Hello Mr . . . . I guess you must have a name?'

'Martin Staunton, madam at your service.' He bowed and saluted mockingly.

Some of them giggled again but Grace asked him about his two children. He threw back his head and laughed at this.

'You have the wrong end of the stick there now. I'm not the father of any children—well none that I have been told about anyway,' he joked. 'I was just buying them an ice cream for services rendered,' he added.

Again a few of them giggled which was driving Martin mad. One of them said, 'You're not a dirty old man, are you?'

At that Martin really lost his patience. He turned around and muttered, 'ah fuck the lot of ye anyway' and walked out the door. He stood outside to cool off. He was never so insulted before in his life by women. He had always known he was a bit hot headed, but he never had any reason to be so in the company of women. He was annoyed with himself for losing his temper.

He was so deep in his own thoughts he had not heard the half door opening behind him, but suddenly felt a hand on his arm. He looked down and saw Grace had left the bunch of girls and had come out to him.

'I must apologise for the rudeness of my friends Martin. It was uncalled for. Your private life is your business. Can I make it up to you at all?' Martin could not help noticing how very polite this little person was and so cute too. She was looking up appealingly to him and he felt such a softening of his mood. He could not stay mad any longer and anyway it was not her that had hurt his feelings. Maybe it had turned out all right. After all wasn't this exactly what he wanted to happen. He was here on his own with Grace Summerfield! Martin decided to make hay while the sun shines as the old *codgers* often phrased it!

'You could make it up to me if you came to the dance tomorrow night in Jordan's house and save at least four dances for me,' he laughed.

'Well now Mr . . . Martin, that won't be much making up to you. I can certainly manage that if it would please you. I'll be there with bells on, as they say in the States. You have got yourself a date. Cheerio then Martin.'

She skipped back through the half door as quietly as she came out. Martin could hear the others laughing and clapping their hands as he walked away, but he did not care now. He had bagged his catch for today! His step was light going down the street and as he ran his fingers through his hair it reminded him he needed a haircut badly. No time like the present, he thought. He wanted to look his best tomorrow night. He headed straight for the barbershop, with a smile on his face, like he had just won the Irish Hospital Sweepstake.

Chapter 24

A Burial in Chicago

John Joe Staunton was just finishing setting the last few drills of potatoes. There is a lot of pressure on a farmer this time of year. It was a very good spring and everything was growing rapidly. If you fell behind for a few days, you ran late with everything. The turf had to be cut next and he had no help. Poor Maggie was taken up with their two children, and she was not the most robust of women. At least she was able to look after them without much help from him. Being of a quiet temperament, he tried to manage without any fuss.

Sometimes he wished he were a bit more like his brother Martin; he got things done before others even thought of doing them! He had often heard Eddie complaining about him being too forward. It got him into trouble alot over the years. Of course Martin was living in the home place until recently and Eddie had seen a lot more of him. John Joe was remembering the last time the three of them were together bringing in the hay. Martin was blabbering, as usual trying to be funny at someone else's expense.

'Do you and Maggie still eat your dinner off of the one plate?' he asked John Joe as he was handing up a fork load of hay to him.

'Shut up Martin' called out Eddie. He well knew where this could lead. Martin was not the most sensitive of men and no matter how many times you told him that he was out of order, he never seemed to learn. John Joe had left home a good many years now. He knew Maggie was the woman he wanted to spend his life with, and it did not take him long to make up his mind to marry her. Everyone knew poor Maggie was not the pick of the bunch, but she was the one for him. He knew well Martin had no respect for his wife and every chance he got he belittled her. Nowadays, the brothers only all got together when there was some big job to be done on their farms. Mostly that ended in a row before the day was out, and the coolness could last for a year.

John Joe knew Eddie had got himself a wife. He only heard that at Christmas when Anthony was home from America and came to visit him. There had been an almighty row amongst the three brothers last autumn bringing in the hay. To the onlooker they would appear to be as thick as thieves working away together, but before you could say Jack Robinson they were at the point of sticking the hayfork into each other!

Straightening his back to relieve the ache, John Joe was surprised to see Martin coming down the hill towards him. He appeared to be rushing, as usual. When John Joe asked him if there was anything wrong, he replied happily 'Devil a thing wrong only everything right, how's things with you?'

‘Aah, sure there’s no point in complaining. Who would listen to me anyway?’ answered John Joe.

‘Well I’ll tell you now why I came to see you. I have a favour to ask of you. I’m about to take a big step. I’m going getting married and I came to see will you be my best man?’

‘Well leave it there man,’ answered John Joe, reaching out to shake his hand. ‘I didn’t think there was a woman in the country good enough for you! I thought we’d have to make one especially for you. Who is she anyway and does she come from around these parts?’ asked John Joe.

‘She’s a returned yank, and her name is Rose Summerfield. What do you think of that John Joe?’ Martin was ecstatic.

John Joe was silently thinking to himself ‘There’ll be no stopping him at all now! He was bad enough before this, but God help the poor woman. I wonder does she know what she’s letting herself in for?’ It had nothing to do with him anyway and sure the man was over the moon about it! He agreed to be best man, and whenever the wedding date was fixed Martin said he’d let him know. He said he had not told their mother yet but sure Nora would surely be pleased for him. Isn’t that what all mothers want for their sons! He had never mentioned a word about meeting Grace to Eddie and Catherine either. He was silently looking forward to seeing their faces when he told them. They would think he was a fast worker! There was no point in beating around the bush. Grace was giving him all the signs he needed, and he prided himself that he didn’t need a matchmaker to get a girl to marry him. He would now be able to put in a bid for 'Mouse McGowan's' fields next to his own, and at last he would have a substantial farm of land.

He let a week pass before he decided to break the news to his mother. The postman had just gone down to Eddie's, so he'd wait till he had gone. He could not remember the last time he was as excited about anything! Well, yeah he could! He felt really excited the time he bought Dolly, the brown mare, at the horse fair in Castlerea. At last now he had something as good as Eddie. Fanny was the pride of the village, but now they could have a team working together for the ploughing and pulling in the haycocks. He would be able to get the work done even sooner.

The postman was on his return journey and waved his hand going by Martin's house. He mustn't have any post for him. He decided it was time to make his way down to break the good news to them all. He burst in the door without knocking as usual and called out. 'Are ye all ready to hear the good news I have?'

He wasn't prepared for the scene before him. Mother was holding an opened letter in her lap, and Catherine had her arms around her shoulders. He could see by the blue and red striped envelope it was a letter from America. Eddie was leaning against the mantelpiece looking into the fire. He did not even look around when Martin came in.

'What's up with ye all at all?' shouted Martin.

Nora looked at him and said, 'the postman just brought us bad news Martin *agra*. It's your brother Anthony. He had an accident. He got knocked down by a bus in the streets of Chicago.'

'Aah Jesus no Mother,' said Martin shocked at her words, his own excitement now forgotten, 'he's not dead is he?'

'He is dead and buried.' Eddie said quietly. Their mother started wailing now. 'Never did I think I'd live to see the day that one of my sons would be buried in Chicago. Wasn't it enough that I should see my poor Tommy buried at the age of twenty-one? No mother should have to live to see this,' she cried pitifully now.

Martin tried to console her by telling her at least Anthony had a very nice time with them all last Christmas. But instead of improving matters, it was worse she got, wailing away torturing herself that we didn't do more for him while he was at home. This had been his last Christmas!

'Someone should tell our John Joe,' Nora suddenly called out through her tears.

'What's the rush mother? Who needs to hear bad news anyway? There's nothing he can do any more than any of us.' Eddie called out from the far side of the room.

'We must tell Father Gibbons to call it out at Mass on Sunday and we'll get him to say a Mass for poor Anthony,' Catherine spoke then too. She was just as shocked as the brothers. She at least could identify with the awful situation of getting knocked down and killed on the busy streets of Chicago. It's a terrible way for anyone to meet his or her death.

'Seeing as we are all here now together let us say a decade of the Rosary for poor Anthony's soul,' Nora suggested.

She now seemed much more in control. They knelt down and bent their heads while Eddie started the prayers. They all joined in automatically, but their minds were on his last visit home at Christmas. Each one had their own personal regrets. Could they have done more for him? Could they have made him more welcome and not dreaded his homecoming! Did he notice they were glad to see the back of him when he said he was leaving? It was too late now. Oh regret is a terrible thing! They all had one thing in common at this moment. They were all thinking of the last time they saw Anthony alive.

Chapter 25

Jealous Martin

Grace Summerfield could not believe her luck! Since the first time she had seen Martin Staunton in the ice cream parlour, she felt this was the man she had waited for to come into her life. He was tall and handsome and even though she was small in stature, she was also aware that she would be considered a very good catch!

Two years ago she had come home hoping to meet a prospective husband, but it was not to be and so she returned to Chicago. She had worked as a cook, in a grand stately house with a very rich employer who had been kindness itself. He was so reluctant to let her go, but knew she had her mind made up. The homeland was calling her, as he had discovered many times with his Irish staff. She was a grand little cook though, he thought to himself, and told her if it did not work out in Ireland, there would always be a position for her if she wished to return.

So after nearly four months at home, being vetted propositioned and offers made to make a decent woman out of her, she returned to Chicago and crawled back to her former employer and asked for her old job back. There she settled once more and saved money like never before. She wasn't interested in meeting anyone with a view to marriage in Chicago. She wanted to settle down in Ireland. She had a growing fear of being left on the shelf! The years were slipping by and she wanted children. Soon it would be too late and no man would want a wife who could not breed some sons for him!

Now Grace felt her luck had turned at last. Martin Staunton had asked her to be his wife. He had not beaten about the bush either! This suited her down to the ground, as she was about to engage a matchmaker to look out for a suitable man with the right prospects. Of course this could take time, as she had to admit she was terribly fussy. Now there was no need for such a course as Martin was all she wanted, even though he had confessed his farm was small, but he had his eye on neighbouring fields, which would make his holding a more respectable size.

Grace accepted gladly. Martin was to arrange a meeting with his mother and brother and wife to break the good news to them. This did not happen as soon as Martin had planned. He had to bide his time, as news had just come from America that their brother had been killed on the streets of Chicago, and they were all very grieved over the tragedy. Grace had to be patient. She was looking forward to meeting his brother's wife Catherine, as she too was in America for several years. They should have a lot in common, and she understood they would all be living in the small village. She could not wait. Imagine having your in-laws, as your neighbours!

'I sure as hell hope we all get along!' Grace thought to herself. Martin had told her Catherine was already pregnant, so this would be wonderful having another young woman to discuss such things with, especially as she hoped to get pregnant herself. It was all so exciting and they must soon set a date to get married.

Martin was already rushing her in more ways than one! But a girl has to have time to get her trousseau, and a lot of other plans have to be made for such a big event! Men never seem to think further than their trousers!

Martin seemed to be very keen on having the wedding reception at his house. He reckoned he had to match the wedding reception Eddie and Catherine gave when they got married. He still talked about the lively *hooley* it was. Also Catherine stole the show with her beautiful singing voice. 'Well' Grace said to herself, 'I'll show them I have talents too.' She would put her own stamp on this reception, she promised him.

So far Martin had no idea what talents she had. He knew she was a cook in America and that greatly improved her suitability as his wife. He did not know she was a very good melodeon player, and could rattle out the jigs and the reels as good as any man. She would keep that a secret from him and make it a wedding present and surprise him on the day. She had other tricks up her sleeve for the night too!

Martin said his mother was a great help to Eddie and Catherine altogether. Maybe if she got along well on their first meeting with her future mother-in—law, she might be willing to help out with their big day too. Surely she would be happy for Martin to have met someone with a good dowry. Isn't that what every Irish mother wanted for their sons?

At least that was what Grace's parents were always drumming into her head, and her sister Mary. She could never understand why her brother John did not have to save every penny of his money. He was advised to be on the lookout for a girl with prospects—whatever that meant! It wasn't fully explained to Grace when she questioned it, but she got the gist of it, and it all boiled down to money.

'Martin can I ask you truthfully,' Grace asked one day in a fit of devilment and a twinkle in her eye. 'Would you by any chance be marrying me for my money?'

'Ah now Grace, don't be putting such daft ideas into your head. Tell me now my little woman, how would I know if you have money or not. Sure I've never seen the colour of it. I only heard you're a great little cook! And if you think you're taking on too much having to feed a big fellow like me, sure I suppose you have time yet to back out.'

Grace looked to see if he was serious or not, but with the twinkle in his eyes and him ready to burst out laughing, she knew he was not taking her question seriously. He even came up behind her and gave a playful pinch to her bottom, and from the frisky way he caught her bosom as she went by, she realised he was not thinking of money at that moment anyway. She felt she got her answer and was content enough with that.

'Would you like to talk about setting a date so Martin for the wedding?' she asked him. He was surprised at the suddenness of the question, as the last time he brought up the subject Grace was very hesitant.

'You go ahead and choose. I'd marry you in the morning if you want! When were you thinking?

'Well seeing as you would like to have the wedding breakfast in your house, I was thinking of a date after your brother's baby is born. Let things settle down with them, and then maybe your mother would help with the preparations. And Catherine would have her strength back again to enjoy it too. So that would be about September. Will we say 15th, that's a Wednesday? As the rhyme says 'Wednesday the best day of all.'

'Whatever you say Grace will suit me,' Martin agreed happily. He kissed her passionately there in the middle of the street and did not care who was looking. Grace had to push him away from her playfully. She felt he was forgetting where he was and it was not the first time she had to cool his ardour.

He felt like shouting the news to everyone. He was long enough watching other men getting wives, and they were not as good looking as him at all! He often wondered how some of them got on with their new wives on their wedding night! He knew he would not have any such worries about things like that. He was well experienced there and he knew Grace would be very pleased with him. He was having a hard time keeping himself in control, but he already knew he would have to wait till his wedding night.

She seemed to be very strict and old-fashioned with that side of their relationship. Anytime he tried to put his hand up under her dress, she would slap him away.

At first he found it exciting and he would turn it into a game, but he soon found out she was very serious about not having any sexual encounters before marriage. She could be such a tease! He told himself he could wait. He would take his mind off it by getting the summer work done in good time.

For the first time in his life he felt he was at last getting what Eddie seemed to take for granted, but he still had a lot of catching up to do. Eddie was soon to be a father and no doubt produce a son. Only another couple of weeks and he would be an Uncle. Well all he could hope for now would be that Grace would also want children. He would like to have some sons.

They had not discussed it. Not many men do. When it happens everyone is delighted but it was not the easiest of subjects to approach. In fact if she did start talking about it Martin felt he would be so embarrassed. He was happy to be getting on with the marriage for now, and sure these things happen naturally he told himself.

Chapter 26

The New Arrival

'It's a girl' the nurse calls out. 'A perfect little girl! Well done Mrs Staunton and congratulations.'

Catherine heard the cry of her firstborn and lay back on the pillows exhausted. Eddie and Nora heard it to. A few minutes later the nurse came down to the kitchen carrying the little bundle and placed her in Eddie's arms. He could hear the little groans and sucking noises she was making. Poor Eddie never held a baby before. He was shaking holding her. He offered her to his mother for fear of dropping her.

'Any news yet?' shouts Martin with his head halfway in the door. He didn't need to be told he was an Uncle. He could see his mother holding the little bundle and crooning. 'Well is it a boy or a child?' he guffawed in his usual loud manner.

'It's a little lady we have here Martin,' Nora replied. 'Aren't you going to congratulate your brother now on doing a fine job?'

Martin spat on his hand and rubbed it against the other hand. 'Leave it there Eddie my lad, I never thought you had it in you! Sure I thought you'd need me to help you,' he laughed aloud again at his own joke.

Eddie blushed as usual when Martin talked like this in front of their mother. Nora noticing poor Eddie's discomfort, told him to get a few glasses and the bottle of whiskey she kept under her bed.

'Come in Martin, and will you for once in your life keep your big gob shut. Where did I get you at all?' she pretended to groan. 'Will you fill out a drop of whiskey to wet the baby's head and make yourself useful.' She was still holding the new baby and even though she was pretending to be annoyed with Martin, she hadn't felt this happy since she held her own children in her arms.

Nora loved all her children but God knows she could well see that Eddie and Martin were like chalk and cheese! Eddie wouldn't hurt a fly, while that other devil got his kicks from watching his brother's discomfort, especially with his sexual innuendos. She also noticed in the last year that Catherine showed some signs of agitation when Martin put his head in the door. She politely told him one day, he ought to knock in future before entering. Little notice Martin took of that! He still walks in at the most in-opportune moments!

I'll bet my money on Catherine marking his cards for him if he enters when she's feeding her new baby! Nora chuckled at the idea and hoped she'd be there when it happened. He needs taking down a peg! Someone needs to put a bit of manners on him! He never took any heed of me, she told herself.

Martin was a relieved man tonight. On hearing the news Eddie was to become a father he was consumed with jealousy. If Eddie had a son he would be the apple of Nora's eye and Martin would be on the hind tit! The family name would be handed down and with it came great respect. Now Martin's wish had come true. Maybe he will be the first yet to hand down the family name! He could only hope Grace would produce sons! He would have to work on it! A smile came on his handsome face at the thoughts of such pleasure.

'Share the joke with us Martin,' called out Nora as she made her way to the bedroom where Catherine was. She couldn't be bothered waiting for his reply. It was sure to be another jibe at someone's expense! She had heard them all anyway! She was in great spirits now the baby had arrived safely and she promised herself she was going to be a great help to them.

'What are ye going to call her Eddie?' Martin asked when his mother was out of the room.

'I'll leave it up to Catherine' Eddie answered. 'We were talking about Mary if it was a girl. Sure the first girl in every family is called Mary. I don't think we're going to be the ones to break the tradition. It might be unlucky. Sure we'd be only calling her after our sister Mary in Chicago if we do. She'll hardly marry now so wont be having any children of her own. If she's as pretty as her she'll do well. Of course Catherine has her sister Mary in Philadelphia too. Sure we cannot go wrong with another Mary.'

'Can I do anything to help? Do you want me to tell the priest you have a baby to baptise? I suppose you'll want it done next Sunday,' Martin asked.

It wasn't like Martin to be so helpful, but he had his own ideas for getting on with the christening. He wanted everything out of the way before he announced the date he was getting married. He wanted the limelight for himself and to get on with his own married life. He had sown enough of wild oats now, and he wanted what Eddie had! Wait till they hear I have landed a returned yank as well. At least I didn't have to get the help of a matchmaker, like Eddie he was thinking to himself.

'Are you gone deaf or what Martin? How many times do you want me to ask you?' Eddie was saying as Martin came out of his reverie. 'Do you not want to be the God-father?' asked Eddie.

'Oh Jesus, Eddie I was miles away there! Oh I do, I do. I will of course.' He spat on his hand and said to Eddie 'Leave it there man' and they both shook hands again. Eddie added that Catherine had talked about having her sister Bridget to be Godmother.

Catherine was awake when Eddie joined her in bed. She had slept after her ordeal and the little one was sleeping peacefully in the cradle Eddie had made. All the chores were done for tonight and they were both very content at how well it all turned out. As he kissed his wife he told her he was a lucky man the day he met her.

'Sure now that we know how its done and we have found out you're a dab hand at having a child, we'll have plenty more of them! You have a natural *knack* for it Catherine,' he said laughing.

'I'll give you *knack* Eddie Staunton' she replied laughing, giving him a right nudge in the groin. He pretended to be injured. 'Ah Catherine what have you done to me now at all! Now poor little Mary will be an only child. There was me thinking, we might get a mate for her before too long.'

Catherine was too happy and too tired to care. She picked up a bolster feather pillow and stuffed it down between the two of them in the bed.

'Good-night Eddie' she called out meaningfully! 'I think I'll have to enlighten you about this baby making. There's more to having them than you realise. Oh, did I hear you say little Mary? It didn't take you long to make up your mind on a name for her. Mary it is so 'Dad,' she said contentedly.

Eddie didn't answer. He was already fast asleep.

Chapter 27

Ten Years Later

Catherine was busy stacking the turf trying to get ahead of the workload. Eddie was drawing it from the bog with the donkey and cart, and expected each load to be put away by the time he arrived back with the next one. They were experiencing a heat wave and if the turf wasn't brought home, it would shrivel up in this weather.

July is a busy month on a farm but Eddie and Catherine had plenty of little helpers. Mary nearly ten now, was a great help with the smaller ones, always eager to feed them before she ate a mouthful herself. Young Patrick was a great help at eight and a half. He could milk a cow as good as his father. Catherine could always trust him with his younger brothers Francis and John aged seven and six. The three boys were with their father at the moment, collecting up the clods of turf and putting them into the cart, and then hopping up into the cart for a ride home.

'Nora will you make a pot of tea, we're all parched with the thirst,' Catherine called out to her Mother-in-law. Nora was minding the two little girls and Tony who were playing hide and seek in the maze of boxwood in the garden. Angela was four and a half and little Tony was three and baby Teresa was almost two. Sailor the sheepdog was lying in the shade pretending to be asleep. Even though his hearing wasn't the best now he didn't miss much. It was hard to sleep with so much going on. He wasn't able to follow the donkey and cart down the fields anymore, but he would still ramble around the yard after Eddie.

Catherine straightened her back to ease the tiredness. The heat was overwhelming her, but that wasn't the only reason. She was keeping some news to herself till she found an opportune time to tell Eddie and Nora. God knows, she was thinking to herself, I've played this old fiddle often enough to be able to tell it without embarrassment. She asked the Doctor to give her some advice on how to avoid getting pregnant again. His only remark was 'keep your distance from Eddie in the middle of the month.' She also had a good chat with Grace, who had married Martin nearly ten years ago. They had three little girls, but none in the last four years.

Of course Grace is a lot older so probably is past childbearing age. Catherine was mulling it over in her mind as she stacked sod after sod of turf. She knew Martin wanted a son badly, but it wasn't God's will. When she first got married she was well aware he was jealous of Eddie but it was more obvious than ever now. She would often notice him giving little clips around the ears to her boys, while he would pinch the girls' bottoms. Odd habits indeed, thought Catherine!

YoungMarywasn'tputtingupwithitanymorethough! One day when bending over sowing potatoes in his drills, he came up behind her and pinched her bottom. She told him off in no uncertain terms. Catherine pretended not to notice but was secretly proud of her oldest daughter! When this little lady grows up, she smiled to herself young men had better keep their hands in their pockets! She must remember to tell Eddie about it. That night Mary told Catherine she was never going to help Uncle Martin anymore. She was quite indignant and her final words were, 'and mammy don't ask me to, cause I wont do it.'

Eddie loved every one of his children but Catherine was not sure how he would react to another mouth to feed. With the war on at the moment there was talk of food being rationed. There was going to be a shortage of tea and tobacco. Eddie liked his pipe especially in the evening when he had all the chores done. She enjoyed watching him puffing away, seemingly content with his lot. She hoped he would still able to get his ounce of 'Bendigo' every week.

They would all have to be careful and spare things. She would just have to give the smaller ones cocoa instead of tea, if the rumour was true about the rationing. They would have their own milk, butter, vegetables, eggs and plenty of potatoes. The chickens will be a great source of meat, and when they kill the pig there will be lots of varieties of meat dishes. There were plenty of apples growing in the orchard, so she would be making apple tarts, to fill the empty little stomachs coming in from school. If flour remained plentiful they would manage. They would not starve.

Keeping shoes and clothes on the children was the hardest. She handed them down as best she could, but the shoes were worn through by the time the boys had outgrown them. Catherine spent every night altering the clothes to make them fit for another few months. Nora knitted socks for the boys and Eddie all year round. She was there whenever Catherine needed a second pair of hands. Winding skeins of wool into balls for knitting was tiresome and required two people to do the job. You could get by, in a pinch, using two chairs back to back, placing the skeins around the chairs and winding away till you had a ball of wool ready for knitting.

Catherine was still only thirty-eight and expecting her eight child. If we keep this up we'll have a football team, she mused to herself! Her sister Mary was a slow starter compared to her. When she returned home from Philadelphia she had high hopes of settling down with a nice man. It was not happening. She wrote letters to Catherine telling her she was planning on returning to America.

She couldn't hang about any longer.

She was disillusioned and disappointed. She was not as lucky as Catherine in finding a husband. With her trunk packed and ready to go, Tom Coyne, her second cousin, who finally got the courage to ask her to stay and marry him, approached her. He lived only a quarter of a mile away from her home. She accepted and they were married straight away.

Poor Mary wasn't blessed with the same robust health as Catherine. She found pregnancies wore her out, and had two mis-carriages and a stillborn little boy in their first two years of marriage. Tom was inconsolable and took it out on poor Mary. She often wrote letters, which made heartbreaking reading for Catherine. Reading through the lines, he seemed to be blaming Mary for not being able to carry children. Their lives turned out very different from their days in Philadelphia.

Mary was coming to visit tomorrow. Catherine was so excited at the thoughts of it but was wondering how in the world was she going to tell her another baby was on its way. She felt she had to tell Eddie tonight, before she told Mary. I'll get around to telling Nora another time. After all she had ten children herself so understands how these thing happen! she thought to herself. She was the luckiest woman in the world to have a mother-in-law like Nora, so understanding and never a cross word spoken between them. The poor dear was so helpful over the last ten years with the childrearing and the housekeeping.

Catherine's life wouldn't be the same if Eddie's mother was not here. She was nearly eighty-five years old now and Catherine dreaded the day she wouldn't be with them. She was as healthy as a trout, and apart from an odd puff of the white clay pipe, and a drop of whiskey she kept for special occasions, she didn't cost them much extra in the house. She was more than generous with her pension of ten shillings weekly. She would hand Catherine the price of a new pair of shoes for one of the children from time to time. This was a Godsend and Catherine appreciated it more than ever with each new arrival. Since the pension was increased from five to ten shillings when Ireland became a free State, all older persons in a house now became an asset instead of a liability! Catherine always considered Nora an asset, even without her pension.

Her husband had died many years ago but she never complained. She had worked very hard on the farm with help from her large family, until one by one they left home. She was not a great cook but she used always say if you were able to boil an egg you would never go hungry. Nora loved her duck egg for breakfast every morning. She shared a lot of old cures handed down through the years. When any of the children were poorly with a bad chest, she would boil *carrageen moss* and lemon juice and dose the child with it.

The house was never without Epsom salts and was used for cuts and grazes when anyone got injured. It was also used to relieve constipation. Half a teaspoon dissolved in hot water and drank fasting relieved many a blockage! A dock leave was rubbed on a nettle sting and if you could get a child to drink hot milk that had been boiled with a clove of garlic, it cured all coughs and colds. Nora always washed her hair in rainwater with a good pinch of baking soda at the end to give it softness. She also said it helped to keep the grey hairs away. Could be something in it, Catherine thought to herself as Nora was showing only little signs of grey. Catherine promised herself she would remember to keep that little trick up her sleeve, as she grew older.

She was never miserly but she was very economical and didn't abide wastefulness. Because she had such a large family she devised ways of making do. Of course she would have loved linen sheets for the beds, but the only linen she owned came from the eight-stone bags that the flour came in. They were made of coarse linen and when the flour was all used, she would wash them and open them up and sew four together to make a good size sheet. She showed Catherine how to crochet little lace collars from the fine white thread, which she gathered from the flour bags when she ripped them open. Nothing was wasted.

She was a wonder at making butter. Catherine's own mother never turned out butter like this. It could have been she did not have the right type of creamy milk needed for good butter. Some cows were better than others. Or it could be she did not have the same technique as Nora. There was no easy way to make butter. Each day after milking Nora would collect the fresh milk and leave to cool in the dairy. By evening, the cream would have come to the top and she would skim it off and collect it in a special utensil, and repeat the process everyday till there was enough cream to make a churning and that was the hardest job of all. The dash churn had to be kept pounded non-stop. Depending on the temperature this could take anything up to an hour. Churning would be done on a day when there was plenty of help around. People in the house would take their turn at the handle, as the previous one got tired. A visitor calling to the house while this chore was in progress, would have to take his turn, otherwise it would bring bad luck to the house. You couldn't wait to hear a mild thump inside the churn as this meant the butter had finally appeared. You still had to continue churning till the lumps had collected together and then you would stop.

Everyone would look inside to see the good return and say a prayer of thanks and make the sign of the cross over the churn. Taking out the great lumps of golden butter made the chore all worthwhile. The butter would then be washed several times in cold water till the water ran clear and salt added. Nora would make several slabs and wrap in muslin and greaseproof paper and there would be enough for a household for a week. The process of collecting the cream started all over again! Towards the end of the week Catherine and Nora would be heard saying 'spare the butter' as it may be running out before churning day. Some days were either a feast or a famine. Still they were grateful for what they had and never a day went by the didn't say 'thanks be to God.'

Chapter 28

A Welcome Visitor

Catherine was sizing up Eddie with the corner of her eye as he sat drinking his mug of tea, and drawing shapes in the turf mould, quizzing the boys about his drawings. He was a great father and had good fun with all of them. When rows broke out amongst the young ones, he was firm but fair and had good reasoning powers with them. They looked up to him.

Today he looked flushed. It's probably the heat, she thought. They would soon finish working with the turf, as the evening chores had to be done. They each had their own chores to do every day. Mary had to go and collect the eggs in the henhouse, and feed the hens, making sure the gander didn't eat all the food on them. Patrick had to feed the mare and put fresh water out for the cattle in the far field. Francis and John had to go and bring in the cows for milking. They would also have to feed the calves with the milk Eddie and Patrick took from the cows. Nora would have made a head start on the tea for everyone, and would help Catherine get the three young ones ready for bed.

Eddie didn't seem to be in his usual form at teatime. He left his tea half finished and got up from the table. Later Catherine found him lying down on his bed with his clothes still on. This was not like Eddie at all! He had a bit of a lingering cough lately but it didn't stop him working. She sat down beside him and asked him to tell her how he felt.

'I'm burning up and at the same time I'm shivering,' he answered.

'Let me send for the Doctor for you Eddie,' said Catherine. Eddie was feeling so bad he didn't care. Catherine made her way to the kitchen and told Patrick to go up to Uncle Martins house and ask him to go to *Drumoneen* for Doctor Murphy. 'Tell him your Daddy is poorly and to hurry.'

Catherine was trying not to make much of it in front of the children, but she whispered to Nora she didn't like the look of Eddie at all. She busied herself going back and forth to his room, putting cold wet cloths on his forehead, and at the same time wrapping him up with extra blankets. She was shocked at how quickly he got to this stage. Had she neglected to notice him or were there some signs she should have seen earlier? She knew her mind was elsewhere since finding herself pregnant again and keeping the news to herself.

She heard the Doctor's car coming down the lane and ran to open the door. He looked around at the bunch of small children but quickly followed Catherine to the bedroom. Poor Nora was trying to keep the children occupied, so they would not notice how worried their mother was. Often enough she had seen the roles reversed with Catherine in the room giving birth to the babies, while Eddie was here in the kitchen, showing his anxiety.

It was not long before Dr Murphy put his head through the doorway. He put his hand on the foreheads of all the children in turn and looked into their eyes, pulling down the lower lids, as if to diagnose their condition.

'Your daughter-in-law will tell you the news, Mrs Staunton. How are you keeping yourself Mam? You look well. I'll see myself out, don't go getting up now, I'll be back again in the morning. Catherine knows what I want her to do,' he rattled on as he made his way out the door.

Nora made her way to the bedroom. Poor Eddie was wet with sweat and Catherine was busy mopping his brow and looking very flustered and worn out. 'It's pneumonia, Nora,' she whispered, 'it will be a long night. Will you prepare the small ones for bed and I'll be down to help as soon as I can leave Eddie. Say nothing to the young ones about their Daddy being so sick. Just say he has a fever.'

Martin stuck his head in the door asking how the patient was. Nora made light of it in the company of the children, but he knew when she gave him a knowing wink, there was more to it. He stayed and helped get the young ones to bed, giving them little tickles under the arms and making them squeal with laughter.

Nora was glad of the way he was distracting them. Normally she would have run him from the house. She would not want them to be getting this excited at bedtime, but this was not a normal evening.

'I hope poor Eddie will be all right Martin,' she said to him when they were finished putting the children to bed. 'The Doctor said he has pneumonia. Where in the world now did he get that?'

'Oh Jayus mother that's a bugger of an ailment. I have seen strong men in the Army dying from that. I'll go back and take a look at him and see if there's anything I can do to help,' he said.

He was not prepared for the state of affairs in the small room. Catherine was trying to get the wet sheets out from under Eddie and replace them with dry ones. Eddie looked like he was burning up, but he still couldn't stop shivering. Martin was galvanised into action and lifted Eddie straight off the bed, giving Catherine a chance to make up the bed again. She appeared exhausted and his heart went out to her. She thanked him for his promptness in going for the Doctor. 'Can I count on your help tonight Martin if things get any worse? The Doctor is coming again in the morning, but I've a feeling it will be a long night for me. It's best if he keeps sweating it out of him, but it will mean changing the sheets and vests throughout the night. Where in the world did he get this at all? she said, more to herself than to him. 'When you go home Martin will you tell Grace I could do with her help. Ask her if I could borrow more sheets from her. I haven't half enough for something like this.'

They sat in silence for a long time listening to Eddie's uneven breathing and agitated state. 'He couldn't die on me Martin, could he? Surely God wouldn't expect me rear eight children and look after an old woman and a farm at the same time' she moaned almost to herself.

Martin looked at her and quick as a flash calculated she must be in the family way once again. He hadn't heard a word from Eddie or his mother about this. Maybe Catherine hadn't told anyone yet. He was filled with mixed feelings. He had never before seen her so vulnerable in all the years he's known her, yet he was secretly envious of Eddie, already having four sons.

It was not looking like Grace would have any more children. She is past it now, he though to himself! He decided to keep his mouth shut for once and pretend he hadn't heard what she said. Of course he may be wrong. It could be a slip of the tongue.

By morning, when the Doctor arrived he was very pleased with Eddie's condition. The worst was over and his temperature was more normal. A couple of days in bed were all that he recommended and plenty of chicken broth. The children were allowed to see their Daddy and all lined up one by one, quiet as mice, to stand by his bedside. It was a Saturday morning and Catherine was grateful for that at least. There was no school to go to and they would help Martin with the chores.

He was already outside milking the cows. It was good of him as he had his own work to do as well. She would suggest he take young Patrick to help with his own chores after he had finished. Even though he could be a right nuisance at times, she was very glad he was living so near last night. She must remember to thank him. Eddie was sleeping peacefully now, but every time Catherine went to check on him her eyes were drawn to the mountain of wet sheets piled high in the corner of the room. The water was boiling in the big black pots over the fire and there were more pans on coals in the hearth. At the best of times, washing day was the most dreaded day of the week. Catherine hated all that steam coming from the pots, and leaning over the washing board even when you weren't pregnant. It was very hard work indeed. She could hardly remember a time when she wasn't pregnant these days. Wringing out the sheets with the mangle was another day's work. By evening, her arms ached if she overdid it, but it had to be done.

There was no time for self-pity. While she left Nora keeping an eye on the little ones, she proceeded to tackle the washing. She felt weak even before she had begun the dreaded chore. Keeping watch through the night, and giving Eddie medicine at regular intervals, she didn't think she slept at all. If she did, it was only for moments. After about an hour of scrubbing, and bending over the washing board, she straightened herself up for a rest, when lo and behold, she saw her sister Mary cycling down the lane looking cheerful and what a sight for sore eyes! Catherine cried both with exhaustion and delight at the sight of her. Here she though is the help I so badly need.

'Oh Mary, thank God you've come. I completely forgot you were to visit today. We've had a terrible time here. You went clean out of my mind,' cried Catherine.

'Come on now Cathy it can't be as bad as all that. Sure there's nobody dead, come on now,' Mary coaxed as she hugged her tight. This wasn't at all like Catherine; she was always the strongest of them with a level head on her shoulders.

Mary took off her coat and hat and sat down on the wall to hear all about it. After Catherine told her all that had happened in the past twenty four hours, she decided it was time to take Catherine in hand, and the first thing to be done was to get her into bed for a few hours sleep. She could see her flagging before her eyes and Mary was never so glad to have come when she was needed.

She did not have to persuade Catherine at all! She was content to be led to bed and knew things were in good hands with her sister Mary about. Last instructions before giving in to the tiredness was 'take a look in on Eddie and see if he's ok Mary.'

Mary was more than happy to oblige. After all, she had so much to be thankful to her sister Catherine for, all those years ago in Philadelphia and never got any opportunity to repay her. Now she was getting her chance.

Chapter 29

Post Pneumonia

Almost two years had passed since Eddie's illness and Catherine noticed a big change in his behaviour. He was a different man. He was more contrary and hated any form of noise. The children cowered when he'd shout at them for the least commotion. When little Jamie was born six months after Eddie's pneumonia, he couldn't bear the baby's cries. She was never sure if he was unhappy with another mouth to feed or that he had been left with a legacy related to the illness. There were odd times he seemed more like his old self, but they were few and far between.

When she discovered she was pregnant again ten months after little Jamie was born, Catherine kept it to herself until he noticed her bump. She noticed him watching her one evening when she was in the middle of combing nits out of the children's hair. They had come in from school with a note from the teacher, saying there was an infestation in the school, and every mother had to inspect their own children and buy lotion to eliminate the lice. Catherine had the creeps all evening.

'God knows Eddie haven't I enough on my plate without this,' she moaned near to tears. He could see her distress and realised the terrible chore it was, especially with the girls. He asked her if she would like him to cut the three boys hair very short, and she agreed it was the easiest way, but she didn't want the girls cut short. They had lovely heads of wavy hair, a legacy from her. Baby Jamie had none worth talking about, but she still washed his head in the shampoo prescribed.

'Are you planning on surprising me one morning with a new child, *a gra?*' Eddie whispered to her when the children were out of earshot. Catherine saw the twinkle in his eye and thought she had her old Eddie back again!

'There is plenty of time left to tell you, Eddie. Maybe I should have said this before but after this one we'll have to call a halt! We cannot go on like this. It's wearing me out,' Catherine added watching him closely.

At least he took that in good spirits she thought to herself, when he had gone out to the barn to check on the cow that was due to calf. She could not depend on him like before. His mood could change like the wind. She remembered the windy winter's night he got all fired up; collected up the set of tin draughts the kids were playing with, went outside and hid them. They were never to be seen again and the poor kids were distraught. Catherine tried to intervene and begged Eddie to go out and get them again, but all he would say was he couldn't bear the noise they were making.

It was useless to mention a Doctor, for he felt there was nothing wrong with him. Even Nora noticed the change in him, and commented that he was almost as unpredictable as Martin now. She was not as lively herself lately, but still noticed all that was going on. They had good kids, but Eddie couldn't bear noise anymore.

One consolation for Catherine was her sister Mary was also expecting a baby. It was looking good that she would carry full term. She was due a month before her. It will be lovely to have her very own child at last. She looked after enough in Philadelphia and she had been such a help to Catherine all along when special occasions came, like first Communion and Confirmation. She deserves a break now. Catherine would be there with advice but would be of little general help, with so much to do for her own family. There was never an idle minute.

Last year, when she was eight months pregnant with little Jamie, Catherine's mother died. She was over 90 and died as peaceful as she had lived. At the funeral her brother James had said if this were a boy maybe ye would call him after him—James. Catherine's boys were in great demand! Martin had just the three girls and James had two so far. Martin said he would be Godfather again to this one if it were a boy. So to keep everyone happy they called him Jamie and Martin was the Godfather.

When Catherine was down in Owenboy at the funeral, she made arrangements for John Ivers, a dancing teacher to come up and teach her children Irish step-dancing. He was busy going around to the local villages in the winter months, but he said he would come to Catherine's in the summer months. It was a long journey on the bicycle, so he wanted the evenings to be bright. She said she would have a crowd of local children collected up in her house for lessons. She wanted to give her children every chance to get ahead. She had it all planned out. The summer months were the best for her too, as the trashing barn would be empty at that time, and it was clean and had a nice concrete floor.

Of course Eddie wasn't too keen. He had no love of dancing at all and couldn't see what was to be gained from it at all. Catherine tried to persuade him it was a nice hobby, good exercise and would be no load on them!

'What if they have two left feet like me?' he enquired from her one day.

'Well, sure Eddie it won't be the end of the world if they do. Some of them are bound to have taken your side, but sure we'll have fun finding out,' she laughed and was glad to see he was smiling too.

Catherine wanted her children to have whatever was going. Occasionally, a man by the name of Albert would bring a travelling comedy show to the village in the Hall. The whole family would go, and there were prizes to be won and good fun for everyone. Punch & Judy shows came to the school too and the children would know in advance, so they would have their pennies with them to pay for it.

The travelling dentist was another excitement albeit not a pleasure. Most of the children had a fear after the first encounter with the dentist, and often invented excuses to stay at home whenever they heard the dentist was coming to the school.

News came in a letter one morning that Catherine's sister Mary had at last delivered a baby girl. They were calling her Olive and Mary wanted Catherine to be godmother. The christening was to be next Sunday.

Catherine was so excited as she was never honoured with such a request before. She told Eddie to hire Kenny's Hackney car and she was already planning she would take Mary and Patrick. They could do with a day out as they were always helping her around the house. She would have to take little Jamie anyway and I'd better bring Teresa, as she's a bit of a weasel by times, she said to herself. She didn't want Eddie to get out of sorts while she was gone, so between Nora and him they could manage the rest of the clan and have the chores done by the time they got home.

She had only a month to go herself before the birth of her ninth, but she was keeping up good. At least it had been the winter months and work was slacker outside when she was at her heaviest. She would have her strength back by the time the spring work had to be done. There were many chores that Eddie liked her to help with on the farm. He was beginning to be a bit of a pet really, always in need of someone by his side when working in the fields. God knows I'm producing enough helpers for him, though Catherine, but the poor children need to go to school too and have a little time for recreation.

The winter's nights were spent with the whole family busying themselves doing their own thing. As soon as the evening meal was over, and often before all was tidied up, Eddie was on his knees starting to say the Rosary. Everyone had to grab their Rosary beads and stop what they were doing! He couldn't wait to get the evening prayers said. He would then spend the night making his own creations. He could make the loveliest potato baskets and *ciseogs*—made from willow rods. These rods were grown in the sally garden behind the house, and when Eddie had a day with nothing specific to do, Catherine would help him collect the rods and tie them up in bundles. She often did this with her father too before she went to Philadelphia. She knew they would be needed for the thatching of the roof for the winter. Eddie was a wonder at thatching too.

It was a joy to watch him create his baskets, while she sewed or darned the pile of socks that the Wellington boots had ravaged at the heels. She never knew what he was making, and he wouldn't tell her, till the very last piece was secured. Then he would show it off to all of them—proud as punch, asking Catherine what she thought she would use it for.

Catherine would have conjured up an image of something altogether different while it was in the making, but she never failed to have an answer for Eddie. Depending on the size of it, it could be used to store potatoes in the kitchen, eggs in the larder, turf beside the fire, straining and serving the dinner potatoes.

Her favourite was a rectangular shaped basket, relatively high, and so safe and secure, especially for harbouring an injured animal till it was well again, or used for a bed for a stray puppy till an owner was found. If a sheep had three lambs this basket was perfect and would be booked for weeks until the pet lamb was big enough to jump out of it. Catherine found it the perfect place if she purchased a dozen yellow and red chicks in the factory, on a spur-of-moment whim.

While the older children were busy with their books and homework, Nora sat in the corner taking an odd puff of her clay pipe, and busied herself knitting more socks. Sometimes she would crochet a colourful shawl with lots of bits of left over wool. This would turn out to be a Godsend on a cold night when one of the children felt poorly and couldn't warm up.

Catherine herself could never master the art of crochet until Nora patiently, showed her a number of times. She had so many other things to do anyway there weren't enough hours in a day to do everything. Buttons were always coming loose and sewing was her biggest chore. She often wondered what the men were doing with their trousers anyway! Hardly a day passed that the arse of a trousers hadn't split! If a man's trousers were about to fall down a nail was often produced to perform the service of a button. Only temporarily of course till nigh time came when Catherine would be called upon, at very short notice, to repair it for tomorrow.

She recalls with dread the time she left a huge darning needle dangling inside the seat of Eddie's long John's! It was about two weeks later; when she was going to wash them she noticed the needle and thread still intact. She had forgotten to cut it off! She went weak at the knees! She shivered every time she thought of what the consequences might have been. She vowed never to tell Eddie about it. He would never trust her again!

Long winter nights were Catherine's favourite time of year. Watching her big family all safe, healthy and happy together. The younger children would pass the time playing the game of marbles in the little hole in the floor. Sometimes there would be an odd scrabble amongst them when one decided the marbles belonged to him, and someone would have to referee before peace was restored. If they got fed up with that they would play a game of 'hopscotch' marking out the squares with chalk on the flagstones. The cat was beside the fire and the dog Sailor was at the end of the room, sleeping but alert to any commotion. He knew his time was short lived in the house but enjoyed whatever length he was inside. He knew it was out to the barn for him when everyone retired for the night!

Watching her big family all safe, healthy and happy together, and content with their lot, Catherine wished she could hold on to this time forever. She was no fool she knew there would be changes and when the war was over who knew what was to be. Her family were growing up so quickly. Mary was almost twelve now and poor Nora was nearly ninety.

Now and again when she took the time to think about it, she knew it was imminent that she would soon be without her mother-in-law. She had to be sensible about it. She never mentioned it to Eddie and neither did he! Nora still had all her wits about her and even though she was not much help nowadays, she was no trouble either. The age was there though and Catherine dreaded the day she would die on them. For now she was content knowing she was soon about to give birth to her ninth child, and please God the war will soon be over.

Chapter 30

Jamie's Accident

It was a lovely crisp October morning and Eddie was heading for the potato field. He liked this time of year as all the other chores were complete, and all that was left before the winter set in was to get the potatoes out of the ground. Even with all the help he had, there was nobody he could call on to day! The seven oldest were gone to school, and young Jamie was only three and Alanna only eighteen months. Catherine's hands were tied minding them and poor Nora had to be minded now too. Martin, as usual was always ahead of him, and had all his potatoes dug and in pits. When Eddie asked him to give a hand in case the weather didn't hold out, he was heading to town to get a tooth out.

As Eddie walked the path to the far field he planned his day. He would dig all day and in the evening when the youngsters came in from school, they would all come out and pick everything he had dug. It was by far the best plan. He had brought a bottle of tea and some brown bread and had his pipe filled with tobacco, and Sailor was at his heels. He would have a little nap at the headland around noon, after his tea break and wouldn't bother going back to the house till evening. He never felt alone when the dog was with him, but he would be glad to see the young ones coming out the gap, he'd know it was around 4 o'clock then. As well as getting the help they would be someone to talk to. A man could start talking to himself in a big field like this with not another soul in sight, he thought!

Catherine told him she was going to busy herself with the laundry chores to day. Often he watched her at work and knew it was hard going. Bent over at the washboard and wringing those sheets would be hard work for a man! He blessed the day he got her—a fine strong healthy woman. Nora was making extra washing of late, having little accidents in the bed, so sheets were the main priority. Catherine was a dab hand at opening up the flour bags and sewing four of them together for sheets. That woman was a miracle worker, he thought happily, always planning ahead and not wasting anything. He was a lucky man the day he met her.

It must be mid-day. He heard the Church bell ringing and blessed himself and said the Angelus. He sat down to eat and had a relaxed smoke before drifting off with the mid day sun shining on his face. He had no idea how long he was there, but he thought he heard Catherine's voice calling in his sleep. He looked over at Sailor, expecting to see his ears cocked if he heard anything, but he wasn't there. He spotted the tail end of him going out the gap heading for home.

That wasn't like him at all! Eddie listened again. There were only the birds singing, still Eddie was uneasy. He could trust that dog with his life even though his hearing wasn't as sharp as it used to be, and by times Eddie thought his sight was failing too. Something made him head for home though! He decided to go back to the house.

As Eddie approached the house his first thoughts were that it too quite. He went in to find Catherine bending over a white bundle on the settle-bed. She was crying so much he couldn't make out what she was saying. He looked to see if it was Jamie or Alanna for he couldn't see either of them about. Catherine turned around and said 'Alanna is asleep in her cot, but poor Jamie got scalded with the pot of boiling water. Eddie he backed into the pot on me. I had turned my back to get the sheets. He had been sitting on the floor playing with his toy soldiers, and must have got up to admire them, and backed into the pot. I pulled him out immediately but the water has splashed up his back and the skin is all melted. I've wrapped him with a sheet but I don't know what else to do. He has passed out Eddie. What are we going to do at all?' she wailed clinging to Eddie.

'I'll go for the Doctor straight away.' Eddie said

Thank God Eddie was good in a crisis. It's later on she was dreading! He tended to be calm when it was necessary to deal with a crisis, but Catherine knew the repercussions would come. She never felt the time so long waiting for the Doctor. She tried to remove the sheet, but every time she lifted it, she took a piece of Jamie's skin with it. 'If only Mary were here,' she wailed to herself. 'what can I do at all, what can anyone do, what can a Doctor do?' she wailed to herself. 'Oh dear God don't let him die, not our little Jamie.'

She knew Eddie would blame her. He wouldn't be able to take the crying. That is if little Jamie survives! Right now Catherine would give everything she owned just to hear that little boy cry again! Times like this she wished she were a Nurse. She felt utterly helpless. Nora was lying down having a morning nap with Alanna, so she would not dream of waking them. She had enough on her plate without a little one running around in her way.

When the Doctor came he had the Nurse with him. Clearly, Eddie described the horror of Jamie's injury. They immediately got to work on him and told Catherine they would call her if she were needed. She went outside for a breath of air and to greet Eddie when he returned. She didn't know what else to do. She was begging God to spare her little boy when she heard a familiar cry. 'Oh thank God,' she whispered looking skyward. She ran into the house even though she had seen Eddie turn the corner on his bicycle. Jamie was lying flat on his stomach and the bandages were all around his back and stomach. He slowly reached out his hand to her and wailed "Mammy it hurts."

Catherine thought her heart would break! She couldn't hold him or cuddle him and knew in her heart it would be many a day before she would be able to comfort him in that way. The Doctor explained he was a case for the Hospital, but because of his age, the separation from his mother would be too traumatic and he advised her if she could manage to looks after him, it would be in Jamie's best interest to be at home. The Nurse would call every day to check the burns and change the dressings when necessary, so Catherine wouldn't have to worry about that side of it. Between him and the Nurse, he assured her, Jamie would get as good of care as if he went to Hospital. They would have to make special sleeping arrangements for him, as he will not be able to lie on his back for a very long time. He had given him an injection that would make him comfortable for now, and he would return in the evening to give him another that would see him through the night. Catherine had to be content with that and said she would abide by their decision.

Eddie had stayed outside after getting back home. He tried to imagine what poor Jamie was going through and shivered at the thought. How quickly did Catherine grab him from the pot of boiling water? he pondered to himself. He knew how soft the skin of a three year old was! Would the shock kill him? 'Oh, great God spare our little man!' he prayed. He turned to Sailor who had been watching him since he got back and said 'this one is too big for you old boy.' He was remembering the number of times Sailor was called upon to lick a wound when the children fell and cut themselves!

The Doctor interrupted his thoughts and told Eddie to be patient with Catherine. She will have a hard time ahead of her now. He told him the extent of Jamie's burns and added 'If it's any consolation to you he will never be called to do duty in the Army when he's a young man.' Eddie did not know how to comprehend this statement, but made no comment. He thanked the Doctor as he departed, and went inside.

Catherine was bent over a sleeping Jamie whispering how sorry she was. She looked up at Eddie and he could see how much she was aching. He tried to comfort her but no words would come out. He felt so inadequate. He had never seen her so vulnerable. She was always the strong one. What could he do at all? 'I know,' he thought. 'A cup of hot sweet tea might help her,' so for the first time in their married life he proceeded to make a pot of tea. It was foreign to him. Having two women in the house for the last fifteen years had spoiled him. As he handed her the mug of tea he sat down and coaxed her to drink it, as she had done many times in the past for him. 'We'll get through this, *a grá* he said.

'With the help of God,' she quietly answered.

Chapter 31

Nora's Demise

When youngsters got a bee in their bonnet there was no stopping them! Young Mary wanted to be a nurse, so when she finished her schooling, she knew she had to bide her time till she was old enough to go to England to train for nursing. You had to be eighteen years old to be accepted, so she got herself a housekeeping job in a grocery shop in town, living in the premises and getting her meals with the family. She saved her earnings for her journey to London but gave Catherine five shillings each week. This was a godsend as there was one less mouth to feed and Catherine could buy little extras with Mary's contribution.

Young Patrick had taken a job with a local farmer who had no family. He too was only interested in getting enough money saved to go to England. His first job didn't last very long. If the truth were told, it was really Eddie's fault he lost it. He got work in a quarry when he was just sixteen, and Eddie knew young lads were always given the worst jobs to do in the first few days. He had advised Patrick not to fill the wheelbarrow to the top with cement, as he could hurt his back. So Patrick took the advice of his father.

The foreman noticed he was going back and forth with just half loads in the wheelbarrow, and told him he would have a better days work done if he filled the barrow each time. So Patrick told the story over dinner that evening, and Eddie said 'take no notice of him, sure he wouldn't know what a good days work is.' The next day Patrick continued to only half fill the wheelbarrow, and when the foreman approached him and said, 'I thought I told you yesterday you'd have a better days work done if you filled up the wheelbarrow.' Poor young Patrick replied, '*sure you wouldn't know what a good days work is!*' He was called to the office that evening and given his marching orders!

Francis had also got a job in a public house in Midfield and lived in the premises. He would be only coming home once a month. He had planned to buy a bicycle with his first few weeks' wages. He too was planning on going to England when he would be old enough.

Eddie's help was dwindling, but Catherine felt the extra space in the house made up for it. The youngest, Alanna was nearly four now and Catherine was feeling so grateful to have got this long without getting pregnant again. Her sister Mary had another baby girl—a pal for Olive and called her Monica. She was the happiest woman alive to have at last two healthy little girls.

Nora was fading away slowly. They felt it was only a matter of time now. At 94 years old what could you expect? Catherine tried to tell Eddie it was inevitable. She knew he would miss her but if the truth were told,

Catherine would miss her even more. She knew the house would have such a void without Nora's presence.

Poor Jamie was mending nicely. Catherine thought she would never get over the days and nights she spent with him in the beginning, trying to keep him comfortable and making sure he stayed on his tummy all night. Oh it was a terrible scald and would leave scars on his back forever. Poor little fellow! He was a good patient most of the time. Catherine hoped he wouldn't become spoiled because of this. Grace and her three girls were always fussing over him too and buying him little presents.

Sometimes Catherine felt Eddie was different since Jamie's accident. She couldn't quite put her finger on it but she felt he was colder towards her. She wondered if he was jealous of all the attention she was giving to Jamie—sleeping with him for months, in case he turned over on to his back. It could also be that he couldn't forgive her for neglecting him, allowing such a horrible thing to happen him. It haunted her day and night!

She confided in Grace one day when the men were out in the fields. Grace was the heartiest of people, always in good form and wouldn't hesitate to scold you if she felt you were being ridiculous. In this case she too had noticed Eddie's coldness.

'Men can be peculiar creatures right enough, Catherine,' she said. 'It will only eat into you if you dwell on it and if he won't talk to you about it there's not much you can do. He must realise accidents will happen. With a big family you must expect things to go wrong sometimes. You have been blessed with good health, all of you up to this.' Catherine agreed and had to be satisfied with that for the moment.

'Grace, will you take a look at Nora while you are here and tell me should I send for the Priest to anoint her?' Catherine asked. 'She's on fluids only for the past few days and has lost the talk now too.'

It only took Grace a moment to see that Nora's breathing was very shallow indeed and her skin looked very waxy. She had seen the same happen to her own sister before she died. She advised Catherine the time was very near and they had better prepare for things to happen. She said she would go back to her own house and send young Maureen for the Priest and get that part done anyway. She told Catherine she would return with linen cloths and some good sheets she always kept for emergencies. The candles and the holy water were already blessed since Candlemas day.

They wouldn't alarm Eddie or Martin just yet, but when Maureen went to tell the priest she would get her to go to Uncle John Joe's house and prepare him for the worst. He might want to see his mother before she dies. He hadn't visited last Sunday. It wasn't like him. He always arrived with his little Jack Russell in the basket of his bicycle. Maybe he had a cold and wasn't feeling up to it.

Young Alanna was playing with her rag dollies and wasn't listening to them at all, but when she heard Uncle John Joe's name mentioned, she cocked her ears. She loved to hear he was coming. He always treats her special because he is her Godfather. Every time he visits he gives her half a crown! Not that her Mammy would let her keep it. She would hand it up when he was gone, and take what ever she got back for ice cream the following Sunday. She felt very special. It was her very own money. She went outside to see if he was coming, and as she climbed up onto the stile she heard the piper a long way away. She loved the music he played. Her Daddy always gave him money after he played a few airs for them, but he would say after he'd gone up the *boreen* 'I hope it will be a long time before he calls again.'

She ran inside and shouted excitedly 'Mammy, the piper is coming. I can hear him up at the back of the wood.' Catherine was not very impressed. They had noticed whenever he came by there was always bad news afterwards. Last time a cow died trying to give birth, and the time before that her own mother died. It was looking like he was coming again for poor Nora!

As it was springtime there was plenty to do in the fields. Eddie was helping Martin with the ploughing and opening the drills for sowing the potatoes, and tomorrow it would be Eddie's turn. When he came in tired and sore from the newness of the work, Catherine warned him about Nora's decline all day. They said the Rosary with all the children around her bed, and felt this may be the last night they would have her with them.

After, the younger ones were told to kiss their grandmother good night, and when they were tucked up in bed Eddie and Catherine stayed by her bedside. They felt very close at this moment. This was something they had to get through together. Eddie talked about the time his father died. He didn't remember much but he knew he died out in the yard, and was found by his older brother Pat before he went to America. Nora didn't keep his memory alive, having never talked about it again and they didn't like to upset her by talking about him.

When they both agreed it was time to send for Martin and Grace, they knew it was near the end. As Eddie was putting on his shoes to go for them, John Joe put his head in the half-door and had Martin and Grace with him. Thank God they were all here now, Catherine thought. They started a decade of the Rosary and while they were praying a thought came into Catherine's head.

She took down Nora's clay pipe and asked Eddie to fill it with tobacco. He lit it as she asked him to do, and handed it to her without a word. Catherine propped Nora upright, holding her in her arms and held the pipe to her mouth. She took two puffs of the pipe and lay back on the pillows and drew her last breath. It was so peaceful, and for the first time in their lives, the three grown men were stunned into silence. Never having witnesses such an experience before, all three were very vulnerable and felt closer than they had for years. They were so grateful their mother got such a happy death.

The three sons left the room in silence, leaving the women to do what was necessary. They told the older children who were still awake that Nora had passed away, and watched in silence as they cried for their grandmother. Eddie told them they wouldn't be going to school tomorrow, in honour of their Granny.

The three men started discussing the arrangements for the burial—who would dig the grave and who would do the undertaking? Eddie took out a bottle of whiskey from the top shelve of the dresser and half filled three glasses. They toasted together and thanked God for a great mother. Each had their own memories of her, and had to agree she had a hard life but was one of the best.

Martin was thinking to himself how lucky he was to have got the field ploughed today before she died. The trouble was he would be loosing a few days now, with all this, before he would be able to set the potatoes. The more he thought about it the more he realised it was only foolish to be idle. He could get up early in the morning and quietly put out the manure in the drills. He had heard Eddie telling the boys there would be no school tomorrow for them. That was music to his ears! He now knew how he would accomplish the task before the funeral time. Those three lads were great workers for Eddie! He'd get them to put in the potatoes for him. It was a quiet enough job and if he told them to keep the noise down, nobody would even know they were working at all. Anyway half the job would be done before anyone heard Nora was dead at all.

He knew if Eddie realised what he was thinking, he would be in the bad books! So he would keep quiet about it till morning when the young lads would be outside, he would nab them before they could refuse! He wouldn't mention his plans to Grace either or she would scold him for having no respect for the dead.

Martin had spent some time in the Army and had seen men die, so he had very little feelings for dead people. As far as he was concerned, life is for living and when you are gone, you are gone! Those who are left behind must get over it and move on. And that is what he intended to do. Life is for living!

Chapter 32

Immigration

The September morning dawned dull and misty. It suited Catherine's mood as she hurriedly dressed and got the fire blazing under the kettle to get the breakfast ready. She had not slept well, waking every hour in case she slept in. Mary was catching the train to England, and Catherine thought her heart would break. It's not that she wasn't happy for her. Mary was going to have a career—something Catherine never had. Being a chambermaid in Philadelphia was very enjoyable, but it was classed as one of the lower positions.

Catherine would miss her eldest child. She was always so helpful with the smaller children, dressing them and polishing their shoes, brushing their hair and feeding them before she would take a bite of her own. It was only a matter of time before three of lads would be off too. No doubt all her family would be emigrating. It was in the times. If you wanted to become anything, and earn a good living you had to immigrate. There was nothing to keep youngsters at home and very little work around. The farm wasn't big enough to keep grown men busy, and Eddie was content with a small amount of help.

'Catherine, are you trying to make butter out of that saucepan of porridge?' Eddie called out making her jump. She hadn't realised she was stirring the life out of the porridge for the last ten minutes. She was in a world of her own!

'I hadn't realised you came in Eddie, I was dreaming away and feeling sorry for myself. Aren't you feeling it too this morning? I'm going to be so lost without Mary.'

'Come on now my dear, and cheer up for her sake. Remember when you left home. I'm sure it wouldn't have helped to see your mother so sad as you were leaving. She's going to better herself. And won't it be nice to have a nurse in the family?' He put an arm around Catherine's shoulder. 'We are going to have to get used to them leaving. I heard Patrick telling young Francis that he's going to head off to England soon where there is plenty of work. They need to have work and get paid a decent wage. There's not much around here. They need space of their own too. It's getting a bit cramped now. The old *settle-bed* wasn't meant for grown men, you know Catherine,' he said laughing down at her.

At times like this she knew why she had chosen Eddie. Nineteen years had passed since she met him. They had a very good life even though the work was hard at times and not a lot of money to spare. Catherine's dearest wish in time was to build a new house. She was secretly saving money, and hoped when the older children went to work in England they would send money home. She wouldn't have as many mouths to feed either and her little *nest egg* would grow faster. Eddie had no idea of her plans, but she would get around him. She would pick her time when he would be in good humour. He usually let her have her way, but for now it would keep her going thinking of it.

All the family gathered after breakfast was over out in the yard. Eddie was getting the horse and trap ready to take Mary to the train station in *Drumoneen*. They hugged and kissed and cried, and made all sorts of promises to write to each other every week. As Catherine watched her lovely children, loving and caring for each other, she realised she wouldn't want to be without one of them now. She also knew they would have to go through this ordeal many times in their lives. As she bravely hugged and kissed her firstborn, she was to find out that parting from your child is the hardest thing, but loosing her to a foreign country is heartbreaking. Suddenly, she though of her own mother. How brave she seemed that day when Catherine left for Philadelphia, all those years ago, but perhaps she too was doing a good job of hiding it all.

There was only one cure for what ailed the lot of them today, Catherine thought. Work! Everyone was feeling downhearted, so Catherine conjured up ideas for everyone. She didn't know how long Eddie would be or what he had planned to do today, but by the time he would come home, he would find everyone busy with their own chore.

She decided to start with the youngest. Alanna was only six but well able to muck in. And young Jamie was seven and a half. Those two were as thick as thieves, so Catherine gave them two small shovels to dig the tufts of grass from the paths leading to the house. It got so overgrown lately with the damp weather. It was nobody's favourite job, but when those two got together they could make it interesting. They would turn up worms and slugs and feed them to the chickens that always gathered around when this job was being done. She had to be very careful giving chores to young Jamie. Although his burns healed up, the skin looked so thin on his back, it looked like it would tear at the slightest touch.

Next she decided the dresser needed a good turnout. This is a feature of most farmhouse kitchens, where a housewife displayed her crockery. Poor Nora had kept a lot of rubbish in there. It was time to sort out the good from the useless. There were some items that were neither useful nor ornamental. She had a lovely set of well-known willow pattern jugs that were very eye-catching, but on closer scrutiny, you found the good sides were on display, but the insides were all cracked and chipped. It was time to be ruthless. She called Angela and Teresa aside for this chore. At ten and twelve they could be trusted with delicate crockery, but they sure will get great satisfaction from smashing the ones that are to be discarded, and there are plenty of them.

Francis and John were kicking a ball, commentating as they did so. "Toe-to—hand, toe-to-hand up the field" you could hear as they tried to side track each other. 'Come on you two lads,' Catherine called out, 'I've your jobs lined up too. You are not getting away that handy. I'm sure even the best footballers had to clean out the barns at some time. The cow house and the hen houses need a good going over lads. Your Dad will be proud of you for having it done when he gets back.'

'Tony, I want you to take Sailor to the river and give him a good wash. Bring the water buckets with you and bring me up fresh water for the tea when you have finished. Don't let him chase the sheep. You know how frisky he can be when he's shaking off the water when he's drying himself. There's a good boy!'

'Patrick you and I are going to do the dirtiest job of all. The oil lamps need a good clean. I hate doing them but if you help me, sure we can be talking and it won't seem as bad. The storm lamp is in a bad way and if your Dad has to go out to see to the cow when she's calving, he needs a good light.'

Patrick was pleased to hear he was going to be able to spend time with his mother. It wasn't very often he got a chance to talk to her on his own. There were always so many around all the time. He did not know how he was going to approach her with what he had in his mind for some time now. He was been planning on going to England. His friend had gone a month ago and had said he would write and let him know the story there. With Mary going to London, he hated to upset his mother further by telling her he too would be leaving home soon. He felt he had to make room for the younger ones growing up in the house, and the money was supposed to be good and plenty of work there. He would take any job he got, but he would wait till he was seventeen. That would be in January. So it would be a few months yet, but he wanted to prepare his mother and not spring it on her.

Patrick had been expecting it would be a shock to her to hear he was leaving home, but to his surprise she took it very calmly. 'Thank God for that,' he though to himself. He would be so sad at leaving but it had to be done. He would try and make a go of it. Francis was secretly hoping to go too but was not old enough yet. Patrick would have a job got for him and have a place to stay.

Everyone was busy with his or her chores. Catherine kept an eye on them but at the same time never stopped thinking of Mary and wondering where she is now. Eddie would soon be home, but she was sure he would not come home without having a visit to the pub. He would also have some lamb chops from the butcher for their dinner. She hoped he would have a bag of *bull's eyes* for the children too. After tackling all those long overdue chores they deserved a treat. Catherine decided to make jelly and custard to cheer everyone up after the dinner. She only made it on Sundays, but to day was a milestone in their lives.

So engrossed in her thoughts, Catherine hadn't realised it had gone so late. The lads were out playing pitch-and-toss us the *boreen*, and the girls were busy putting waves in their hair. Everyone was happy the ugly chores were done for a long time to come.

'Where in the world is your Father?' Catherine said to the older children, as it was getting nearly dark. 'Patrick and Francis, will you take out you're bicycles and go over the road and see is there any sign of the horse and trap coming. Something must have happened.'

Catherine was fully focused now and kept peering out the window, and trying not to look too worried in front of the younger ones. She could not concentrate on what she was doing. Just as she was about to peer out the window for the umpteenth time, Francis burst in the door shouting, 'Mama, Daddy is asleep in the trap and the mare is eating grass along the side of the road. The reins are hanging loosely on the mares back. I brought home Patrick's bike and he's bringing the mare and trap home now. Daddy wouldn't wake up for us.'

Catherine could not believe her ears. Eddie must be scattered with drink! She knew he like his porter on fair days, and there was one of them every month! Secretly she dreaded fair days, but it was all part of the bargaining, handshaking, keeping your word and sealing the deal with a drink. But to day was different. Could Eddie be that down about Mary's leaving for London? He did not show much emotion this morning. She didn't think he had much money on him either. After all he was only going to the train station to buy Mary's ticket.

Catherine realised she was jumping to conclusions. What if Eddie wasn't well? Maybe he was not drunk at all! She called out to Francis to come in and tell her how his father looked. 'Was he pale or did he open his eyes at all? Is he dead?' Francis assured her he was not dead. 'He had a big red nose on him and his shirt and tie was all stained with porter!' The younger ones laughed at this, but it was no laughing matter to Catherine.

She hurriedly gave them their supper and got them ready for bed. She certainly did not want them ever to see their father in this state. The three lads would be needed to help Eddie into the house, and onto the bed. Her mind was in turmoil. What in the world possessed him to behave so, today of all days?

Catherine was on the verge of tears, but she had to be strong for the others. There was no point in creating a scene tonight, but 'Eddie my boy, you'll have some explaining to do tomorrow,' she told herself under her breath.

Chapter 33

Eddie's Dilemma

Eddie was gone out milking the cows the following morning when Catherine woke. She could smell the fresh milk wafting up from the barn when she opened the back door. She could only think he must be feeling guilty and could not face the family this morning.

After the young ones were all ready for school with their lunches packed, she made her way to the barns to collect the buckets of milk that would be left for the household. The majority of the milk had to be fed to the young calves. As she drew near the door she heard Eddie give a shout "you hoor from hell." She heard the rattle of a stool and a cry of pain. As she opened the door she saw Eddie on his back holding his leg, the stool on top of him and the bucket of milk spilled on the floor.

She already knew the worst. A kick from a cow can be very damaging. Eddie was in agony she could see. All thoughts of her coolness towards him for his behaviour yesterday were forgotten, and she quickly called Patrick from the kitchen where he was making his sandwiches. They helped him into the house. She could see already his leg was getting quite large and could only think the worst.

Luckily Patrick had not left for his work yet and Catherine sent him for the local Hackney car, which was only half a mile across the fields. She knew Eddie would have to go to Hospital to have his leg X-rayed. She felt sure it must be broken. While she was waiting she gave Eddie a cup of sweet tea and a slice of brown bread. He was in great pain and found it very hard to keep still.

'What in the world made that hussy kick you this morning Eddie?' she asked. 'You have been milking her every morning. You must be hurting her or squeezing her teats too much for her to lift her leg like that.'

'Maybe I was a bit rough with her, but she got her own back on me now, the bitch!' Thank God you know how to milk a cow Catherine. If this has to have a cast I won't be able to sit under a cow for months. I cannot be holding up Patrick or Francis in the mornings to do the milking, or they will be late for their own jobs. They will be home by milking time in the evenings though. Oh, Christ the pain of this is woeful.'

'Don't be worrying about that now Eddie till we see what the Hospital says. We'll manage somehow. It's not the end of the world,' Catherine tried to sound cheerful.

But she knew it was going to be a hard couple of months ahead of them. She knew Eddie would prove to be an awful bad patient. 'How is he going to pass the time at all? He's a dead loss at reading and apart from listening to the news on the wireless, he won't listen to anything else and turns it off. If he cannot walk out the fields he will go pure mental!' Catherine exaggerated to herself.

The Hospital confirmed Eddie had in fact a very bad break, and was sent home the next day with a plaster cast above his knee. What a heavy lump of plaster poor Eddie had to carry around and two long crutches for support. It was pathetic watching him trying to hobble around with the aid of the crutches that he found nearly impossible to manage. Co-ordination was never his strong point!

He was like a bear with a sore head. Everything was wrong! When Catherine handed him a mug of tea it was either too hot or two cold or not sweet enough. He was miserably cold and kept poking the fire with one of his crutches and calling out to get more turf. The pipe was his only consolation, and that kept him quiet, cleaning it and cutting up the *Bendigo* tobacco, and trying to light it. The days were long on him, and watching everyone doing their work and able to get about, was indeed very hard on Eddie. Catherine felt so sorry for him in the midst of all the extra chores that were landed on her lap, through Eddie's misfortune. Silently she blamed Eddie. He must have hurt that poor cow to make her do such a thing. No doubt his head was throbbing after his drinking the day before. She was not going to bring that up ever again. He was going to have plenty of time for reflection, she thought to herself!

Eddie of course felt too ashamed to ever bring up the subject at all. He would like the ground to open up and swallow him when anyone mentioned the day Mary went to England. He really never remembered a thing after he passed the Railway gates. He also tried to imagine what it must be like for the lads seeing their father in such a drunken state. 'If this doesn't make me a teetotaller, nothing else ever will,' Eddie was thinking to himself. 'God dam and blast the cursed drink,' he moaned under his breath, several times a day when he was struggling with the crutches, especially when he was trying to relieve himself! 'Carrying this awful load into the bed every night will be the death of me,' he muttered. 'How will I get through these months of torture at all?' he asked Catherine over and over.

He begged her not to tell Mary about his accident with the cow. He knew in his heart it would not have happened if he had not gone drinking the day she left. That poor cow was not to blame at all. Certainly he was not going to sell her off as the lads had suggested. You could not blame them for their reluctance to approach her again. Animals instinctively knew who was kind to them. He knew he would have to get them to trust her again but in the meantime Catherine would milk her. He would reassure them when the time was right that it was safe to continue milking the cow. Eddie knew it had all been his own fault. It sure was a lesson to him, and a sobering one. "God damn the bloody drink," he would say to himself in the many months to come, as he was struggling with the big plaster and the crutches.

Catherine could not ever remember a time when Eddie was so contrary. She came to realise he was a very poor patient indeed. 'Just as well it wasn't him that had to have the babies,' she mused to herself. He may be responsible for the next generation of Staunton's, but were he the one having the babies she felt they would never have had nine children. One day she would get around to saying it to him but this was not the time.

God knows Catherine could do without the extra chore of milking a cow every morning and evening. 'Have I not enough on my plate?' she thought to herself every day. She used to hear her mother saying, "these little crosses are sent to test us." So she had to be content with that and keep the bright side out, even though she knew that by bedtime, she would have such an ache in her legs from on her feet all day. With the various amount of things that had to be done around the farmyard and in the house all day every day, Catherine had a tough time of it. And now she had Eddie under her feet, moaning about how he was suffering. It wasn't easy now and Catherine often wondered if she would have had an easier life had she had stayed in Philadelphia!

She daydreamed, as she rubbed the butter into the flour when she was making the bread for her large family. Thoughts of the lovely big house she worked in with only the bedrooms to be seen to every day, made her a bit disgruntled the odd time she let herself get carried away. Still there was no point in going down that road. There was no turning back. Her family came first and they were all very healthy. This is just a set back for a few months with Eddie. They'd get over it with the help of God! Sure nobody died!

Chapter 34

Wedding Fever

The 4th September 1957 dawned warm and sunny. A perfect day for a wedding! Catherine and Eddie stood out on the steps of their new bungalow and felt the proudest of parents. Today they were having their first wedding in the family. Mary was getting married and had wanted the wedding to be at home. She was marrying Jim Hegarty from Sligo. They had met in London where she had spent 7 years nursing. They would be going back to live there again after the honeymoon.

With her large family Catherine knew this day would come. Her longing to build a nice new bungalow with a bathroom and running water was her dearest wish. Since the boys went working to England, she was able to save and add to her nest egg. She had been building it up, unknown to anyone.

The white registered envelope was a familiar sight coming out of Tommy Rumley's postbag. Catherine knew the day it would arrive and would always make sure she was around the house to sign for it. They sent her money every week and never asked what she did with it. Angela and Teresa were also sending money home, but girls usually earned less than boys. Mary sent money home when she first went, but as the boys followed her soon after, Catherine told her to save her money for herself. Nurses did not get a lot when they were training.

With only Jamie and Alanna at home now, it was much easier to make ends meet. Eddie left all that side of things to Catherine, but she was not sure how he would take to the idea of building a new house. It was a huge undertaking and she knew he did not like changes. Sometimes he could be old-fashioned in his thinking and Catherine could almost hear him saying 'didn't this house put up ten of us before you came to it?' It was going to take a lot of courage to approach the subject. He was not always agreeable to her ideas, and she knew it would have to be the right time.

She broached the subject light-heartedly one evening when they were out rolling up the wool, after shearing the sheep all day. You could hear the little lambs bleating, each one looking for their own mother, as they looked more like goats than sheep without their thick wool coats. Catherine always felt sorry for them at this time of year.

Eddie was relaxed and happy with the great days work. You couldn't approach him when he was in the middle of a tough job—he could be like a weasel! He was not always like that but since the pneumonia he was a different man. He was grand if he got ahead with his many chores around the farm, but his patience was tested many a fine day with Martin. His tools and equipment were often gone just when Eddie needed them for himself.

Catherine knew Eddie's many moods and made allowances for them, so when she asked him who did he think would be the best contractors to build a house, she was amazed when he answered "Well we wont be giving it to Joe Murphy's gang anyway—they are too high and mighty and think they can charge any price. There's plenty more out there that can do the job as good and cheaper. I'd be in favour of Johnny Heneghan and Pakie Gibbons. They do a nice neat job. Are you sure you have enough saved to give them a few hundred to buy the blocks and cement?"

This was music to her ears, as she now felt he was going to be agreeable. He then told her he had an idea she was saving up to build a new house, although at first he thought with six of the family now left home, sure hadn't they more space than ever! But he knew they would be coming back visiting, and maybe bringing husbands and wives home with them, so if that was what she wanted, he wouldn't stand in her way. "We might as well move with the times, Catherine," he said as he put an arm around her shoulders.

Catherine assured him she had enough put by. When Nora died just over six years ago, Catherine found a tidy sum of money in the lining of an old handbag belonging to her. She had almost thrown it out! She knew Nora was always fumbling in it, but it never looked as if there was anything inside. She blessed her silently and felt Nora would approve of what she intended doing with it. So she never said a word about it to anyone, not even Eddie, but knew it was going to be a Godsend for the blocks and cement, to start off the building she so very much longed for. Eddie said he would have the six large bullocks ready for the fair next month, and the lambs and the wool will fetch a nice price too.

And so after 26 years of marriage, they were the proud owners of their lovely bungalow. It boasted four bedrooms, one bathroom, parlour, kitchen and back-kitchen with running hot and cold water. Catherine thought she would burst with joy. If only she had this kind of luxury when she was rearing the kids! How on earth did she manage she asked herself over and over as she got accustomed to all this space?

Of course Eddie ended up with a windfall too. When they moved into the bungalow, the thatched cottage became a shed for the cows. One of the rooms was kept for storing the corn, the dog found his own corner beside the fireplace, and a cat would have her kittens in a cosy spot secretly chosen by herself. On a wet day Eddie would be nice and warm inside fixing punctures or repairs to bicycles, or whatever repairs needed doing to horse equipment or tools for the farm. All in all he felt life was good to him and all thanks to his good wife of nearly 26 years. He had discovered very early on into his marriage that Catherine seldom made a bad decision. She never rushed into things and had a level head. He couldn't always say that about himself!

Catherine had written to Aunt Anne in Philadelphia telling her about the new bungalow they had built. In her reply she said she had made up her mind to make a trip home. With Mary's wedding coming up, and Catherine and Eddie's wedding anniversary in a few days after that, sure it was a cause for a double celebration, and if she didn't make the trip now, she never would. She wasn't getting any younger. She would stay in Goulboy with her cousin Mary as there would be less going on there, and they would all be together on the wedding day. Her P.S at the end of the letter said 'I hope you don't mind me inviting myself to the wedding.'

Catherine gave a sigh of relief as she stood beside Eddie on the top of the steps. All their family were together for the big day. She was relaxed now but the drama of yesterday still hadn't fully evaporated. They thought at one time the wedding would have to be called off!

Father Gibbons called unexpectedly to the house in his car at 3 o'clock He announced that no 'letter of freedom' had come from Mary's parish in London and that he could not marry her without it. Having lived in England it was necessary to have documentation to prove that she had not been married before. He apologised and said he could not perform the ceremony without that letter of consent! Poor Mary didn't know what she would do.

For a few hours everything was at a standstill! What was the point of continuing with all the preparations? The chickens were roasting in the ovens and the gammons were boiling in their pots. Eddie had gone to Tuffy's with the ass and cart for the barrel of porter and minerals for the younger ones. Grace was busy baking all sorts of cakes and tarts and trifles in her house next door. The wedding dress was hanging up on the outside of the wardrobe, and Angela was busy sewing a dainty bit of lace on the front of her blue bridesmaids dress. Catherine said she was showing too much of her bosom, especially when she would be above at the alter. What would the Priest say!

He wouldn't know where to look! She'd be distracting him from the holy Ceremony!

Young Alanna seemed to be the only one not too put out by this news. For days now she was showing everyone the beautiful new white dress with the big blue polka dots that Mary had brought home from London for her to wear. She was taking the news very well. When Teresa questioned her about it she said if the wedding did not take place then she would be able to go to school. She hated missing the first day at Secondary school, and felt if she did not enrol on the first day she wouldn't be able to go at all!

Patrick, Francis and John and Tony were all gone out fishing. It was their greatest thrill, even better than playing football, and they missed it when they were in England. Catherine missed the trout for the dinners although Eddie would go fishing an odd time but he didn't have the patience. He never seemed to come in with the same haul as the boys did! He admitted he could never get the hang of creating a dam of stones across the river, making a barricade so the fish couldn't swim through. With this method you could catch a big shoal all together in a fishing net. When they got home they would make a fuss about the big one that got away!

And so it was, when Father Gibbons dropped the bombshell the women were on their own with the exception of Jamie who was practising playing his black button accordion in the back bedroom. He was improving every day and Catherine was so proud of him. He was going over the tunes for a few waltzes and half-sets and Catherine had hummed the Stack of Barley for him to practice. Grace was to play for the wedding on her melodeon and she never refused to sing a song. John was well used to playing the accordion in England, so between the three of them they knew the music would be good enough. It was the dancers that Mary was worried about! If all men were like her Dad, then there would not be any demand for half-sets!

That was the least of her worries now. What on earth was she going to do? Should she go to the Post Office and get them to send a telegram to Jim and his family telling them the marriage cannot take place. Telegrams usually gave people an awful fright. Catherine's advice was to 'take your time yet till we see is there anything we can do.'

They decided to send for Grace. She was always good in a crisis. Whenever there was a row brewing between the two brothers, Grace was always able to abort it before it got out of hand. She had a lovely calming way with her. Young Alanna ran across the field and dashed into the kitchen breathless. 'We have a crisis that Mammy wants you to fix.' Smiling to herself, Grace took off her apron and went with Alanna.

She listened while all of them at the same time started telling her what Father Gibbons had said. 'Wait, wait now ladies, one at a time,' she laughed. 'I can't make head or tail of what any of you are saying.' So, word for word, Mary repeated what the Priest had said. They all sat in silence waiting to hear what Grace would make of it. She took her time thinking it through before she answered. 'Mary if I was getting married tomorrow and got this news, I would be on my bike to the Parish Priest and get him to ring Westminster Abbey to see if this 'letter of freedom' is in the post. They all have phones nowadays. Even if they have to look it up, wait there till they ring back. Please God they have it sent and will allow Father Gibbons to go ahead with the marriage, pending the arrival of the letter. Go now Mary, and Angela you go with her for support.'

And so it was, that by the time Mary and Angela got to the Priest's House, Father Gibbons had already made a call requesting the matter be looked up, and was waiting for a call back. He made a cup of tea for the girls while they were waiting as he could see how flustered they were. They sat looking at the telephone willing it to ring, and at the same time dreading what might be the outcome.

When it did finally ring both girls were so startled, the cups rattled in their saucers. They nearly devoured the Priest gazing at him, to see his reaction as he held the phone to his ear. He kept saying, 'Yes, yes, very good, yes I'll do that, thank you. Goodbye.' He left down the phone slowly and carefully and from his expression, neither of the girls could hazard a guess as to the outcome of the conversation. When he spoke his next words were 'Mary, my dear, this time tomorrow you will be Mrs Hegarty.'

'Are we going to stand here all morning Catherine?' Eddie quietly said in her ear. 'I thought this marriage was at 10 o'clock. Isn't it time to call them all? I know you are not going to the Church but them women need time to get all their glad rags on. It won't take us fellows very long to get dressed. Did you give a rub of a wet rag to the tongs, just in case it hits the end of the wedding dress when I throw it after Mary?'

Catherine had forgotten the old custom of the Father of the bride throwing the tongs after her as she made her way out of her house to the Church. This was to bring good luck. She'd better do it now! There would be plenty of time when the family were at the Church to tidy up the house and get herself presentable. She was looking forward to wearing the new sea green dress with little red roses scattered here and there. It had a nice white peter pan collar that reflected on her rosy cheeks. She hoped she would be able to stay calm today, as recently Doctor Murphy checked her blood pressure and told her it was pretty high. She would have to take it easy. He prescribed tablets for her to take.

Alanna was staying at home to help her. They would have the house tidy, the kettles boiled for the tea and everything laid out for the wedding breakfast. Someone had to be at the house in case some of the guests turned up instead of going to the Church. When Mary returned with her brand new husband everything was going to be as she had wished. With the help of God it was going to be a wonderful day that they would always remember.

Chapter 35

Double Tragedies

Tony Staunton stood watching while his men worked away steadily on the building site. He was a project manager for the past twelve months. He had a good head for business and was picked for promotion from a bunch of good skilled men. The first thing he did was to write a letter home to his parents. He knew Eddie and Catherine would boast to the neighbours that their son was a project manager on a building site in Southampton! Tony did not mind as long as they were happy. This was news they could boast about—unlike the news he broke to them four years ago. He wrote and told them he was getting married to a Scottish girl, whose husband had died from a fall in the building site he was working in. She had a young boy aged ten and a girl seven. Catherine did not take the news very well. She pointed out the pitfalls of rearing another mans children and he only twenty-nine years old! Letters were sent back and forth, till in the end Tony won his mother around! As long as he was happy, then she would be happy for him and gave her blessing!

Right now he was very proud of his achievements. He was not altogether surprised the day the foreman called him into his office. He had heard through the grapevine there was a promotional job on the horizon, and as Tony had worked all the hours God sent, he felt it would all be in his favour one day.

When he was sixteen years old he went to work in a pub at home. He heard a lot of stories behind the bar from drinking men home on holidays from England. They had made it good in England by working long hours, showing initiative, giving an honest days work and showing an interest in the business. It was a *feather in your cap* at home to have bettered yourself in '*John Bull's*' country! Many ended up in the slums. Tony was taking it all in. He admired these well-dressed drinking men, sporting wads of money especially around Christmas. He could not help comparing them to his father. He knew how hard his parents were working to survive, and feed nine children on a small farm.

He had got a good start when he first set foot in England. He had his brothers Patrick and Francis there before him with digs and a job to go to when he arrived. Not every young Irish lad had it so lucky! He intended to make money and send it home to his mother to help with the young ones. She had often mentioned she hoped one day to build a nice new house.

As Tony stood watching his men working, his mind was in turmoil. He had a huge decision to make. He loved his job and he was blissfully happily married to Betty for four years now. There were the odd disputes when he would try to discipline young Roger who was fourteen, and getting 'corners'. When Betty failed to get through to him and Tony would intervene, Roger was quick to remind him with a retort 'you are not my Father.' Times like these Tony remembered his mother's words about 'rearing another mans child.' Roger was becoming rather wilful and Tony had to remind Betty he was at an awkward age. Maybe he would grow out of it! Maybe he was missing his father!

Pamela, now eleven, showed no signs at all of any effects from the death of her father. She was a most pleasant child to have around and was a great little 'mother' to baby Sally, who was born a year after they were married. Sally was the light of their lives, although Betty suffered terrible post-natal depression after she was born. There were days she did not want to get out of the bed at all! This was something very foreign to Tony. He never noticed his mother taking to the bed. She was always up before them in the mornings and never went to bed before them at night! Betty assured him she never experienced this after Roger and Pamela were born. The Doctor said it must be because of the bereavement.

Tony wondered if the move they were contemplating would set her back again. They discussed it night after night when the kids were in bed, with still no definite conclusion. Tony's boss, Mr. Munford-Jones who owned the company he worked for, offered him the job of manager of his lately acquired stately home in The Isle of Sky. His father had passed away and he had inherited it all—lock, stock and barrel. He was not prepared to live there till he retired. He said he knew Tony had a good head for business, and would trust him with the smooth running of this mansion and one hundred acres of land. The staff that had been there in his father's time would assist him, but he would have the final word on any decisions or changes made. He would have the living accommodation for himself and his family. The sum of money he was prepared to pay was extravagant to say the least. The more Betty and he though about it, the more they knew it would foolish to turn it down. They discussed it with Roger, who said he didn't care where they moved to—he would be leaving home as soon as he turned sixteen anyway!

Betty was an only child and both her parents had passed away before she and Tony met, so she didn't have any roots and had no problem moving. As long as she had Tony and the children, she said she didn't care where she lived. Her in-laws lived in America where she had met her first husband George while on holiday. After returning to England there were lots of letters and phone calls back and forth, till he surprised her one evening when she got in from work. He was sitting on her doorstep with two big suitcases. He asked her to marry him and she accepted without any hesitation. He was now happy to live in England with her. They kept in touch with his parents and Betty still likes to keep them informed of their grandchildren's whereabouts, and sends them photos as they grow up. Roger chats on the phone to them and recently said to Betty after one long conversation, he would like to live in America. George's parents were bound to be heartbroken after the accident and no doubt felt close to their grandson. Maybe he would compensate, and fill their void if he did live with them when he is older. Unless Tony puts a stop to it when the time comes, Betty has no fear of letting him go. She knows he will be in good hands.

They finally made up their minds to move at the end of the month. They left their house in the hands of a Solicitor to be sold, and headed for a new life. They were excited but apprehensive too. Catherine and Eddie thought it was a wonderful chance for them and so proud of their son to be trusted with such an important position.

At first, everything seemed to be going well. The workforce was mostly from an older generation, with some of the men having sons working there who were the same ages as Tony. They settled down quite well. Tony was a likeable young man and the older men did not appear to resent taking orders from him. Occasionally, he would ask their advice on certain matters that were foreign to him, and they willingly shared their knowledge with him.

Betty and the children loved the space and the freedom of the outdoors. Living in the countryside held such excitement for all of them. There were two tame horses on the estate and Roger and Pamela learned to ride them in the evenings after school. When they were exploring the sheds one day they found an old unused sidecar. They asked Tony if they could paint it and polish it up and see if one of the horses could pull it. They could see themselves trotting down the avenue in the evenings after school and maybe venturing to the local small town for errands for their mother.

Roger changed from a surly, bad tempered adolescent to a most pleasant young man, chatting away to old Jock Mc Coy after school and would come in with stories for his mother, often making her laugh even though half the time she didn't know what she was laughing at. She was just happy to see Roger in such good spirits now. The change was remarkable. She felt a different woman herself too. Looking after Sally kept her busy and she enjoyed organising meals when Tony was expected in from the fields. She would help him with the wages for the men as she had a good head for figures. It was so safe for Sally, even when she wandered off down the long avenue, picking bluebells and daffodils in the spring, and any other wild things that grew on the hedges. She would call Betty out to see a little birds nest in the ivy and ask her to lift her up, to see if there were any eggs or birds in the nest.

Betty would often sit outside in the long ornamental seat under the large trees, listening to the birds singing and keeping an eye on young Sally. On a quiet day she could hear the gulls circling over the lake that was about a hundred yards away at the end of the cornfields. At ploughing time they would congregate looking for upturned worms after the tractor had turned over a sod. The peaceful surroundings were such a balm to Betty after losing her husband, and she did not care if she never seen a city again. It didn't hold good memories for her and she was so happy in the knowledge that her depression seemed to have lifted at last.

Tony had noticed the change in her too and normally would discuss work matters with her, but what he was noticing lately from the younger members of staff, he felt was not something he should share with her. He heard some rumblings of the men going to demand a raise in their wages, and if they did not get it they would all go on strike. Old Jock Mc Coy told him discretely one day, that the younger members of the staff were very peeved that a stranger with no experience was brought in to dictate to them. He telephoned Mr. Munford-Jones to see if a raise was appropriate but he was not interested in the demand, and not at all perturbed by the threat. That evening Tony held a meeting and told them there would be no raise forthcoming at this time. Needless to say Tony was now less popular than ever! The younger men left the building very disgruntled, and he could hear their mumbled tones as they made their way down the lane.

He was a quiet type of person and did not like any kind of confrontation. When Old Jock discretely told him a couple of days after the meeting that they were brewing up something, it troubled him greatly. He took to taking a walk to the lake after work was finished most evenings and enjoyed a leisurely swim. It was very soothing and it relaxed him. Betty joined him one evening just to see what he was going on about. She did not know how to swim and hated getting even her big toe wet! It was a heavenly setting she had to admit. The sun sinking in the west, reflecting on the water in the mid-summer evening, with not a sound around but the screeching of the gulls circling overhead was like another world. They wandered back to the house hand in hand and Betty turned and impulsively kissed Tony, and told him she couldn't remember a time when she was this happy.

One evening, a week later when Tony had not returned by dusk, Betty got concerned and asked Roger to go and see if there was any sign of him coming up the lane. He returned almost immediately with a look of horror, calling out to send for the doctor quickly. Betty didn't ask any questions till she had made the call. She then ran out with Roger to where he had found his stepfather. He was almost beyond recognition. He was covered with blood and was croaking something like 'they ganged up on me.' She asked him to try and say it again as she couldn't understand what that meant. He tried but blood was gurgling out his mouth. By the time the Doctors car drove up the lane, Betty knew her beloved Tony was already gone in her arms.

Outwardly, Betty seemed to be coping with the trauma of the funeral arrangements. She wanted Tony to be cremated. She couldn't bear to bury a second husband. Was she jinxed? Was she bringing them bad luck? How was she going to tell his poor parents? She decided not to tell them until the cremation was over. There was no point in putting them through that, as she felt it would be against their beliefs anyway. She was not able for any confrontation. Old Jock McCoy couldn't do enough for her. He was there whenever she needed advice and she never felt she was imposing on him. Roger and Pamela was a great strength, but as Tony was not their father they did not feel the loss and grief she was experiencing. Poor little Sally was too young to realise what was going on at all! She would spend her days outside foraging for any thing that moved slowly. She would stay all day poking at a hedgehog or singing 'pookie, pookie put out your horns' to a snail with a house on its back!

Betty prayed to the Lord to get her through this once again. Some days she almost wrenched her hair straight out of its roots, asking him "why me, why me again? What did I do so wrong to deserve this?" Nobody was ever found for the death of her husband. Investigations were carried out for weeks, with the police no nearer a solution than when they started. When all the staff on the estate were questioned, nobody had seen anything, everybody had an alibi and children even said their daddies were at home that evening! The police did not close the case, but Betty could see they were slackening off with their visits and had no fresh information for her.

As grieved as Betty was, she realised their time was limited in this lovely place. Six weeks after Tony's murder, Mr. Munford-Jones called to see her. He was kindness itself and told her she would be compensated for the loss of her husband, but they would have to find a home elsewhere. He gave her a month's notice to vacate the living area. He and his family were going to have to come and live on the Estate sooner than he had planned.

Betty rapidly went into the depths of depression. She would go for walks to the lake each evening just before dark, leaving Roger to listen for little Sally. She never spoke when she came in only went straight to bed. One evening after coming home she suggested to Roger he should ring his grandparents in America. She said it would be good for him to chat with them. He thought it a little odd as she often scolded him for his lengthy overseas calls.

Pamela was trying to keep household chores done and would spend her evenings washing and ironing clothes, for her mother didn't seem to have any interest in doing anything for them anymore. When Pamela questioned her one evening after dinner about where they will live when they leave the Estate, her mother answered her with a question "would you like to go and live in Ireland with Tony's parents?' Pamela was shocked, as they had never gone there before. It's not like they are our real grandparents, Pamela thought to herself. Well, yes they are Sally's real grandparents; she had to admit. She was thinking little Sally was too young to notice where she was or what was happening, so nothing was mentioned to her.

Betty told her she had a letter from Catherine during the week saying they would have room for them if they wanted to come. All their own family were now gone abroad. It would bring great comfort to them and they would get to know their grandchildren. As Pamela was starting Secondary school in September, this would be a good time to move to Ireland.

Pamela didn't give her mother an answer at that time and Betty didn't demand one. She pondered on it all evening after her mother went for her walk to the lake. It sounded like a rather nice idea and she had known they had a farm with lots of animals and fowl. Tony had told her alot about his life on the farm when he was growing up. She liked him and missed him very much. She didn't say it to anyone, but knew in her heart she missed him more than her real father.

A week before they had to move, Betty never returned from her evening walk to the lake. After Roger raised the alarm that his mother hadn't come back after dark, they searched with torchlights, but had to abandon the search till the morning. At first light they found her body floating on the edge of the lake. She was fully dressed and her walking boots were still on her feet. She never knew how to swim. She hated to even get her big toe wet!

Chapter 36

Sally's Awakening

The tears were rolling down Sally's cheeks. She thought her heart would break. 'Why, oh why did I not leave well enough alone? I tried so hard to find out about my parents and now it will haunt me for the rest of my life,' she told herself over and over again. She wished she had never found out. She now realised why nobody wanted to tell her. She was so young and innocent. Why would anyone want to spoil that? Maybe if she had been told when she was younger it might not be as painful. She will never know. Poor Gran. She covered it up so well whenever Sally broached the subject. Her poor heart must have been breaking all those years. Sally sat with her arms folded and her head bent. She was trying to memorise the many times she had asked about her parents. Everyone was very tight-lipped. She couldn't blame them. It was too tragic.

A realisation suddenly dawned on Sally. Every night when the rosary was finished, Grandad and Granny had an odd habit of standing in front of the mantelpiece, quietly murmuring more prayers. On that mantelpiece, amongst all the other condiments jars and vases stood a brown urn shaped ornament. Sally neither found it interesting or attractive, so never questioned it. Now she was seeing it with a new interest. Did it contain the ashes of her parents? She shivered momentarily, and wished Ian was with her today for comfort. Her head was spinning with all she had taken in, and Gran had fallen asleep once again. The nurse told her yesterday, she has been sleeping a lot more during the day of late. They felt she was getting more worn out and her senility seemed to be getting more advanced.

Sally felt a wave of nausea and decide to take a walk outside for some fresh air. One of the nursing staff stopped to ask her if she was feeling ok. Sally felt like answering she would never be ok again, but her good manners came to the fore and she just said she was taking a little walk in the fresh air. She sat on a bench under the large oak tree. She thought her heart would break. There was so much going on in her brain and so many questions she wanted answered. She felt deprived. Not having the ability to remember anything up to the age of four was enough to drive you insane. So much seemed to have happened in that time.

As she sat thinking she tried to recall her first memories. A pair of red shoes was very exciting, but also tinged with disappointment. She remembers Granny coming home from town on the bicycle and handing her the new shoes but they wouldn't fit. She must have got another pair but Sally couldn't remember anything about them.

She could recall her first communion day very easily. Grandad was not able to go to the Church. He was in bed with a cold. The first thing she did when she came home was to run down to his room for a big hug. She could still hear him say 'my blessed little girl!' She must be about seven years old then. She was wearing a long white lace dress and a veil, and her Granny told her that all her own daughters had worn it on their first communion day. Did my sister Pamela wear it too? Gran never mentioned that. Sally sat pondering it over and over. Enlightenment dawned! Pamela would not have been living in Ireland when she was seven. Maybe their Mum wasn't a Catholic and Roger and Pamela never made their First Communion at all! 'Oh dear, so many questions to be answered!' moaned Sally as she held her poor throbbing head in her hands.

'I suppose I must have been a great reminder of my father to Granny and Grandad,' a new wave of though rippled through Sally! To bring up the little orphan daughter of their son who died so needlessly, must have been some comfort and Sally hoped she helped to ease their loss. Now she had her own little boy Jack, she could visualise the feeling of losing a son. She also realised it could not have been easy for them to start all over again, when your own children had grown up. She wished she could thank Grandad for all he had done for her, but he died four years ago. He was a wonderful age, almost reached his ninetieth birthday. He contacted pneumonia when there was a bad flu epidemic raging before Christmas. He held out till 2nd January. Sally was surprised when it happened that Granny didn't appear to be too shattered by his death. She wasn't by his side when he died. Uncle John, Auntie Angela and Auntie

Alanna were all called in that day, as the Nurses knew he was very poorly. Granny had gone to the rest room in the Hospital for a break after spending all day with him. Sally was with her when Alanna came out to tell her Grandad was gone. She blessed herself and said "thanks be to God." She said he had a great long life and that it was inevitable and she was prepared for the parting. She was glad that Eddie was taken first, as he would be lost without her if it were the other way around. So it gave her some consolation that she got her wish. Knowing the way she prayed for everything Sally guessed she would have prayed for that too!

At his funeral Sally got a chance to meet all her Aunts and Uncles together. Lord knows she knew them by name and address, remembering all the nights she addressed the envelopes while Granny wrote the long letters to all her children. Some times she would ask Grandad to add a few lines at the bottom of a letter. Sally smiled now and felt a warm glow at the thought. If she had asked him to climb Croagh Patrick he would have done it more willingly than write those few lines. She would coax him by saying the youngsters were fed up looking at her writing, and two lines of his would mean more to them than the whole letter she had written. In the end he would give in and as Granny handed him the pen, Sally could see that poor Grandad would be more comfortable holding a shovel or a spade. She knew the routine so well that now she could almost hear his words as he took the pen "What am I going to draw here now?" Granny would then proceed to tell him word for word, what to write till a couple of lines were complete.

Oh how she wished those times were back again. She closed her eyes and lent herself to the very happy years she lived with her Granny and Grandad. For a moment Sally thought she could smell the fresh milk coming from the cows at milking time, and she was sure she could hear the piper playing in the distance!

As she came out of her reverie, another depressing thought descended on Sally! Roger and Pamela are not her real brother and sister at all! They are really only half-sister and brother. Not that she feels any different towards them but how do they feel towards her? She always felt Roger very detached and now it made more sense. He never wrote a letter to her and she has no idea where he lives. It gives her great comfort to realise that Pamela is no different in her eyes than if she were her real sister. In fact she was always more like a mother than a sister, Sally reflected. At least now Pamela will be able to relax when she finds out I know the whole sad story. Sally felt very sympathetic towards her, now she knew what Pamela must have gone through. Well at least she won't have to live through it all again telling me, Sally thought.

Her thoughts were momentarily interrupted by the arrival of a robin perching itself at the far end of the bench. She could almost touch it if she reached far enough. She must tell Gran there will be good news today! Sally jumped up suddenly. She had better return to sit with her for a while before she had to go home. She had so much to tell Ian tonight!

The fresh air helped her feel better and equipped her to return to her grandmother's bedside. As she approached the bed she could see her eyes were open. They were glazed and her skin was very waxy. Sally didn't think she knew her at all. She had so many questions she needed answers to, but would have to be careful not to wear her out. She was very fragile now. Her family had no idea that Granny had told Sally everything lately. They probably would not have believed it, as she made very little sense anytime they visited. Sally felt so privileged to have had this time with her. In fact she was seriously considering not telling them a word of what Granny told her. She will keep it to herself for the moment, apart from Ian of course.

"Granny I just seen a robin, we'll have good news today," Sally whispered.

There was no recognition in her eyes. Sally kissed her forehead and told her she would be back in the morning. She had better get on home. After little Jack was tucked into bed, it will be good to share the whole sad story with her husband who was very understanding. She knows he will be there to comfort her. It will be a long night with all she has to tell him. She also needs a good cry. He too will be relieved, as there will be a certain amount of closure to her past life, and they will be able to move on to enjoy their own future at last.

Chapter 37

The Golden Jubilee

'Who did you say I married anyway, Sally?'

'Oh no, I can't take anymore of this,' Sally moaned under her breath.

She felt surprisingly good this morning considering it was so late before she finally fell asleep last night. She told Ian everything, as best she could remember, going back and forth with the sorry details, forgetting some and repeating more, but left nothing out in the end. He was very patient and sympathetic, as she knew he would be. She was so blessed with a dependable husband. Relating it all took its toll on her, but she knew it was no easy ride for him either, as he watched her cry like she would never stop. Thank God Jack didn't disturb them as they talked and talked into the night. Even when they had retired to bed she still couldn't switch off, and would think of something she had forgotten just as they were drifting off to sleep.

'Sally, do you hear me a grá? Did we have a big *hooley* with all the children and grandchildren home for it?'

Sally realised her grandmother was getting their wedding day and their Golden Jubilee all mixed up, so she had better put her mind at ease.

She looked around for the little bottle of brandy that she knew was kept for special occasions, and gave a few sips to her grandmother to relax her. She sat down and took her fragile bony hands in her own. She told her to close her eyes and she would tell her the story of the most wonderful day of their lives. Sally felt she owed it to return the compliment and tell her adorable grandmother the story of her Golden Jubilee!

It was 8th September 1981. Mass was being celebrated with renewal of their marriage vows at 7pm in the Church in *Drumoneen*—the same place where the matchmaker took her to meet a man called Eddie Staunton over 50 years ago. The sun was low in the sky and the thrush and blackbirds were singing their evening song as all the family headed for the Travellers Rest Hotel where the party would begin.

Mary was home from London with her husband and two daughters. Patrick was home from Southampton, with his wife, son and daughter. Francis was home with his wife and three sons. John was living in the homestead with his wife and four children. Angela had returned from London in the sixties and married a local farmer and has six children. Teresa was home from Milton Keynes with her husband and five children. Jamie was living in Chicago and didn't make the long journey home. He had never married. Alanna had also returned in the sixties from London and married a local man and they were at the party with their five children. Their sixth child was due in December, so baby Kevin was at the party that evening, but keeping a low profile!

John, who had played for Mary's wedding, provided the music for the dancing. His daughter assisted him on the fiddle, together with Martin's granddaughter on the accordion. Martin had died four years ago and Grace was deceased some years before that. Grace would have liked nothing better than to sing and play her melodeon if she were alive. Catherine's beloved sister Mary had died years ago, and in fact Catherine and Eddie were the last of that generation left.

Photographs were taken and the cake was cut and shared out. Sally remembers the pantomime it was trying to get a photo of all twenty-eight grandchildren together. After assistance from almost every adult, they were all rounded up and stood together for a precious photograph. Catherine would be proud to gaze at it when this day had ended and everybody had gone home.

Eddie and herself were called on to dance a few steps for their grandchildren to see. Poor Eddie was mortified. He had two left feet when he got married and that hadn't improved with the years! Catherine still could manage to dance a waltz and she had big sons now to dance with her, thank God.

"*Oh Danny boy, the pipes the pipes are calling.*" Catherine sang out feebly.

Sally jumped at the sound. She had been so carried away reliving that wonderful memory of the Golden Jubilee where all the family had been together, that she almost forgot why she was telling it at all. There was only the odd little smile of recognition as Catherine heard a familiar name. Her eyes had opened a couple of times but closed again just as quickly.

"Is that you Eddie coming for me?" she called out again. "Come on and we'll have a dance. *Daisy, Daisy give me your answer do. I'm half crazy all for the love of you,*" she was singing away happily and smiling.

Sally was getting scared now. 'What is going on in her head at all? Sure Grandad died four years ago.'

She was happy to see her smiling, but knew in her heart it wasn't she that put that smile on her face. Whoever she could see it was not Sally. There was no point in staying any longer, so she gave her Gran a kiss goodbye and said she would see her tomorrow, but she already knew Catherine didn't hear her. She was gone into her secret world again.

The following morning as Sally was coming in the door of the nursing home she was approached by her Auntie Angela and Alanna, who looked like they had been crying. They told her the nurses had rang early this morning and told them to come in. Catherine has died in her sleep. She was at peace now and with Grandad and Tony. They said she was a great age and at eighty-seven you couldn't expect her quality of life to be improving. They hugged Sally and asked her to try and not to be too upset. They knew how devoted she had been to her. They said they would take care of all the necessary arrangements, but if she would like she could go and see her grandmother before the undertaker took her away.

Sally wondered how much more she could take. She never knew her own mother and her feelings now were that of a mother lost. She knew she made Catherine very happy lately. Lovely memories brought up from the past that brought many a smile to the poor fragile face, which nobody else but her had seen of late. Sally had no regrets when it came to her beloved grandmother.

The one regret she did have though was she had not got around to telling her the good news she was savouring. She was pregnant again and had not found the right time to tell her. Catherine would understand all about that, Sally consoled herself. Sure she couldn't always find the right time to tell the same news to Eddie!

One thing Sally knew for sure, that if this baby is a boy they will name him Edward. If it's a girl they will be proud to name her after Catherine. This new life inside her will be Sally's salvation and give her something to look forward to and not to continue dwelling in the past. She closed her eyes and repeated the very prayer she heard her grandmother say every day of her life—*thanks be to God.*

Glossary

a grá	=	dear
babog	=	baby
banshee	=	fairy woman
boreen	=	a little lane
cailleach	=	a bed
cailin	=	a girl
ciseogs	=	baskets
codgers	=	eccentric people
craic	=	fun
meitheal	=	gang
poiteen	=	homemade Irish brew
seanachai	=	a storyteller
slainté	=	cheers
smig	=	chin

About The Author

Born in 1944, the youngest of eight children, married to her husband Tom for 43 years. They have three daughters and three sons and nine grandchildren. She currently lives and works in Castlebar. Co. Mayo. This is her first novel.

Donations

Western Alzheimers, Main Street, Ballinrobe, Co. Mayo provides a complete service of care to families affected by dementia in the Western Region of Ireland. Nancy is happy to "Share The Care" by giving donations from royalties received from this book; to help support hundreds of families receive "home from home" care that suffer from Alzheimers Disease in the West of Ireland.

Overview

- In April 1924, the Carmania set sail from Cobh, Co. Cork bound for Philadelphia. Catherine Brennan was one of many passengers on board who hoped to make her fortune. Her life story unfolds at the age of 22. Meeting the bold Maurice Fitzgerald on board ship—her 6 years in Philadelphia living with the rich and returning to the west of Ireland, to seek a husband through a matchmaker. This novel tells of the ups and downs of rearing a large family through 50 years of marriage. It features the fascination and reality of matchmaking, written as was spoken, full of Irish wit and natural humour, in times when entertainment was free and kissing the opposite sex had to be confessed to a priest!
- In 1965, Sally Staunton was left an orphan. Now married with a son, she desperately needs to know what happened to her parents. Reared by Catherine since she was four, all she was told was they died in tragic circumstances. It was a time shrouded in secrecy. Sally tries to get Catherine who now suffers from Alzheimers disease, to tell her life story before total senility takes over her beloved grandmother,

Lightning Source UK Ltd.
Milton Keynes UK

176358UK00002B/2/P

9 781456 785437